Family Affair

Saxon Bennett

Bella
BOOKS
2009

Bella Books, Inc.
P.O. Box 10543
Tallahassee, FL 32302

Printed in the United States of America on acid-free paper

First Edition Bella Books 2009

Editor: Katherine V. Forrest
Cover designer: Linda Callaghan
Cover art: peanutty designs

ISBN-10: 1-59493-150-X
ISBN-13: 978-1-59493-150-5

Biography

Saxon Bennett lives in New Mexico with her beloved partner and three fur kids. She is the author of ten novels.

Dedication

To Lin for her amusing and enlightening stories which serve
as the stuff fiction is made of.

Acknowledgments

To the real Annie and Jane for their cameo appearances—
you will be paid in biscuits.

Chapter One

"Rumor has it you're holed up here pouting," Lacey James said as she stood in the doorway.

"I am not. I'm working. I have a lot of editing to do and it's not going well," Chase Banter said as she sat at her desk. Chase's two dogs of mixed origin, sat next to her with mournful looks on their doggy faces as if mimicking the mood of their mistress. They had been taken into her custody while she nursed her hurt pride and her smashed aorta. They seemed to ache for new company as Chase had been so quiet and self-absorbed. Fortunately for them, Lacey had appeared like their fairy dog mother.

Lacey scooted Annie, the black dog, away from her crotch. "Damn, I swear that dog reaches my cervix when she does that." Chase looked up. "She wants to work for the TSA as an official underwear sniffer in search of contraband."

Lacey laughed.

"What are you doing up here, anyway?" Chase's attention

returned to the task at hand, primarily getting rid of Lacey so she could get back to work.She was now horribly behind because the household crisis had distracted her.

"Gitana called me. She's worried about you. This is the longest you've held out and she really wants to talk." Lacey moved a stack of papers and sat on the blue leather couch. "This place is a mess."

Chase studied her best friend. Tall and thin with brown, shoulder-length, fashionably cut hair, Lacey had an upturned nose and a pointy but not unattractive chin. Her parts taken separately should have made her pretty but somehow put altogether they made her only interesting looking. Lacey rued this fact but worked hard to conceal it. Chase had told her she had what Jane Austen referred to as a not unpleasing countenance. This did not hearten her, having never read Jane Austen.

"I know where everything is." But she conceded that the writing studio was a scary place. It had been a guesthouse of questionable nature. She would never have allowed anyone to stay in it except her mother, whom she loathed. She and Gitana had completely gutted the inside and started over. It was utilitarian pine—wood floors, a coat of sunflower yellow paint, a cast-off couch, a wooden coffee table full of nicks and stains, and three burgundy wingback chairs Chase had dug out of her mother's attic which was filled with unwanted furniture.

"What is all this anyway?" Lacey pointed to the wall and then the ceiling. Cork panels ran the length of one wall at eye level where Chase attached her storyboards. She'd run a cord from the front of the studio to the back where she hung index cards that held her character notes. "It's how I keep track of things."

"I thought you had it all in your head."

"That's a common misconception."

"Oh, you writers are so misunderstood. Now, when you're going to talk to your girlfriend? It's really stupid that I have to drive from Albuquerque when you two are only separated by a few steps."

2

"The studio is half an acre from the house," Chase informed her.

"Yeah, yeah. Why the hell you live in the middle of nowhere, I'll never understand."

"I like the mountain views and my flower garden and it's not technically the middle of nowhere. It is thirty-eight miles north of downtown. A mere forty minutes from the conveniences of New Mexico's largest city."

"You sound just like the realtor that sold you the house eight years ago. You live up here because you hate people. Just admit it."

"You know me so well we could be kindred spirits." Chase glanced down at her notebook and thought of *Anne of Green Gables* and wished she had been as fortunate as that vivacious orphan in the kindred spirits department.

"Don't be so hard on Gitana. I'm sure there's a good explanation hiding in there somewhere."

"Like immaculate conception. You can tell her they used to stone adulteresses in the virgin birth days. I'd like to know how you'd feel if your significant other had been puking every morning for a month, finally goes to the doctor and comes home to tell you she's pregnant."

"You're overreacting." Lacey scratched Jane's head as the dog climbed up beside her on the couch. Annie was napping at her feet.

"Go away." Chase turned back to her desk and tapped her pencil.

"I can see where I'm not wanted. I'm going to talk to Gitana." Jane licked her face. "At least you like me."

"She's not home."

"For someone who doesn't care you're sure keeping tabs on her."

"Don't you have a Jazzercise class or something?" Chase opened another of her notebooks and began scribbling.

"This is my rest day. Why don't you call me when you're done brooding."

"I'm not brooding. I'm working."

Lacey gave the dogs another pat on the head and left.

Chase's notebook blurred as her eyes filled with tears. She quickly wiped them away. She never cried unless something incredibly painful occurred like the time she fell off the pump house roof and dislocated her shoulder. She had cried and then puked.

She could cry, she told herself. First, she'd been angry and now she was depressed. How had this happened to them? Gitana wasn't one to stray. She had been pursued a time or two but that was to be expected owing to Gitana's very pleasing countenance, but she laughed them off as idle infatuations. No one could ever replace Chase in her heart. Or so she had said.

The dogs woke up and barked at the French doors that opened up onto the small deck. Chase saw Gitana's white Land Rover pull up in the driveway. That used to be a happy sound. It meant an end to her solitary day. The orchid nursery that Gitana ran was just outside the small town of Cedar Meadows ten miles away. They decided when Gitana started the business that having it on the property wasn't a good idea—too close to home. The nursery employed people and Chase disliked most of the human race. She was certain that she was a modern descendent of the anchorites that lived in caves—communing only with God so the story went. She figured it was just their excuse to steer clear of people.

She looked over at the dogs. "You're staying put. Don't be traitors to the cause."

Annie sat down obediently. Jane took one look at the door and sailed out the loose end of the screen that had served as a doggie door ever since they broke through it to chase a rabbit. Chase had never bothered to fix it. Annie followed suit.

"Come back here you Benedict Arnolds!" Chase yelled.

They were on the stairs and across the front yard by the time Gitana was in the gate with a bag of groceries.

"Hi, girls," she said, before they floored her and she dropped the groceries.

"Girls, girls, get down," Chase yelled as she ran across the yard. The dogs had crushed a carton of eggs and were licking the yolks with great fervor. She stuck her fingers in her mouth and let out a piercing whistle. Both dogs stopped licking the sidewalk and sat at attention—Alpha had spoken. "You're grounded. Report to your room immediately." They slunk, tails between their legs, to the sunroom.

"They'll both get sick now," Gitana said, her beautiful almond shaped eyes not meeting Chase's. She pulled back her disheveled long hair, twisting the dark mass into a French knot like she so often did—the gesture broke Chase's heart. She tried to pick up the egg shells while Chase salvaged the rest of the groceries. Gitana started to cry. "I can't live like this."

They were still kneeling. Chase saw her wretchedness. "Hey, don't cry." She reached out and held her.

"I miss you. I miss the dogs."

"I miss you too." Chase brushed away her tears. "Come on, let's get the rest of this inside then I'll hose what's left of the eggs off the sidewalk."

Chase didn't know if going back to the house was her anger caving in or the simple resignation of her depression. She couldn't live without Gitana, anymore than Gitana could live without her, whatever this was they'd get through it.

They carried what was left of the groceries into the sunroom where Annie and Jane were sitting like perfect angels who had no prior memory of their transgression.

"Right. You two are still in trouble. Five minutes of grounding." She held up five fingers. Not only did the dogs understand voice commands when they deemed fit, they also responded to hand signals, because those most often supplied treats. Both dogs went to their beds. Chase put the milk and butter in the fridge.

The phone rang and Gitana picked it up. "This is she. Hello, Dr. Bertine."

Chase reached over and clicked on the speakerphone.

"We regret to inform you that it appears that your chart was mixed up with another woman with the same last name. You were both scheduled for the same time slot last month on the second. This produced some complications as you were scheduled for a pap smear and she was scheduled for artificial insemination. This is most regrettable. If you decide to keep the baby we will, of course, pay all medical costs."

"How about a fucking college education for the kid, you moron? And how come it took you so long to figure out how it happened? Were your files like the lost Dead Sea scrolls?" Chase shouted at the phone.

Dr. Bertine cleared his throat. He appeared to realize his ass was in a sling. Chase savored the moment. She'd spent four days in relationship purgatory. Now, it was his turn to sweat.

Gitana pointed to the living room. "Go sit. Right now."

Chase stomped off toward the living room, but not before she turned around and scowled at the phone.

"I'm sorry. My partner is a little upset by all this."

"A little?" Chase shouted from the living room.

Gitana finished the call without the speakerphone. She came and sat on the couch next to Chase. "He says I can terminate it."

"I'm sorry I doubted you." Chase felt the weight of ultimate contrition.

Gitana took her hand. "I didn't mean for this to happen."

"I know. It's not your fault. It's just so…unsettling." It was the only word she could think of to describe this. She liked things ordered and settled. She chewed the cuticle of her forefinger. There had been incidences where mix-ups occurred. Mark Twain used it in *Pudd 'nhead Wilson*. It was the entire premise of the book, but then one had to adhere to Coleridge's willing suspension of disbelief. She couldn't see how it would work in this instance. If she had used this premise in one of her novels her editor would have tossed the idea as preposterous, yet what didn't ride in fiction was here in fact. "I just don't understand it. Didn't you think something was odd? I mean a pap smear and artificial insemination are extremely different procedures."

"Not really. I mean, you sit on the exam table, spread your legs, scoot down like they tell you and relax like they tell you, which is virtually impossible, and the doctor sticks something cold up there. The nurse did wish me good luck, but I just thought she hoped that I didn't have cervical cancer." Gitana frowned.

Chase took a deep breath. "It's a horrid mistake. What, one Ortega is as good as another? Oh, it's just another Hispanic woman with long dark hair—you all look alike. That's racist. Someone should have checked."

"I know. They were busy that day and they made a mistake."

"A major fuck-up is more like it." She looked over at Gitana who appeared more miserable than Chase felt. "It's all right. We'll get through it. We always do." She took Gitana's face in her hands and kissed her softly.

Chase got up to go. She needed to go to the writing studio and think. She did her best thinking there, like Winnie the Pooh, who sat on a log and thought, usually about honey.

Gitana pleaded, "Don't go."

She gave her that look which would make Chase chew off her own arm if Gitana asked her to. She sat down and tried to look cheerful. Gitana wrapped her arms around Chase's neck and then kissed it. Chase's nether regions did a loop-de-loop and thoughts of Gitana's warm body reminded her of the four days of deprivation. She kissed her, their tongues getting reacquainted.

Gitana kissed her harder. She pushed Chase down on the couch and reached for her. She pulled off Chase's T-shirt and ran her hand up her stomach, sending shivers across her body. Gitana reached under her sports bra and caressed her nipple, taking it in her mouth and running her tongue around it. She undid her shorts, slipping her hand under Chase's underwear.

"I missed this," she said, pushing her fingers inside Chase who wrapped her legs around her and moaned.

"Me too." She struggled with Gitana's jeans. Gitana helped

her with her free hand until Chase found what she was looking for. They moved against one another with the precision of years of practice. Chase came first and Gitana followed up momentarily. Chase liked that. It made her feel like they were in sync.

They lay there for a moment in a tangle of clothes. "Want to take a nap?" Chase asked.

"I'd love to. I haven't been sleeping well lately."

"Me either. If you're not there to steal all the covers I don't feel right." She got up and took Gitana's hand helping her up.

"I don't steal the covers. You throw them off when you're hot and then roll on top of them."

"And then you steal them," Chase said, as they climbed the stairs.

"I'm going to get a video camera installed in our room."

"I didn't know you were that kinky," Chase said, raising an eyebrow.

"Not for that! I only wanted one so I can prove my point."

Chase pulled back the covers. She watched as Gitana took off her T-shirt. She'd never tire of her body, her round firm breasts, her curvy hips and her flat smooth stomach.

"What?"

"I love you," Chase said.

Gitana pushed her back on the bed and then climbed on top of her.

"More?"

When Chase awoke, pink and yellow covered the mountains outside the bedroom window. Twilight had set in and she knew they'd had a good long nap. She rolled over. Gitana was on her side and she was crying. "What's wrong?"

Gitana turned to face her. "I don't want to kill the baby."

Chase wiped away her tears. "Oh, that." She hadn't given it much thought. She was still basking in their reuniting—the other problem had taken a back seat. "Well, we don't have to go that route, exactly," she said, although she couldn't think of another route. She didn't like the idea of Gitana being some sort of baby-maker that turned her baby over to someone else after it was born. It didn't seem the correct choice for them.

Gitana started to cry again. Between sobs, and she said, "I know this isn't what you wanted, but he or she is here now, with us."

Chase rolled on her back and studied the ceiling. The bedroom windows were pumped full of setting sun. She would suck at parenting. What if it was a boy—how was she going to teach him to pee? Did boys inherently know how to hold it? This was big—far bigger than she'd ever be ready for. Of course, everything they'd done so far was a risky adventure that always panned out in the end. Why not this?

Gitana sniffled. "Chase?"

"I'll have to take parenting classes because I'm not going to be good at it."

"No, you won't. You can do anything you set your mind to." Gitana wiped away her tears and suddenly looked resolute.

This made Chase apprehensive. Gitana had sallied forth and it was her duty to follow. She gathered up her limited things-I'm-good-at-resources and said, "Can I pick out the clothes and read to him or her?" Aside from writing, those were the only two things that came to mind. She loved to shop and loved to read. This kid would have everything, including a well-stocked library, but not be spoiled. She didn't know how she'd work that one out, but she was certain there must be a way.

"Anything you want." Gitana kissed her.

Chase rummaged around for her own clothes. "My mother will be ecstatic." She found Gitana's underwear and one sock.

"I hadn't thought of that."

Chase heard trepidation in her tone, but then anything to do with Stella gave trepidation. "Do you think the dogs have figured out they're no longer grounded?"

"I'm certain Annie can count." Gitana handed Chase her bra which was under her pillow for some reason.

"I can just see her, one-one-thousand, two-one-thousand."

Gitana hugged her. "I love you."

"You're not so bad yourself."

"Chase!"

"I love you, too." Chase knew that this might turn out to be the best decision of her life or at least she hoped so. She wasn't necessarily a believer in happy endings. Perhaps it was all those Brothers Grimm fairy tales her mother had read her as a child. Stella had odd child-rearing methods.

Chapter Two

"How the hell did that happen?" Lacey screamed into her cell phone.

"Clerical error," Chase replied, as she flipped through the Lands' End catalog for kids.

"I thought it was a biological thing."

"They got her mixed up with another woman." Chase earmarked the page with the cute flannel baby outfit. Yellow would be good—a nice gender-neutral color.

"Like when the surgeon cuts off the wrong leg?"

"Something like that." That cutting off the leg thing certainly stuck in everyone's head, Chase mused.

"Can I decorate the baby's room?" Lacey asked. There was a gasp. "Next week she'll be two months along. We better get going."

"I think seven months will give us enough time." Interior design was one thing Lacey was good at. She'd done wonders with the furniture purchases and placement in the unusual floor plan of Chase and Gitana's house. Classified as passive solar, the house was a long rectangle with large windows along the entire front of the house which made furniture placement a difficulty, but the house was energy efficient and that made Chase feel very hip and green. Chase closed the catalog and spun around in her chair to look at her early blooming flowers in the jewel garden. The daffodils and crocus were beginning to flower, dotting the garden with bursts of yellow and white.

"When you coming to town?" Lacey inquired.

"Tomorrow. I have to go to the shrink."

This didn't appear to faze Lacey which Chase thought was good. Not everyone handled having a crazy person for their best friend. Chase could have been going to the dentist not the Behavioral Science building.

"Call me when you're done and we'll go shopping. I'll work out a color scheme. Have you told Stella yet?" Lacey asked, effortlessly switching gears.

"No, but I will." She was going to try for that night, but wanted to see if Gitana was up for it and didn't want to commit if she bailed. Potentially unpleasant activities could, in all good conscience, be put off. She did it with Ariana, her editor, all the time so what was the difference.

"I wish I could be there."

Chase heard pining in her voice. "I'd invite you, but this is a private family moment and I don't know how Stella is going to take it."

"I know." There was a heavy sigh.

Chase felt bad. "I'll give you all the details."

"Swear?"

"Girl Scout's honor." Chase held up two fingers.

"You got thrown out for being a belligerent anarchist."

"I know, but I was a kid then. As an adult, I make oaths with complete sincerity."

"Right. Well, I'm off to Jazzercise."

"Have you seen Jasmine at class lately?" Chase inquired as Jasmine had missed their last meeting.

Jasmine Carter was in Chase's writing group. She compulsively exercised and wrote thrillers, but her protagonists always ended up in the gym and the story got stuck there.

"No, her husband is keeping close tabs on her. Her shrink advised cutting down on her exercise classes because she's excessive. She says she's concentrating more on her writing."

"We'll find out next group meeting." Which, come to think of it was her turn to host. This meant she'd have to shovel out the writing studio and soon.

Chase clicked off and got back to work. To keep on schedule, she had to write fifteen pages a day. She turned to her notebook and began scribbling, letting her imaginary world take-over. It was more comforting than the real world. In her world, she controlled everything.

Gitana was home from work. The dogs dashed out the broken screen doggy door and were across the front yard before Chase had shut her notebook, got up and stretched. If anyone thought the writing life was glamorous they were sadly misinformed. Sitting was difficult for the hyperactive. Her back hurt, her fingers cramped up and her mind was tired from creating an entire universe in her cerebral cortex.

From the front yard, she heard Gitana cooing and fawning over the dogs. Chase imagined Gitana as a mother. She'd make a great mother, a perfect mix of love and discipline. She herself was the one who needed serious reconstruction. One of her writing manuals purported that any subject could be mastered by spending sixty days in a decent library. Was the same possible with parenting?

Chase made her way down to the sunroom and kissed Gitana.

"How was your day?" Gitana asked, as she scratched first Annie's ears and then Jane's.

"Well spent and yours?"

"Profitable."

That was Gitana's keyword for she sold a lot of orchids or she got a wicked deal on a shipment of orchids. She looked radiant. Had her pregnancy already given her that glow people always talk about?

"Are you still willing to have that chat with Stella?"

Gitana smiled. "No time like the present."

She said it without cringing. Chase was impressed. "We'll feed the dogs and then pop over during her cocktail hour."

"Is she more amiable then?"

Chase nodded. "More like less argumentative. Her combat skills are slightly impaired." She bounced a tennis ball for Jane who caught it in midair.

"At least that's in our favor," Gitana said, as she opened the kitchen door.

Chase followed her in. The dogs came in behind them. Gitana set her bag on the counter and retrieved two biscuits from the treat jar. She indicated down with her hand and both dogs sat. She gave them their biscuits and patted their heads.

"Let's get it over with," Chase said, filling the dog bowls with kibble and trying to look cheerful.

Chapter Three

Stella Banter lived in an enormous house in Four Hills. The silos of the missiles that were part of Kirkland Air Force Base were ostensibly in her backyard. She liked it that her property was protected in the finest manner. It went well with the rest of her well-deserved privileged life. Every time Chase pulled up in the circular driveway with its automatic black wrought iron gates—the letter "B" prominently displayed—she wondered about all this privilege and how much of it was truly deserved. Not that Chase had not benefited from the money—but she saw it as fortuitous, not a right. Novels of the horrors of the poor often popped into her head: *Jude the Obscure*, *The Grapes of Wrath* and Sinclair's *The Jungle*. She was simply a member of the Lucky Sperm Club and guilt welled up.

"Her gardens always look so beautiful," Gitana said, as they passed through the poplar trees that lined the drive. Behind them lay manicured lawns and flower beds. There was a pond and a stone wall section lined with topiaries.

"Yeah, and it takes two full-time gardeners and a lot of water." She parked in front of the house—a brick colonial something like Martha Stewart's Turkey Hill. They'd driven Chase's car, a steel gray Volkswagen Passat. The car irritated her mother because it wasn't flashy. It was 'the People's car,' Chase had informed her.

"People without means, kind of car," was her mother's retort.

She didn't want her mother to think that just because she was going to be a grandmother that their mother-daughter feud had come to an end. Driving the Land Rover might have signified that.

Rosarita answered the door. "What a surprise!" She hugged both Chase and Gitana, her brown face beaming with delight. "She said nothing about you coming."

"We wanted it that way," Chase said.

"She's in the living room having her medicine." She ushered them through.

Chase gazed at Rosarita with affection. She was from El Salvador. She saw Stella as her glorious benefactor. Stella could do no wrong. Her mother, quite out of character, was amazingly kind and generous to Rosarita, who in turn excused any of Stella's bad behavior. Subsequently, the evening cocktails were referred to as "medicine" versus a problem with the bottle.

They walked down the statue-lined marble hallway to the living room. Rosarita offered to bring iced tea. "Is that good?"

"Perfect," Chase said, as they entered the completely white living room decorated in what Chase referred to as overdone heaven.

"To what do I owe this honor?" Stella said, waving a hand. Lithe with aristocratic facial features and bobbed platinum hair, Stella was still beautiful at fifty-seven.

"We have some news," Chase said, taking a seat next to Gitana on the white leather couch.

"Oh, yes. I wondered when you were going to tell me. You know, Gitana, we will have to sue." Legs crossed, Stella sipped her martini and studied them from where she sat on the barstool before the white vinyl wet bar.

"Lacey told you. I'm going to kill her," Chase said. "She couldn't be here, so she beat me to the punch. That little bitch."

"You'll do no such thing. She couldn't help herself. When she first found out she was afraid you'd be mean and keep it to yourself as some sort of punishment." Stella narrowed her eyes, as if to test her theory.

"Now, why would I do that? We're here aren't we? I told her we'd come tonight," Chase said.

Rosarita brought in a tray with the pitcher of iced tea and two glasses. She gave Chase that warning look she always did when beverages other than vodka were being served in the white room. Chase nodded. "We'll be careful."

Rosarita withdrew from the room. Chase poured them both a glass and squeezed in lemon from the little silver bowl on the tray. Rosarita thought of everything.

"We didn't intend to leave you out," Gitana said. She sipped her tea and was silent. They'd decided that this was Chase's gig and that she should handle it.

"We had some things to sort out. It wasn't exactly like Gitana chose motherhood," Chase said, getting irritated. She got up and grabbed three of her mother's favorite Fabergé eggs from the sofa table. She juggled them. Stella pretended not to notice. Over the years full of arguments, Chase had become adept at juggling.

"Motherhood is never chosen," Stella replied.

"Gag me," Chase said.

"We're still going to sue," Stella said, calmly sipping her drink.

"They offered to pay all medical expenses," Gitana said.

"Poppycock. Raising a child is an expensive endeavor. Don't I know." She pointedly stared at Chase who scowled back.

"I don't remember you working at Circle K trying to make ends meet," Chase said.

Stella waved her off. "We're going to sue for damages and

enough money for a well-financed trust fund. That child will be going to Harvard when I'm done."

"I don't think that's necessary," Gitana said, running her hand through her hair.

Stella ignored her. "I'll take care of everything. I called Owen."

Owen was their nasty, slimy, family lawyer. Chase loathed him.

"And your fucked-up years are over," Stella said, pointing at Chase.

"Excuse me? Please, not in front of the child," Chase reprobated.

"Child?"

"The shrimp in Gitana's uterus. She'll have eyes and ears any day. She could have them now for all we know." Chase threw the Fabergé eggs higher. Long-distance juggling required more skill. If she ever quit writing she could join the circus.

"How do you know the baby is a she? And as a matter of biology, he or she doesn't have ears yet," Stella said.

"But he or she will, so we all have to watch our language," Gitana said, looking at Chase who had the filthiest mouth of them all.

Stella got off the barstool and slid the ottoman over, propping up Gitana's feet and fluffing a pillow to put behind her back. Chase, who had never seen her mother give a flying fuck about anyone, was astonished. Although Gitana did look a bit like a rag doll her mother was playing with, Gitana smiled, did not speak and sipped her iced tea. She has the class of the ages, Chase thought. She studied her mother carefully.

"As I was saying," Stella said. She put one hand on her hip, jutted one foot forward and clutched her martini. "Your fucked up years are over. You're going to be a father. It's time you behave and live up to your responsibilities."

Chase stopped juggling in shock at this revelation. She managed to catch two of the Fabergé eggs. They all watched the third one go sailing off. Gitana stuck out her hand, and like the lucky spectator at a baseball game, caught the egg. Chase placed the other two eggs in their stands. The gravity of being a parent hit her full force. Her mother was right.

"Can I have a martini?"

"Ha! I knew you'd come around." Stella set her martini down and went to sit by Gitana. "Together, we can reform her. More tea?"

Gitana nodded.

Chase refilled her glass and mixed herself a martini. The drink was vile, but it did straighten up her nerves.

"Supposing my fucked-up years are over what are these next years going to be?" She went back to the white vinyl bar and swung around on the stool.

"These will be the butter years. I've always likened the growing periods of a person's life to bread. First, there is the yeast rising, kneading and rolling—the form your choices make as to the course of your life. Then there's the baking, your life actions brought to fruition. As your life choices bring success there's buttering the bread."

"And then you're toast," Chase said, unimpressed by the lengthy metaphor.

"Where do the fuck-up years come in?" Gitana said.

"Improper kneading," Stella said, pointing at Chase.

"I think it's a bad batch of yeast. That stuff does expire, you know." She grimaced as she sipped her martini, it was awful stuff.

"The center falls in and the loaf is misshapen."

"More like incorrect oven temperature—the cook's fault," Chase retorted.

"Subsequently, a work gone awry." Stella pursed her lips.

"In Binky Land" Chase said, referring to the imaginary world her mother had created. She felt sure this would put an end to the banal metaphors about stupid bread.

Stella smiled. Chase, having thought she'd gotten the best of the debate, was perplexed.

"You remember Binky Land?" Stella inquired of Chase.

"I plan on continuing the tradition." She snagged a cocktail olive and went to sit by Gitana.

"What's Binky Land?" Gitana said.

Stella got up and poured herself another martini. She looked at Chase. If Stella was quiet it meant the floor was relinquished to the next speaker.

"My odious cousin, Cliff, used to visit in the summer. He thought Peter Pan was a fag, so Stella came up with Binky Land to keep him quiet. It was a magical place where good and evil battle—like an amalgamation of *Alice in Wonderland* and *The Chronicles of Narnia* with a little of Kipling's *The Jungle Book* thrown in. It was really quite amazing."

"Maybe you should've been a writer," Gitana said. She was notorious for trying to find a career for Stella. She was always telling Chase that a woman of her mother's intelligence needed an outlet.

Stella waved her hand. "They were just silly stories meant to kill a summer's afternoon, but I think I did instill a sense of storytelling into the children. It's a pity someone's talent is not put towards more serious literature."

Chase pursed her lips. Stella was back to being Stella. Once again, she had thrown away the opportunity to remove the barbed wire that surrounded herself and Chase, squandering it like pocket change with complete disregard for its worth.

"Maybe you should write the Binky Land chronicles. Look at that Harry Potter woman. She's horribly rich. Certainly you could do that instead of wasting your time with these moist mound sagas of yours." Stella threw her arms up in the air like she was at her wit's end with an errant teenager.

"Someone, someone famous," Chase added, "once said that there are two great tragedies in life—not getting what you want or getting what you want."

"Phish. I just think your talents are being wasted." She finished her martini. "Are you staying for dinner?"

"No. We're meeting Lacey to look at baby furniture," Chase

said.

"But I thought..." Gitana started to say, but Chase squeezed her arm. "That's right, she's helping us design the nursery."

"We'll grab a bite out," Chase said.

"Off you go then," Stella said. She hooked another martini and walked out with as much dignity as she could muster down the hall toward the kitchen.

Once in the car, Gitana asked, "Why did you do that to her? She's lonely and wanted us to stay for dinner."

Chase started the car. "I'm punishing her."

"Why?"

"I'll never be good enough. It doesn't matter that I've published eleven books when there's a zillion writers who aren't even published. She doesn't like what I write so all my efforts are nothing but a cipher in her opinion."

"You could tell her you branched into mystery novels and it's coming along nicely," Gitana suggested.

Chase shifted the car into reverse. Gitana put on her seat belt and firmly placed her head on the head rest. Chase slammed her foot down on the gas pedal and screamed down the driveway. "It shouldn't matter and besides it would ruin all the fun."

"How long is this feud over your career going to go on?" Gitana glanced at her side view mirror.

"Ever heard of the Hatfields and the McCoys?" Chase steered a hard right and barely cleared the stone pillars of the entrance gate. She checked her skid marks. They were impressive enough. She nodded her satisfaction.

Then her cell phone rang. The ring tone was the Charlie Daniels song, "The Devil Went Down to Georgia."

Gitana frowned. "You told me you were going to change that."

"I did, it used to be "Devil with the Blue Dress On." She clicked on her cell phone.

"Three words, baby-on-board," her mother said.

"Right."

"Bye, bye, Papa." Stella hung up.

"Dammit," Chase said, as she drove carefully down the street. "Let me guess, no more racing down the driveway backward."

"You got it."

Chapter Four

"What on earth?" Gitana said, rubbing sleep from her eyes.

"I went shopping." Chase was wearing a stethoscope. She pulled at Gitana's arm, rolled up Gitana's pajama sleeve and put the blood pressure band around her bicep and pumped the rubber ball.

"Chase, I'm fine really."

"We're not taking any chances." She put the stethoscope under the armband and inserted the earpieces. She listened intently and watched the dial per the instructions which she'd memorized. "One twenty over eighty. That's outstanding."

"You're crazy, you know that."

"Is that news?" Chase undid the armband and gently wrapped up the device. "Luckily, nature is not at play here, genetically speaking. We'll just have to watch the nurture." She put the stethoscope to Gitana's chest and listened to her heart. "It sounds fine. I couldn't find the thingy-jigger that goes in your ears and up your nose, but I'm sure I can find one on the Internet."

"You scare me. Can I have some coffee?"

"Try being me. At least you can get away. I'm stuck here."

Chase followed her into the bathroom and watched her wash her face and brush her teeth.

"What are you looking at?" Gitana asked.

"I want to see if you're getting fat."

"I'm not. Let's go have some coffee."

They went downstairs. The dogs came flying in the doggie door and jumped at Gitana. "Hey, be careful. Remember there's a baby in there." Chase gave each of them a biscuit. "Now, go play."

"What did you do to the coffee?"

"It's decaf," Chase said lightly.

"What's the point of that?" Gitana peered into her mug with obvious distaste.

"Caffeine isn't good for you or the baby."

"You're going to be a real pain in the ass aren't you?" Gitana poured her coffee down the sink.

"You get used to it." Chase poured herself another cup to make her point. She'd already had four. Usually by now, she'd be having heart palpitations from all the caffeine. "How about we do fifty-fifty?"

"I'm all about compromise." She stuck a Dr. Pepper in her pajama pocket.

"I saw that." Chase tried to grab it.

"I can't function without caffeine. Don't make me go cold turkey," Gitana pleaded.

"All right, but only half a can."

"I promise. Now, what's on your agenda for the day?"

"Shrink's office called yesterday morning. They had a can-cellation, so I can go in this afternoon." She watched as Gitana gulped down as much Dr. Pepper as she could. "A lot of sugar isn't good for the baby either."

Gitana ignored her. "I'm really proud of you for going."

"I'm not sure it's starting out right, though. The receptionist

24

asked for my other Social Security number, because they can't find mine in their database." She rolled her eyes. "I told her I'd have to look for it."

Gitana laughed.

"What?"

"That someone who's bipolar would have two Social Security numbers. One for me and one for myself."

"All right, I guess it is kind of funny. But, you know, I'm a little sensitive about this."

"It's going to be fine. Besides, you might run into your other half someday and we could all have coffee."

"That's not even funny. It'd be like having a twin. Do you really want to have two of me?"

"No. I don't think the world is ready for that." Clutching the Dr. Pepper, a now prized possession, she went upstairs to shower and dress.

"Only half of that," Chase called out to her.

"What? I can't hear you the water's running."

Chase scowled despite knowing no one was around to see it. It was always the conundrum of doing something like burping or farting and saying "excuse me" when you were alone—was it necessary? Maybe it was just good to keep in practice.

Chapter Five

"So you think you're bipolar?" Dr. Robicheck said. She sat cross-legged with a yellow legal notepad on her knee, her pen poised. She looked like a stenographer awaiting testimony.

"That's what they tell me," Chase replied, shifting in the straightback chair. Great for your posture, but far from relaxing. She had considered the couch, but decided it was too Freudian and she wasn't ready for that. The uncomfortable chair seemed indicative of Dr. Robicheck. She was probably a communist from the old days. Chase could tell from her accent she was Slavic. She had sensible short hair, a pinched face and wore a brown polyester business suit with a beige blouse and black square-heeled shoes. Wasn't there a rule about wearing black with brown? She couldn't remember. She'd asked Lacey. Chase wasn't up on fashion faux pas as most of her wardrobe consisted of khaki shorts or trousers and T-shirts.

"I want to ask you some questions. Yes and no answers, only, please."

"You're the doctor."

She nodded. "You have delusions or grandiose ideas?"

"Yes, I guess I do sometimes." Chase quickly ran through her list of mental sins. She harbored a secret desire to win a Pulitzer—that was definitely grandiose considering what she wrote was considered lesbian trash and not high literature. She was convinced that she was entirely responsible for Gitana's happiness and well-being. She desperately wanted to come up with some magical elixir to make her beloved dogs live longer than ten years. Goats, after all, live for twenty-five years. No one loves a goat like they love a dog or a cat. Yes, these were grandiose ideas.

"Excessive drug or alcohol use?" She looked up from her pad and stared at Chase.

"Only on bad days and in moderation."

The doctor frowned.

"Basically, no." She figured that was what the doctor wanted. She must curb her smartass tendencies before she ended up in the psych ward or rehab.

"Have you ever thought you were God?"

"No, well, there was that one time in grade school…" She stopped herself. The doctor didn't have a sense of humor.

"Thoughts of suicide?"

"No." That one she was sure of. She had too much to do—besides it was messy and her mother would bury her in a dress. She just knew it. Her aim was to outlive her mother and bury her in something hideously unfashionable.

The doctor pursed her lips and seemed satisfied. Chase was glad. She hated yes or no answers. Nothing was black and white—except maybe piano keys.

"How'd I do?"

"You have a mild case—most fixable."

"No straightjacket then?"

"That was never a possibility. You're a little crazy. So are a lot of other people. You shouldn't worry. Two pills a day and you'll be normal." She glanced at Chase and amended her statement. "As normal as you can be." She got out her script pad.

Chase kept quiet and busied herself with studying the office decor. You could tell a lot about a person by their surroundings. Being a writer had taught her to look for useful details in the every day. The entire office was a variety of browns—the carpet, the vinyl chairs and table, the print of the copse of trees and, of course, the doctor's outfit. Now, she recalled that Lacey had said brown was the new black. In the doctor's case this propensity toward brown was not about being hip. Chase thought green was supposed to be a soothing color. Maybe brown was the new green. Anyway, she felt she was sitting inside a walnut shell and she couldn't wait to get out. She hoped her dislike of brown, except maybe in potting soil, would not affect the doctor patient relationship. She had a feeling it would.

"You can pick up the sample pack at the Parker Clinic." Dr. Robicheck turned around in her chair. Her Doris Day cut neatly to the chin went with her. Her round spectacles caught the light from the window. "Don't worry about this. This drug will help you and you should not be embarrassed to tell your people."

It was like she knew that Chase was keeping it a secret. Only Gitana and Lacey knew about it. She'd never tell her mother. "Sure, why?"

"It's hard to see change in oneself and sometimes outside intervention is necessary." She handed Chase the script.

Chase disliked the word "intervention." It sounded a lot like incarceration. She wasn't that crazy. Intervention for what? Okay, so she'd been in self-denial about her condition, the mood swings, the ups and downs. But self-denial was in her genes. Admitting one was crazy was like crossing the Kalahari—full of sand with thorn brush and queer creatures and it frightened her.

"So there are no worries. We'll take care of this. You'll be much better." Dr. Robicheck got up indicating the session was over.

Chase got up as well glad to be out of the uncomfortable chair and away from her new psychiatrist. They shook hands.

"Make an appointment for three weeks from now. We'll re-evaluate."

"Sure thing," Chase said, hoping she didn't appear absolutely ecstatic for being dismissed. Three weeks was like spring break for a kid.

She went out to the receptionist to make an appointment. A twenty-something scrub-clad woman with a blond pixie-cut studied the computer screen trying to find Chase an appointment. "Got it," she said. She didn't bother to ask if the appointment worked with Chase's schedule. Instead, she wrote the time and date on the card and handed it to her.

"Great," Chase said, studying the card. She smiled, gritted her teeth and walked out.

Once in the car, she called Lacey.

"How did it go?" Lacey asked.

"Great."

"When you say, 'great' it means it sucked. What happened?"

"My therapist talks like Dr. Ruth and has the sensitivity of Nurse Diesel."

"In the film *High Anxiety*." Lacey loved movies and trivia. It seems she knew stuff that no one in their right mind would bother with. Chase attributed this to Lacey's lack of a full-time job and the need for very little sleep.

During sleep, Chase had read, the brain dumps files, ridding itself of daily clutter. Lacey didn't sleep much, so she didn't dump useless information. Whenever Chase was in need of some particular piece of oddness for a book, she called Lacey, who was happy to help.

"Well, you can always see someone else. The network is huge." Then, Lacey changed tactics. "Shopping will make you feel better."

"You're right." Chase backed out of a parking space and turned onto Wyoming Street.

"You want me to get you a Chai to go?" Lacey asked.

"Sure." She was picking her up at Starbucks—Lacey's second-home. "We'll have to go to the Parker clinic first to get my drug sample pack."

"A sample pack? To see if you like it or not?"

"How the hell do I know?" She stopped at the light. "I'll see you in five." She clicked off and got on the freeway. She really didn't want to be a lunatic on her way to get a sample pack, but she couldn't live on a roller coaster either.

Chase wondered if extending herself in the writing department had anything to do with it. Perhaps all the subdivision of self that her many imaginary worlds demanded was getting the best of her, stretching the limits of her mind and it was starting to crack.

Perhaps, she should consider telling her people to keep an eye out. They could watch her. She would choose Gitana and Lacey for starters. She felt as if she were electing a bipartisan committee to keep her normal.

She got off the freeway and drove into the mall parking lot. Lacey was waiting outside holding a Chai and looking benevolent and understanding. She flounced into the car seat, glanced at Chase and said, "You look the same."

"What? Psychiatric evaluations alter your physical appearance?"

"Who knows?" She scrutinized Chase, who didn't move the car an inch.

"I'm supposed to have people watch me."

"And you picked me?" Lacey reached over and squeezed Chase's shoulder, almost spilling her Chai.

Chase watched her. Lacey acted like she never got picked for basketball in PE class and her moment of glory had just arrived. "You've known me for a long time."

"So, I'd be a great observer. Look what I found at Borders." She pulled the book out of her enormous purse and handed it to Chase. "It's Kate Millet's *The Looney-Bin Trip*. She was crazy

30

too—only she took lithium."

Chase exited the parking lot and pulled up to the stop sign. A red SUV ran the stop. Chase honked and flipped off the driver. "That's right, rules are just for stupid people. How hard is it to comprehend that a four-way stop is part of the social compact? You have to adhere to the social compact. If we don't adhere to it, anarchy ensues."

Lacey had tuned her out and was instead tuning in the radio. "Why do you always listen to NPR? It's so boring." She found a hip-hop station.

"Because I learn things." Chase got back on the freeway and headed up town to the Parker clinic.

"Oh, it's my song." Lacey began to sway to the beat.

"Who sings it?"

"Shakira. It's part hip-hop and Latino salsa. I love it."

Chase listened to the lyrics. "My hips don't lie..." or at least that's what she heard. "What the hell does that mean? My hips don't lie. If that's the case the cerebral cortex is located behind the cervix. Just think, we won't be needing pap smears anymore. One's hips could give the doctor the A-OK signal."

"You're so literal." Lacey turned up the music and ignored her.

Chase spent the rest of the drive wondering what kinds of things a cervix would ponder. When she pulled into the parking lot of the clinic, she said, "You can wait here."

"And miss the chance to see some hunk of a doctor? Not on your life."

They made their way to the pharmacy down the hall from the horribly crowded waiting room. Chase handed over her script and the pharmacy tech disappeared into the rows of drugs.

An attractive blonde doctor walked by. She said hello to Chase. She and Lacey watched her walk down the hall. The doctor turned around and smiled at Chase.

Lacey was disgusted. "Why do you get all the action?"

"Because gay people are usually attracted to other gay people."

"But it's not fair. Why did you get the good looks?"

"I don't know what you're talking about." Whenever Chase looked in the mirror to check for toothpaste remnants on her chin or something hanging from her nose she saw a blond-haired woman with good teeth, a slim nose and a tolerably fit body—that was all.

Lacey continued her tirade. "Lesbians don't need to be good-looking. All they need is a large collection of flannel shirts and sensible shoes."

"That's complete and utter bigotry. I only have a few flannel shirts and you make trainers sound like square-heeled oxfords."

"What I meant," Lacey recanted, "Was that women are like chattel to men. Lesbians are interested in the entire package, not just the tits and ass part."

An elderly woman sitting at the edge of the waiting room gave them a disapproving glance.

"Be quiet," Chase said, poking Lacey in the ribs and nodding her head in the direction of the waiting room.

"Geriatric crew."

Chase poked her again. "When did you abandon your PC rhetoric?"

"Since I decided it was all crap and I should speak my mind. I don't use racial slurs. I draw the line there."

"But it's okay to abuse dykes and old people."

"All right, already I take it all back," Lacey said.

"Good."

The pharmacy tech returned. "I'm sorry the drug rep didn't come today with the samples and we're completely out."

"When will he come again?" Chase asked.

"No telling, really." She tossed her brown ponytail and gave the appearance of caring by giving Chase a half grin and a hands up gesture. She gave the script back to Chase.

"What am I supposed to do with this?"

"You can take it to your regular pharmacy and they can fill it."

"Great." Chase turned around and muttered something

unflattering about the inefficiency of HMOs.

"Come on, we'll hit Smith's on Menaul and then we can go shopping," Lacey said.

"I hate that store. It's like grocery shopping in a shoebox and I get really claustrophobic."

"Chase." Lacey took her arm and escorted her to the parking lot. "Let's get the pills you need to be a safer saner person."

"All right."

They drove across town listening once again to Shakira singing about her hips not lying and something by the Black Eyed Peas about my hump, my hump, my lovely lady lumps. Chase rolled her eyes, thinking that this was what the world had come to, songs talking about body parts. And she was the crazy one.

The shoebox grocery store parking lot was full of cars. An old man in a black Crown Vic slowly pulled out of a spot, turning so that the long car was jammed up between the rows and it required much pulling forward and backing up before he got the car straight enough to pull out. Thoroughly exasperated, Chase said, "Why bother with the medication—the baby will be in college before we get parked."

"Chase, it's the middle of the day. These are retired people with diminished reflexes. Just thank God we don't have real jobs and have to suffer the after-work crowd. Now, those people are cutthroat."

Chase pulled into the spot vacated by the geriatric. It was not to her liking being right next to the cart return, thus putting her side panels at risk, but it would have to do. "I have a real job," she contended.

"No, Gitana has a real job. All you have to do is write fifteen a day, keep your editor happy by turning things in on time and kiss your publisher's ass once in a while to keep on her good side."

"I suffer from writer's cramp and chapped lips," Chase said. She puckered her lips and made kissing noises.

Lacey collected her enormous purse and they exited the car. They entered the store, careful to avoid people with diminished reflexes now armed with shopping carts. The line for the pharmacy was long.

Chase glanced at Lacey who was studying the labels of diet foods that lined the aisle. She sighed heavily and then whispered, "This is going to take forever."

"No, it's not. These people know what they're doing. Most of them have four-dollar prescriptions and pay in cash," Lacey responded not looking up.

"How do you know all this?"

"Duh, I have to get my birth control pills every month."

Having never bothered with contraception, this was news to Chase. She studied the older people in line. Waiting was always good for observation. She just had to get in the zone—that place where the person she observed made a picture in her mind, then she logged the details—their appearance, choice of shoes, their hands, the cadence of their voices, word choice, the banal stories they told to others. It all imprinted itself on her mind—stored away for future use.

Lacey broke her concentration. She picked up a Slim·Fast bar and asked, "Do you think this stuff tastes good?"

"No," Chase replied.

"Why not? It says it does."

"If something is supposed to have sugar in it and they take the sugar out it's like a house where you have removed the studs. What happens then?"

Lacey was an avid watcher of HGTV. It was like her college. Her eyes brightened. "Why it would collapse."

"Consequently, sugar-free chocolate bars are studless."

Lacey wrinkled her brow. Chase smiled. Lacey wasn't one for quantum leaps.

A silver-haired well-coiffed woman waiting in line ahead of them turned around. "Honey, that stuff stinks."

She snatched it from Lacey and threw it at the magazine stand. She just missed the redneck with his butt crack showing as he leaned over to reach for the Low Rider magazine with a car and a woman with abnormally large breasts on the cover. He appeared not to notice the flying candy bar as he ogled the magazine.

"Wow, you've got an arm," Chase said. Not a softball player herself, she still admired the sport.

The woman smiled. She had sparkling white teeth and red lipstick—some of which was on her teeth. Chase admired that quality—if you're going to wear it, keep it on your lips and off your teeth. She suspected it was an expense thing—cheap stuff on the teeth, department store on the lips.

"Used to play fast pitch back in the day. I was a first-string pitcher."

Lacey was glaring at the redneck drooling over the magazine. "Could you hit that guy over there with the butt crack?"

"If I wanted to." The woman studied him and then pursed her lips in obvious contempt.

Lacey handed her a candy bar.

The woman smiled. "This is just between us." Chase and Lacey gave her my lips are sealed gesture.

The butt crack man stood unawares.

The silver-haired woman cocked her still lethal arm. "This is for the ladies, you big pervert." She let loose. The candy bar cold-cocked him in the back of the head. He turned around glaring, in search of the perpetrator.

Lacey was studying the label on a Slim·Fast can. The silver-haired woman looked straight ahead and then glanced at her watch affecting impatience. Chase picked up several cans of Slim·Fast as if to purchase them.

Finding no one to blame, he kicked the candy bar, rolled up the magazine tightly in his grubby paw, gave his pants a good yank and started to the checkout counter.

The silver-haired woman winked at them after she got her order. As she passed by she said, "Remember, girls, fight the good fight."

Finally Chase handed her script to a young man with a baby

skin face, round as a pumpkin. He studied the script. "What am I supposed to do with this?"

Incompetence always turned Lacey from nice girl into Cat Woman. Chase could tell she'd already been revved up by the butt crack episode and this poor bastard was going to get the brunt of it. "I don't want to tell you your job but two words—fill it."

Sometimes Lacey reminded Chase of her mother. Even their lexicons had similarities.

"You don't understand. We don't know what a sample pack is." His pumpkin face reddened.

"From what was explained to me, I start with the lowest available dose and gradually increase over a month long period," Chase said, hoping this would speed up the process.

The young man quickly looked up the drug. "This is an anticonvulsant." His eyes got large.

Lacey took full advantage of this. "That's right. Look at her. She could have a seizure at any moment."

Under the counter, Lacey kicked Chase in the shin. Chase doubled over in pain and groaned. "See, it's already starting. Do you want her to turn into a frothing maniac in the next five minutes?" Lacey said.

"I'll call the doctor. Please take a seat. We don't want her falling."

Lacey and Chase took a seat on the hard plastic bench at the side of the pharmacy. The geriatrics studied Chase like they were waiting for something to happen.

"Everyone's staring," Chase said.

"Seizures make people nervous," Lacey said.

"Ms. Banter, your order is ready."

At the counter the pumpkin boy handed her a cup of water. "I think you should take one right now."

Chase swallowed the tiny pink pill, wondering how drug companies decided on the shape and color of their medications. Then she took out her wallet and paid the twenty dollars.

As they walked out of the store, Chase said, "I feel better all ready."

Lacey rolled her eyes.

Chapter Six

"*When are you going to ask her?*" Lacey screamed into her phone.

Chase took her cell phone into the bathroom and closed the door quietly. She hoped the toast wouldn't burn in her absence. Due to the open floor plan and the subsequent lack of walls, sound carried and she didn't want Gitana to hear this conversation. They were probably the only people in the state who could sit on the toilet or take a bath and talk to the other one in the kitchen from upstairs. Thank God they didn't have any neighbors because they certainly didn't have any curtains.

"Today. I'm going to the greenhouse at lunchtime."

"Why there? It's not very romantic."

"Because I'm emotionally detached. I might get too intense and mushy and I'm not good at that. Besides, I'm paranoid and superstitious. All our friends who got married and had ceremonies in which a strange woman in a long burgundy robe muttered

38

marital incantations are split up now. So I figure if I do it in an odd or unusual way we'll last. Hopefully, the goddess of sorrow will be deceived. It's kind of like *Jude the Obscure* during the good parts."

"Are you taking your meds?"

"Religiously. Why? Don't I seem better?"

"You're not as crabby, but you're still not right. Really, marital incantations and the goddess of sorrow."

"All right, I admit that was over the top," Chase said.

"Call me after."

She heard the toast pop. She thought she was behaving better. She hadn't said anything mean to her editor, Ariana, despite the fact they were in the editing stage of Chase's eleventh moist mound saga, *Songs from the Open Window*. Ariana seemed to notice the change, commenting one day that Chase hadn't sworn at her in the last two phone calls.

She'd seen Dr. Robicheck three times so far and she wasn't giving Chase queer looks despite her admission of burying road-kill so in death the poor rabbits and prairie dogs could have dignity instead of ending up in people's tires or being picked to pieces by the ever present crows that sat perched on telephone lines. Dr. Robicheck noted it down on her yellow legal pad, a look of complete stoicism on her face. This lack of expression concerned Chase. She wondered if Dr. Robicheck was really listening or only pretending to the way Chase did when she was bored, letting her mind wander to someplace more interesting.

She buttered the toast, putting peanut butter on hers and marmalade on Gitana's. Gitana's toast was usually cold by the time Chase brought it up, but she didn't seem to care. Chase always got up early. She was like the dogs. Three sets of eyes, one human, two canine popped open like a Jack-in-the-Box triggered by the morning light filtering in through the window. Day had arrived, time to get up. Gitana slept late by their standards. Chase let the dogs out and then fed them their breakfast.

Chase seemed to need less sleep than other people, excepting

Lacey. Dr. Robicheck had asked about her sleeping pattern and she'd lied. Told her that she got a lot of exercise during the day and that she was very tired at night. She didn't tell her that she slept well at first, but then she'd wake up again in a couple of hours like the computer part of her brain had rebooted. Her thoughts would wind themselves around her until exhausted she fell back asleep again. Even then, her dreams would drift in and out and like a film director she ran parts over and over again, editing and rewriting until things turned out to her liking.

She didn't know why she felt she had to lie. It seemed like it was crucial to not let the doctor know about her most sacred place—the shrine of her imagination. Later she figured it out. She didn't want anyone tinkering with her mind. What if it screwed up her most precious possession—the ability to create? This was a room no one had the right to enter. It unnerved her that every shrink she'd met in her life was always very interested in her once they found out she was a writer, a real writer in their eyes because she was published. They were bigots. Being published was not the Holy Grail. She knew writers who deserved to be published more than she did.

A writer was a person who sat down, invented worlds and described what it was like using the best possible words they could find. She was not going to let Dr. Robicheck or anyone else into her fictional house of cards to forage. She invited people into this house and tried to put them at ease while she cooked up some surprises. She certainly didn't want that messed with. Now, the other parts of her life did need a little work and the good doctor was quite welcome to tinker with those.

She poured the coffee and put the toast on the tray and took it upstairs. Usually, the smell of coffee got Gitana's eyes open. She set the tray down and gathered up her medical instruments to give Gitana her morning exam. Gitana had insinuated that the daily blood pressure checking was not necessary, but Chase had ignored her.

Gitana opened her eyes. "Am I dreaming or is that real coffee?"

"Coffee is coffee. Decaf does not smell different."

She sat up and Chase puffed up the pillow behind her. "Ah, but there you are wrong. This is real coffee."

"It is. I looked it up on the Internet. Small doses of caffeine are not harmful," Chase said.

Gitana picked up the cup. She studied it. "It looks smaller."

"Oh, I hadn't noticed." She avoided her gaze. "Cream?"

"I never use cream." Gitana sniffed at the cup deeply and then took a sip.

"Dairy products build strong bones."

"I'm already taking prenatal vitamins." Gitana set her cup down and took a bite of toast.

Chase ignored her and added cream. Then she busied herself with the task of taking Gitana's blood pressure.

"Good, it's one-twenty over eighty." Then she looked in Gitana's ears.

"What exactly are you looking for?" She sipped her coffee.

"I'm not certain, but if something appears different we can immediately go to the doctor. I think it's a sound plan," Chase said.

"Like what exactly would look different? My eardrum would suddenly go missing?" She bit into her cold toast and eyed Chase suspiciously.

"You're not being very cooperative. In fact, I sense hostility."

"We used to make love in the morning, now we check vital signs." Gitana pursed her lips.

"Oh. Well, I can remedy that. It's all right?" Chase asked, having not researched about pregnancy and having sex.

"Yes." Gitana put her toast down.

Chase kissed her and unbuttoned her pajama top. The soft blue fabric fell away from Gitana's shoulders.

"We can do health care and body care," Chase said as she kissed Gitana's stomach.

"I'll agree to that, but you have to tell me one thing," she said, as she pulled Chase's T-shirt over her head.

41

"Anything." She slipped off Gitana's pajama bottoms and kissed her inner thigh.

"Are the coffee cups smaller?"

Chase murmured something as her tongue ran around Gitana's soft pink folds. Gitana moaned and Chase figured she no longer cared about the size of coffee cups.

Later that afternoon, Chase searched her closet for some decent clothes. Finally, she managed to locate a pair of black rayon trousers and a green dress shirt. After further rummaging and a variety of choice swear words, she found her Italian leather dress shoes. Had she known it would take this long to find an outfit she would have began earlier. She fixed her hair, giving it a good brush job, removing most of the snarls. If she could ever decide which of the seven lesbian hairstyles most suited her she would immediately go to a stylist and get the whole snarly mess cut off. Then she could be more comfortable and hip, but she couldn't make up her mind so she tried to remember to brush her hair more often and purchased high quality hair conditioners.

Satisfied with her appearance, she left the bathroom and took a quick peek in the nursery. Lacey had done a great job. The walls were a pale yellow and the baby furniture sky blue. She'd covered the wood floor with a plush rug with a sunflower border. Above the crib was a mobile of the planets. Toy cubbies, already full of safe but educational toys, ran along one wall. Chase went to the dresser, already full of cute little outfits, and opened the top drawer. She pulled out two burgundy boxes each containing a simple white gold ring. She studied the ring meant for Gitana.

"This is for you," she said, addressing the yet-to-be-born, Bud. "I'm not much of a conformist—so this is really hard for me." She wondered how many one-sided conversations she was going to have with her baby. "So I hope you appreciate the gravity of the situation."

She must remember not to tell her shrink about these conversations. She could only imagine what Dr. Robicheck would say. She didn't want any more information than was necessary on the yellow legal pad resting ominously on the doctor's knee.

She gave the dogs a biscuit and checked to make sure all the gates were locked—got to the garage and had to go back and check it all over again because she couldn't remember if she'd done it. Her medication wasn't helping her with her focusing problem. Dr. Robicheck had suggested meditation. She was supposed to find a class. It was low on her list of priorities. She'd have to remedy that before her next session or come up with a damn good excuse. She managed to get to the road before the panic attack hit. The car jostled so much on the dirt road that she couldn't pull up the call list registry on her cell phone. She stopped in the middle of the road and called Lacey as her neighbor Rusty came up behind her in his black Ram Charger truck. She resumed driving.

Lacey picked up immediately as if she'd been expecting this call.

"What if she doesn't accept?"

"What are you talking about?" Lacey said.

"What if Gitana won't marry me?"

"You two have been together forever."

"That doesn't guarantee anything." Chase checked her rearview mirror. Rusty was now way behind her. He drove very slowly on the road. People groaned in secret agony if they got stuck behind him. They all referred to the mile-and a-half- stretch of dirt road as "The Road" like it was an entity unto itself. She supposed it was. In the summer, it was bone dry and the dirt devils reminded Chase of the over-farmed prairies in *The Grapes of Wrath*. In the winter when it snowed, the juniper and pinon trees were frosted and she felt like she was driving in a snow globe. In the spring, when the snow melted off the mountains the road was a muddy disaster and it was necessary to drive very fast to avoid getting stuck in it. Once she found herself bogged down in her Passat and had to be towed out by a neighbor with a tractor. Every season presented its own challenge and getting down the road in one piece was always considered a boon.

Chase, having momentarily drifted off, found that Lacey had moved on to other subjects. "Do you think that boob cream really works?"

"Boob cream?" Chase was now safely off the road and on the smooth pavement of the county road. Her car purred with happiness.

"The one they advertise on the radio. It says it will increase your boobs by three cup sizes and make them look perky."

"Have you lost your mind? Cream can't possibly augment your breasts." Chase recalled that Lacey was obsessed with her breast size. She was convinced that men would be more interested in her if she had bigger boobs.

"But the ad says it's a new drug they're trying out."

"So what if this experimental cream turns your boobs green and they become covered with warts."

There was a silence. "I see your point."

"You have nice breasts. Stop worrying about it."

Chase was now stuck behind a tractor tooling down the two-lane county road at twelve miles an hour. She was going to have to pass.

"I better go. Why don't you listen to NPR? They don't have any of those kinds of ads."

"Boring," Lacey said. She clicked off.

Chase waited for a safe place to pass and then blew past the tractor, barely avoiding the wad of tobacco spittle that exited the farmer's mouth as she passed him. "Yuck!"

In avoiding the spittle trail she nearly hit a rabbit. That would not do. So far so good, no carnage to stop and bury, she thought. She wanted to get to the greenhouse in time for lunch. She'd only left herself a half an hour window. She cursed herself for not leaving earlier, but there had been the scavenger hunt for a decent outfit. It would not do to propose marriage in a T-shirt and shorts.

She pulled into the parking lot with five minutes to spare. The greenhouse grounds were abuzz with activity. May was one of their busiest months. The help, who were distinguished from the customers by their green aprons over white shirts and khaki shorts, were intent on business. Chase cut through the hothouse and toward Gitana's office. The hothouse smelled of earth and flowers and damp. The sweet smells of the various orchids did a little dance across her olfactory system like butterflies landing on flower petals. She inhaled deeply and her contextual memory drew her back to a place and time... She reined herself in.

Nora spotted her and came over. The heat was unbearable. Chase always felt like she'd been transported to some Amazonian jungle while remaining dressed in a traveling suit of good English wool.

"Long time no see," Nora said, her face beaming. She looked larger in her green overalls and straw cowboy hat—a bit like Mr. Green Jeans in drag. Maybe Captain Kangaroo wasn't who he purported to be, Chase conjectured.

The first time Chase had met Nora was in college and it had been a distinctly uncomfortable occasion. She had snatched Chase—after ascertaining she was the offender—from the hallway where she waited for Gitana outside her American Lit class. Nora had been dating Gitana at the same time Chase was spending every afternoon in her arms. Nora, it seemed, had discovered this, and held her by the neck against the bulletin board announcing upcoming readings. Gitana had fortuitously shown up before Chase lost consciousness and demanded Nora put her down, explaining that Chase was her soul mate and they were meant to be together. Nora was a philosophy major and big into existentialism. She dropped Chase who instantly crumpled on the hallway floor.

"You haven't been here in forever not since..." Nora trailed off. She looked at Chase's outfit then down at her own apron. She decided it was clean enough and hugged Chase.

Chase, in the meantime, studied Nora's belt to see if all the tools were properly attached and then hugged her back. Nora had hugged her the last time she'd been at the nursery and a

45

small potting spade had come loose, landing on Chase's foot, which, owing to the Keen sandals she was wearing, had lacerated her big toe. She hadn't cried that time like when she hurt her shoulder, but she had used a lot of swear words in succession that shocked most everyone who happened to be around.

"Did it heal okay?" She glanced down at Chase's foot.

"Yes, thank you. It's fine."

Chase's presence had been noted. The greenhouse cleared out—all employees not helping customers made a hasty exit. "I always seem to have that effect on people here." She frowned.

"Think of the power. Gitana is in her office," said Nora, not meeting Chase's eye.

Chase went to the office. It was a small room painted a pale blue with Victorian lithographs of orchids with their scientific names engraved at the bottom of each frame placed tastefully about the walls. Chase had given them to Gitana for their fourth anniversary. She'd spent hours on eBay trying to outbid other freaky orchid people. It had been most frustrating but her diligence had paid off. Gitana had been delighted. The rest of the office was pure function, and thanks to Chase, very ergonomic with its cherry wood desk and file cabinets. Gitana looked up from her paperwork. "I knew it was you."

"How?"

"I saw everyone running."

"I should be offended by that. Is it because I tried to drown one of your employees in the watering trough because she was making advances on you?" Chase inquired.

"I think that might be it. The employees still talk about it."

"Did you fire her?"

"No, she quit and thankfully we didn't end up with a lawsuit." She straightened up her papers. "What brings you here?" She leaned back in her chair and looked suspiciously at Chase's clothes.

"I want to get married."

46

Gitana sat up quickly. "Don't you think that's a rather moot point?"

"I knew it. You're creeped out." She sat down in the nearest chair, pouted and sighed heavily doing all three things almost simultaneously.

Gitana got up and put her hand on Chase's shoulder. "Now, why don't you tell me what this is really about?"

"I just think with the baby coming that we shouldn't be living in sin. It won't set a proper example. We don't have to have a ceremony or anything because that might jinx us, but I could give you this and you could say 'I do,' and we'd be all set." Chase pulled the ring box out of her pocket. She opened it and peered inside. "Wait, that one is mine." She dug in her other pocket. She'd put them in different pockets so she could keep them straight but had now forgotten which was which. Opening the other box, she said, "Okay, got it all straight now."

Gitana studied the rings. "They look the same to me."

Chase turned it so she could see the inscription on the inside which read, "I will love you forever."

"What does your ring say?"

"Something like that," Chase said evasively.

Gitana eyed her. "Let's see it."

Chase reluctantly handed over the ring. Gitana read the inscription aloud. "Safe, sane and successful."

"I know it's not very romantic, but I saw it as pertinent. Now can we get on with it?"

Gitana smiled. "All right." She stuck out her hand and Chase put the ring on. She peered down at it. "I like it." Then she put the other ring on Chase's finger.

"So I know we haven't had time to write out our vows, but I think this might suffice." Chase pulled out a neatly folded piece of paper from her breast pocket. She cleared her throat. "We promise to love each other for at least another eighteen years, argue as little as possible and not to commit any form of adultery.

And I will stay on my medication."

Gitana laughed, kissed her softly and said, "I do."

Chapter Seven

"I can't help it. My protagonist has to be fit," Jasmine said to the other five members of the writers group sitting in Chase's office. She peered down at her manuscript and back up at the group. "I mean how else is he going to chase down the bad guys?"

Chase took a deep breath. She did a lot of deep breathing when she was in her writers group. Losing your temper with one's peers was poor form according to Gitana, not to mention rude. She'd told Chase, "Remember you're all here as allies to the creative process and not mortal enemies." Gitana was correct, of course. So Chase did her best. She summoned up diplomacy and took deep breaths. "Jasmine, most bad guys sit in dimly lit restaurants and bars where they eat very unhealthy foods. Those guys are a heart attack in the making."

Alma offered, "Why don't you have your protagonist exercise at home? He could have a treadmill and while he's running his five miles have all these insights into the crimes he's trying to solve."

Jasmine pursed her lips. She looked a lot like a grown-up Shirley Temple complete with blond ringlets and the endlessly sweet smile—ever eager for a lollipop. The lip pursing destroyed the image as did the tight, low-cut jeans and the stuffed halter top. Shirley Temple all grown up was hot. Chase tried really hard not to look at her boobs, remembering the T-shirt she'd seen in a catalog that read, "Tell your boobs to stop staring at me." That's how she felt right now.

"I just don't get it," Jasmine moaned. "Everything starts out great and then it's like a beacon, the gym call. I put in the scene and bam I'm stuck with a protagonist doing bench presses. He has great pecs but no soul." Jasmine got up and threw the manuscript in the trash can.

Luckily, Chase had emptied it earlier or the manuscript might have gone missing in the vortex of detritus.

Alma got up and retrieved the manuscript from the trash can. Bo shook his finger at Jasmine. It had taken Alma a good minute and a half to get up because she was sixty-three and slightly arthritic, but she managed. Alma Lucero was a much better person than Chase.

The thought had crossed her mind to go and retrieve it from the dust bin—like all the other things she ought to do—pick up litter when she saw it on the sidewalk, smile at a crying baby at the supermarket checkout counter, or offer assistance to the old woman trying to get a package in her trunk at the post office. She feared being rebuked—told to piss off when all she wanted to do was good. She buried roadkill. No language was required. No permission granted—only a sigh of relief from the Universe that something was being put right by someone who cared. For her this worked.

"Young lady," Alma lectured Jasmine, "need I remind you that every word is precious. A gift from on high. To be so disrespectful is dangerous. To anger the muse is to court a dry spell. To show disfavor with the creative force is to bring down the wrath—"

"I got it," Jasmine said, snatching the slightly crumpled stack of papers.

Alma was writing *The Book of Forgotten Moments*. It was part memoir, part rumination on the mysteries of life and part philosophy on the nature of love. Alma had a lovely wrinkled face, high cheekbones and gray green eyes, her white hair was cut spiky and she dressed in loose-fitting organic cotton shirts and trousers. She wrote the most gorgeous sentences. She had Virginia Woolf's one-hundred and eighty-one word sentence beat by five words. Chase loved when they read Alma's work.

Alma's book was literary and probably would never be published just for that reason. Chase felt like Alma taught them about using words to paint pictures in the reader's mind. The rest of them, Chase included, wrote plot-driven fiction. Theirs were stories where point A led to point B in a quick and concise manner. Alma's stories were filled with images of the garden, the sky, the raging river, the seedy motel with its dirty linen and the lost memory. Their work was a rush to the finish. Hers was a meandering path through a wildflower garden.

"Here, give the pages to me," Chase said. Everyone stared at her with interest. "I need a few minutes with them."

"Why don't I get us all coffee," Bo said. A good-looking, stylishly dressed dark-haired beauty with his cleft chin and aquiline nose, he should have been a model for International Male, but instead while working at Starbucks he wrote guy-to-guy mysteries, as yet unsold, and short porn stories for fag magazines.

"I'll help," Delia offered while gazing with apparent admiration at Chase's soon to be displayed abilities.

Delia had made it more than evident that she was in total awe of Chase and would fuck her on demand. Chase found this slightly intriguing but also repulsive. She was thirty-seven and Delia was twenty-three. She realized that at Delia's age she had been like that, fascinated by older women, but unlike Delia had no confidence to pursue them. Rather she had engaged in hero worship and fantasies of being discovered as a misunderstood genius and subsequently mentored and fucked senseless. She would never admit this to anyone. Time had been a great and brutal teacher and she'd become the older woman.

While Bo and Delia clanked the coffee things around, peering and whispering in her direction, Chase reconstructed Jasmine's twenty pages—slashing and rearranging, until she got a sense of the plot moving in a better and clearer direction. When she looked up, Delia was handing her a cup of coffee and Alma was smiling at her with sagacity.

"Take a look." Chase handed the manuscript to Jasmine.

Jasmine quickly perused the pages while the others waited. She studied the manuscript like an ER doctor ascertaining the patient's cuts and bruises. She looked up indignant. "You cut the gym scene, made my protagonist fat and ugly and put the murder on the first page. How could you?" Jasmine crossed her legs and scowled at Chase.

Shirley Temple was pissed, Chase thought. She looked like someone had just stolen her umbrella drink.

"I think it sounds brilliant. Can I see it?" Bo asked.

"Feel free." Jasmine handed him the manuscript as if it were used toilet paper. "I don't like it anymore."

"That's good," Alma said.

"Why?" Jasmine asked. She sipped her coffee, her eyes still blazing.

"Because you've divorced yourself from it."

"I don't get it," Delia said, as she read the manuscript over Bo's shoulder.

"Now, Jasmine can work on it without being invested in every word. She's too close to it," Chase said. She put more milk in her cup. Bo always brought coffee from Starbucks and she found it much too strong and too many cups gave her heart palpitations.

"Exactly," Alma said. "And making your protagonist so different from you will make you create a character instead of a male version of yourself which is what you are doing."

"Is it that obvious?" Jasmine asked, chastened.

Bo handed the manuscript to Alma.

"Whit Tamberlaine, detective extraordinaire, is pretty much you with a dick attached," Delia said, smiling.

"Oh, my," Jasmine said. She appeared to be contemplating what that would be like.

Chase had had a dream once where she woke up with a penis and spent the rest of the dream trying to convince everyone, Gitana included, that she was still a lesbian. Freud would have had a heyday with that one.

"Jasmine, this can work. Just start from here and move forward. Find a photo of a rotund man, make a bio for him and start every chapter with someone doing something. You'll be all set. You can make Whit into a great character. Pretty people have it easy so make his life hard, make people treat him shitty and it will make the story much more interesting," Chase said. She had learned all of this the hard way from her much respected yet sadistic editor.

"How do you do that?" Delia asked.

"Years of having my editor rip my work to shreds—it makes for tough skin."

"But how can you not care when your creation is a part of you?" Jasmine asked, obviously still smarting from the attack on her manuscript.

"To be a writer you have to be a cannibal," Chase replied.

"Now, I need an explanation of that one," Alma said. She refilled her mug from the decanter on the table. She sat back and waited, her eyes shining with interest.

Chase smiled. They probably thought she was pulling shit out of her ass. She had written her first novel when she was twenty. The first two went unpublished, eleven others had followed that were published. Over a million words in print, but she'd written more than she could care to count. Writing entailed actually sitting down and connecting ideas, stringing together words to make sentences that made paragraphs and consequently pages. In the rewrite, you cut off pieces. You took stuff from elsewhere in your experience, you read everything you could get your hands on and you learned from it, you cannibalized. You had to be tenacious and ultimately vicious or you never got there.

Chase went to the closet on the back wall of the writing studio and pulled the doors open. Inside was a stack of black and white marbled composition books stacked one on top of the other, floor to ceiling, rows and rows of them.

"What's that?" Delia asked.

"Probably every word she's ever written," Bo replied. He got up to take a closer look. "Holy shit."

"And out of all that came thirteen novels." She picked up her stack of published books that sat on top of the notebooks. "That would never have been published without the necessary reduction and distillation of all this."

"Consequently, you cannibalized your own work," Alma said. "You put all your not so well-chosen words, bad scenes and unclear descriptions into the meat grinder and come up with something meaningful and understandable."

"Precisely," Chase replied, shutting the closet doors.

"I get it," Jasmine said. She rolled up her manuscript and swatted her thigh as if the thought were a fly.

Chase swore she saw the glint of savagery, a necessity for any writer, glistening in Jasmine's eyes.

There was a knock at the French doors. It was Gitana. Chase motioned her in. She smiled and said her hello's to the group. "I'm sorry to interrupt, but I need to talk to you for a minute. We've got familial snafu."

Chase nodded. "I'll be right back." She noticed that Delia didn't take her eyes off Gitana. She did look quite handsome in a pair of khaki shorts, nicely displaying her tanned and shapely calves, and a lavender tank top with a white orchid silk-screened on the front and the words, "live simply" in lowercase letters which revealed her nice breasts and strong arms.

They went out to the deck. Chase shut the door. "What's up?"

"It's Graciela. She's in jail."

"What did she do?" Chase hoped Gitana's younger sister hadn't done something horrible like stabbing one of her many girlfriends in a jealous rage. She was the completely out-of-control wild child.

"She got caught cow tipping."

"What the hell is that?" Chase's only notion of tipping involved waiters.

"Cows sleep upright. You sneak up on them and give them a shove and they fall over in such a way that they can't get up. The farmers don't care for this. She and some friends came up from the city to Moriarty and got caught by one of the ranch hands who called the police. Graciela needs bail or she'll have to stay until her court date."

"When's that?"

"Whenever the judge sees fit."

"So she could rot in jail until then. Just think of it, a lifesentence for cow tipping." Chase laughed.

Gitana frowned.

"It would keep her out of trouble."

"We can set bail, but Mama won't do it. She says it serves the heathen right."

Gitana's mother, Jacinda, always referred to Graciela as the heathen if she was only slightly peeved and devil's spawn if she was furious. She lit a prayer candle for Graciela every day at morning mass and another at Evensong. Gitana figured her mother could have sent them both to graduate school with the money she spent on candles.

"So you want to set bail?"

"Chase, the Moriarty County Jail is full of rednecks. I don't think it's the safest place for a sassy lesbian."

"Gotcha. We'll set bail and then hide her up here for the weekend. That means she goes nowhere. Your mother has spies all over town. She'll know what we did and we'll be on the same shit list as Graciela."

"I love you," Gitana said, giving her a quick kiss on the cheek.

"Call one of those bail bondsmen kind of people and they can tell us how to do it. I've never gotten someone out of jail." She smiled at Gitana and went back inside.

"You can put your tongue back in your mouth now," Bo told Delia. She scowled at him.

Chase eyed her suspiciously.

"I totally understand why you don't take me up on my offer. Your wife is hot," Delia said.

"That's enough out of you, young lady. In case you've forgotten, you're talking about Chase's life partner, not some slick chick at the gay bar," Alma said.

Chase smirked. It always seemed so out of character whenever Alma used slang.

"What offer?" Bo asked. He looked from Delia to Chase.

Jasmine was still studying her manuscript and didn't look up, but she said, "Delia wants to sleep with Chase, but Chase declined the offer. That's a good decision, if you ask me." She continued to be engrossed in her work.

Chase threw her mechanical pencil at her, narrowly missing her head. "Big mouth." This time Jasmine did look up.

"How come she knew and we didn't?" Bo asked.

Gay men were the worst gossips, worse than women, worse than women who lived in tiny European villages, Chase thought. "Because she happened to be standing in the hallway when the aforementioned proposition occurred."

Chase had immediately told Gitana lest she be guilty by omission.

Alma picked up the *Writer's Digest* from the coffee table, rolled it up and swatted Delia with it. "Have you no shame."

Delia shrugged. "Never hurts to try."

Alma swatted her again.

"All right, I was out of line," Delia admitted.

"That's better. Now, let's get back to the business at hand," Alma said, picking up her copy of Jasmine's manuscript.

Chase smiled. For as much as they irritated her, she liked the writers group. Writing was a solitary pursuit and it was nice to have fellow travelers from time to time.

Chapter Eight

"How's my favorite un-in-law?" Graciela said. She was dancing with the dogs, one set of front paws of each dog on her forearms and singing, "It's raining dogs, hallelujah," instead of men, her homage to a much played song in the gay bars during the Nineties. "It's raining dogs, hallelujah," she continued much to Chase's chagrin as she entered the sunroom. The writers had left and their new houseguest had arrived.

"I'm fine. How's the incorrigible one doing? Did you like the prison food?"

"Absolutely epicurean."

Graciela was Gitana's spiky-haired younger sister and there was a lot of family resemblance—the same soulful, when it was expedient, almond-shaped eyes, slightly turned up nose and sculpted lips. Graciela was stouter and taller. Gitana had been in charge of their relationship until Graciela grew big enough to pin her down and demand obedience, which was nearly always forthcoming as Gitana couldn't breathe.

Gitana smirked. "She cost us a five pop."

"Five hundred dollars. You hardly look worth it and you smell."

"It's cow shit. Maybe I should go take a shower."

"I think that's a great idea," Gitana said. She shooed the dogs outside. Graciela had wound them up and they needed to decompress. "Go play."

They took off, running a figure-eight pattern around the grove of trees, chasing one another.

"Nice ring you got there, sis. What's the occasion?"

Chase rubbed Gitana's belly. She got the reference immediately. Graciela had a new girlfriend and had disappeared into the land of we're-having-sex-and-can't-be-bothered-with-the-rest-of-the-world so she hadn't heard any of the news.

"You should come around more often," Chase said. She straightened out the dog beds which had gotten dragged around the room earlier.

"Dude, how'd you do that?" Graciela's question was addressed to Chase.

"I grew an extra part like the kits that grow sea monkeys. I bought it off the Internet."

Graciela gaped at Chase's crotch. Chase and Gitana burst out laughing.

"I knew it was a joke. I did."

"No, you didn't," Gitana said.

"For a minute, maybe," Graciela said, coming over to stroke Gitana's belly. "I didn't know you guys were planning on having a baby."

"We weren't," Chase said.

"What the fuck? It's not like Gitana's birth control failed."

"She was having, or rather she was supposed to be having, a pap smear. Next door there was a woman having artificial insemination. The nurse got the charts mixed up."

"Okay, now that's freaky. Mama must be pretty stoked. She

always wanted a grandbaby and with the dyke sisters the forecast didn't look good."

"Well, if you weren't such a copycat," Gitana said.

Chase opened the door and dumped out the dogs' dirt-filled water bowl and refilled it with the hose. Jane often used the water bowl as a ball wash for her muddy tennis balls.

"I couldn't help it," Graciela said.

Gitana, tired of standing, sat in one of the chairs in the sunroom. Graciela lounged on one of the banquets, brushing aside the dirt. The dogs liked the banquets as well.

"But according to most scientific evidence genetics do not play a part in determining sexual persuasion," Chase said, as she straightened out the coatrack. She looked around the room and deemed it tidy.

"I know I've been out of the loop, but Mama would have told me, right?"

"She doesn't know yet. We're going to tell her when we drop you off Sunday night after you're released from jail."

"She thinks I'm still in jail," Graciela said. She pulled her cell phone out of her pocket.

"Yes, which means you're spending the weekend here in our custody. I'm not getting on Mama's shit list. She thinks you deserve to stay in jail," Gitana informed her.

"Oh," Graciela said, looking mournfully at her cell phone.

Chase could tell Graciela was weighing her options. Jail was bad, but the quiet country life wasn't necessarily better. "Tonight, we can watch the second season of *The L Word*, which I'm sure you haven't seen because you're always out living it up and Saturday night I invited my writers group for dinner."

Graciela twirled her forefinger in indication of her enthusiasm.

"One of the women, Delia, writes erotic lesbian stories and her fictional shenanigans put yours to shame. She wants to meet you."

Gitana gave Chase a look. "Please don't encourage her."

"They would have crossed paths eventually. They both go to the bar. At least this way, we can monitor it."

"This is sounding better already. I should text Andrea and tell her I'm out of commission for the weekend. She's not going to like that. I hope you have beer." Graciela wrote a quick text message.

Chase watched her fingers fly across the keypad. "I wish I could type that fast."

Graciela smiled. "Lots of practice."

"Like I don't practice. Come on, let's go get a beer."

They went inside to the kitchen. Chase got both of them a Corona and cut up a lime, inserting a slice into the bottles.

Gitana was counting dinnerware. "Chase, I don't think we have enough plates or proper glasses for a dinner party."

Chase took a swig of beer and went to peer in the cupboard. Graciela sat at the kitchen island and texted her response to what appeared to be a vitriolic message from Andrea. "Boy, is she pissed."

"No fault but your own," Gitana said.

Gitana was right—they didn't have enough dinnerware. They never entertained and over the years things had been broken and never replaced. This had come to Chase's attention from time to time after loading the dishwasher and discovering there was not one remaining plate, fork, spoon or dish to be had in the cupboards.

"We just don't have dinner parties. I mean, usually," Gitana said as she looked in the flatware drawer.

"It's part of my new socialization plan. I don't want the baby to grow up to be a hermit. The kid will be weird before school even starts. We can't have that. I'll take Graciela shopping. She can go in disguise. Do you still have that floral print summer dress?"

"I'm not wearing a fucking dress."

Chase laughed. Gitana said, "Now, that I'd like to see. Mama wouldn't recognize you at least."

61

"I'll go naked before I wear a dress."

"All right, but you are going to wear a ball cap and dark glasses," Chase said.

"No Williams-Sonoma," Gitana said, pouring a glass of lemonade.

"You read my mind. How about the Pottery Barn?"

"That'll work."

Chase sniffed at the pitcher of lemonade. "Is that fresh squeezed?"

"Yeah, she picked them off the lemon tree out back," Graciela said, still texting furiously.

"Of course not. It's one of those powdered mixes."

Chase peered at the pitcher of lemonade. Graciela got a glass and poured it half full and then she added beer. Her phone chimed and she sat back down to finish the texting argument with Andrea.

"That's disgusting," Chase said.

"No, it's not. The lemonade tastes fine to me," Graciela said, smacking her lips.

"How would you know? You put beer in yours."

"What's wrong with the lemonade?" Gitana asked.

"It's full of chemicals," Chase said, snatching the pitcher away and pouring it down the drain. "It's bad for the baby."

"She's going to be a real pain in the ass," Graciela commented to Gitana.

"She already is."

Chase ignored them. She was making out a list of needed dishware. "Do we have a tablecloth?"

"I don't think so."

"Linen napkins?"

"No."

Chase added those to her list. She sipped her beer and peered in cupboards again. "Serving platter?"

"No." Gitana opened the freezer and read the label on a can of frozen orange juice.

"Let me see the ingredients. It might have polysorbate five or something," Chase said. She read the label. "It's fine. Concentrated orange juice. That's good."

Graciela rolled her eyes.

"If you prefer lemonade I'll pick you up some organic lemons," Chase said, trying to be conciliatory.

"What are we having for eats at this dinner party?" Graciela asked.

"Something good," Chase said, not meeting Gitana's gaze.

"Like what?" she asked.

"Oh, I thought we'd have a rack of lamb." Chase didn't look at her. She couldn't cook worth a shit and everyone knew it. Simple fare she could handle, but the exotic usually ended badly.

"Why don't we have steak instead? We could put them on the George Foreman. A rack of lamb would heat up the house," Gitana said.

Although it was late April it was hardly ungodly hot in the evenings, but Chase got her drift. "Good point. We'll go shopping first thing in the morning. You can push the cart," she said, pointing at Graciela.

"I can hardly wait." Graciela went to the pantry.

Chase watched as she raided it, most likely searching for unhealthy snacks that were no longer allowed in the house. She came out with a package. "What the hell are these?"

"Rice cakes. She's going to need an outfit. Her current one is a little too informal."

"For a dinner party with close friends?" Gitana said.

"She's dressed like a Fascist," Chase said, referring to Graciela's Army and Navy store attire. "We'll hit Macy's."

"How about Old Navy? Let's try and keep this within the budget."

Chase watched Graciela munch rice cakes. "We'll have to be thrifty."

Graciela said, "What's wrong with my outfit?"

"Aside from looking like a Fascist, we can't run the washer

right now because it keeps tripping the pump. The electrician gets here on Monday."

"Can I still have a shower?"

"Yes, the water heater works fine. But not a long one," Gitana added.

"I'll get her a nice dress shirt too. She can wear it to the baptism. I'm not having a Fascist show up in church," Chase said.

"Baptism?" Gitana said. "What if we don't want the baby to be Catholic?"

"Like your mother would allow for anything else. When Bud grows up, Bud can decide to be a Buddhist, a Methodist or a Quaker or any of the other saner denominations. You don't want your mother spraying the child with holy water every time we come to visit like she does to Graciela—the heathen. I mean as long as Bud doesn't get into mortification of the flesh, I'm cool."

"Who's Bud?" Graciela said.

"That's what Chase calls the baby. She got tired of the he/she thing."

Chase got them both another beer.

"Can we go sit on the deck?" Gitana said.

"Are you all right? Do I need to call the nurse hotline?"

"I'm fine. I just want to watch the sunset. It's so pretty this time of year."

"Sounds good to me," Graciela said, grabbing her beer and the package of rice cakes.

Chase noticed. "See, the rice cakes are good. They just take a little getting used to."

"No, they're disgusting, but I'm desperate."

"You've should've loaded up on prison food while you were there," Chase said.

"I don't eat corned beef hash."

Chase grabbed a stack of magazines—*Martha Stewart's Living*, *Bon Appetit* and *Sunset Magazine*.

"Going to do a little light reading?" Graciela said. Her phone gave a beep indicating she had a text message. She flipped it open. "Shit, she's still pissed."

"I'm planning the menu."

Gitana sighed heavily.

"I'll keep it simple." Chase opened the French doors that led out onto the deck. The dogs got up from their dirt nap. She pulled two dog biscuits from her magic pockets—or at least the dogs thought of them as such, because biscuits always magically appeared from them. They gobbled them quickly and then went to explore some movement in the tree grove.

They all sat down in high-backed wooden chairs with matching green pillows, something Chase had seen in a magazine on deck life. She was very much into how things looked. The pink and orange of the sunset caught the wispy edges of the cirrus clouds. Chase always thought that the sky and the clouds were the canvas of the Creator who painted watercolor portraits for the delight of his/her beloved creatures. She contentedly flipped through her magazines, looking for ideas on how to decorate the table, which wine to serve and potential side dishes. She wanted everything to be perfect.

In the world of her mind, the weather would be good, the food even better, and everyone would be good-looking and smart. Everything would start like that until her muse—the dark, ironic comedian—got hold of the scene and everything fell to crap. She would devour Chase's beautiful imaginary world, spitting out great chunks of falsehood and making fun of the world's foibles and demonstrating how failure and dashed hopes were much more interesting than perfection.

Chase glanced over at Gitana who looked the picture of serenity as she gazed out on the mountains with the green of the scrub just starting to blossom—the yellow flowers of the rabbit bush and the wild purple asters bursting forth as if afraid of missing their arrival date.

Chase brought herself back to the task at hand. "So got any ideas for side dishes?" She hadn't found anything within her limited abilities in the magazines.

"Go to Costco and get those medallions…" Gitana said.

Chase interceded. "You mean those little round steaks with bacon wrapped around them." She wanted to be clear about this.

"Yes, they're filet mignons but very well priced. Then get two bags of fresh artichokes, a couple loaves of sourdough bread, a tub of spinach dip, a bag of fifty count shrimp with cocktail sauce and a bag of russet potatoes," Gitana instructed.

"Will you write this down?"

"I'll make a list."

"And I can buy all this at Costco?" Chase inquired, hoping she wasn't going to have to run all over town.

"Yes."

"Why do I subscribe to these magazines?" She smacked the cover of the *Bon Appetit.*

Graciela looked up from her continuing text argument and smirked.

"Because we all like to dream. We imagine the possibility and loathe the reality of doing it," Gitana said. She finished her orange juice and smiled patiently at Chase.

"That fucking bitch!" Graciela screamed at the phone while her fingers flew across the keyboard.

"We're going to have to talk to her about her language," Chase said, remembering that she'd said "fuck" seven times so far today.

Gitana nodded.

"Does everyone do this thing?" Chase jabbed a finger at the phone.

"Texting is very popular. I have to reprimand the crew at the greenhouse all the time. They're supposed to be working not texting their friends. I find them holed up in the oddest places—I caught Josh behind the manure pile one day. It was disgusting," Gitana said.

"Why don't they just call instead of texting? It seems like talking would be more expedient than all this finger flying."

Chase bent down and picked up the tennis ball Jane had rolled toward her. The dogs had returned from tormenting the rabbits.

She threw the ball and Jane went after it. Annie rested at Gitana's feet, her long pink tongue hanging out.

"I think it's a form of detachment," Gitana was saying. "Graciela is most likely texting things she wouldn't necessarily say if she was actually talking to Andrea."

"All right, that's it, we're through," Graciela said. She chugged her beer.

"You should train to be a court stenographer with fingers like that," Gitana said. She was always trying to counsel Graciela about finding some sort of lucrative career.

Graciela faked a yawn. "Boring." She looked over at Chase. "Want another beer?"

"Sure."

"How about more concentrated orange juice minus the polysorbate five?"

"Yes, please," Gitana said, handing her the glass.

Graciela had been a waitress along with other sundry jobs—a long list of low-paying, dead-end employment. Currently, she was detailing cars for rich women in the North East Heights. Graciela alluded to other things she did for these women. Chase imagined her seducing older women on the hoods of their Mercedes-Benzes and BMWs.

Graciela's phone beeped. She returned with the drinks.

"Your phone went off again," Chase said. She resumed her reclined position and sipped her beer, musing that life could be quite pleasant at times. The dogs lounged at her feet.

Graciela read her message. "I'm officially done. She doesn't trust me. She thinks I'm out playing around when I've been incarcerated. She says my jail story is all bunk."

"How long with this one?" Gitana asked.

"Three weeks."

"Oh, my God, a veritable eternity," Chase said.

"We'd planned on going to Pride together." Graciela almost looked mournful.

"So you even made long-term plans," Chase chided.

67

Graciela nodded. "I think I'm growing up. Are you two going?"

Gitana choked on her orange juice. Chase got up immediately to pat her on the back or provide artificial respiration if necessary.

"I'm fine really. It just went down the wrong tube."

Chase watched her keenly and then sat back down.

"Maybe I should hang with you guys," Graciela said. "A lot of lesbians think motherhood is hot."

"We never go to Pride," Gitana said. She gently pushed the dogs away. Any form of coughing, sneezing, crying or yelling brought out their nurturing natures.

"I think we should go," Chase said. "It's our culture and we should embrace it. Besides, there might be booths with literature about gay parenting or other mothers we could talk to."

"You hate people," Gitana said.

"I'm going to have to put my aversions aside for the sake of the child," Chase replied.

"I'm definitely going with you. I gotta see this."

Chapter Nine

"Mama, it's okay, really," Gitana said as she patted her mother's head. Jacinda was kneeling, stroking Gitana's belly and making cooing noises.

"Is this good or bad?" Chase asked. She accidently knocked one of the religious candles, the Fatima of Guadalupe. It wobbled precariously for a moment, but Chase caught it before it fell. It seemed she was always having little mishaps in this house of worshipping religious objects. Jacinda obviously had never read the story of the golden calf or ignored it if she had. There were a lot of graven images in this house—small statues of the Virgin Mary, pounded tin crosses, candles, rosary beads hanging from every doorknob in the place and decoupage pictures of Jesus mounted on pieces of wood hung all along one wall.

"Watch out, dude. I've almost lit the place on fire with one of those." Graciela pointed around the room. "God, she's got them all over the house, scenting Saints in the bathroom, like they're blessing your poop. It's like living in the goddamn womb of the Virgin. I mean, look at all these fucking things." Graciela pointed around the room.

Jacinda leapt up and despite her bad hip grabbed a spray bottle containing holy water and doused Graciela with it. Graciela screeched, "Jesus fucking Christ!" Jacinda snatched up one of the rosary beads hanging from the doorknob and chanted prayers like incantations.

"And you thought telling Stella was difficult," Gitana said, as they watched Jacinda, despite her bad hip, chase Graciela around the small living room madly shaking the rosary.

Jacinda's adobe house was in the South Valley, near the Bosque and the Rio Grande River, in an old neighborhood where the adobe homes were authentic. The house had small windows with blue frames, low-beamed ceilings and a kiva fireplace in each room. Chase felt like she was entering one of those made-to-look-real indigenous displays at the Folk Art Museum. Jacinda herself looked like she belonged in the display. Her long black hair was tied up tightly in a bun and she wore a woven skirt of blacks, blues and pinks and a white peasant's blouse.

That this diminutive, incredibly religious, old-fashioned woman had ended up with two gay daughters convinced Chase that God truly had a twisted sense of humor. Maybe Jacinda tried too hard. She'd personally performed three exorcisms on Graciela, to no avail. If anything, it made Graciela more blasphemous.

"Maybe we should have waited until Graciela wasn't here," Chase said.

"It'll be over soon. Mama can't keep up this pace for much longer."

Graciela ran to her room and locked the door. Jacinda grabbed a crucifix off the wall and jammed it in a looped hinge that was attached to Graciela's door. Graciela was locked inside.

"Is that legal?" Chase asked.

"Probably not. You know, for as much as they torment each

70

other they also need each other. Graciela threatens to move out once a week and Jacinda threatens to throw her out every other day, but neither of them follows through."

Jacinda returned to the couch, sitting down heavily and fanning herself with a paper fan depicting the Last Supper. Chase didn't even know they made things like that.

"That child will be the death of me." She patted Gitana's arm. "But you, you make me very happy."

Gitana smiled at her.

"Oh, but where are my manners. I get you lemonade and then we talk of the baby."

"I'll help," Chase said, getting up quickly and giving Jacinda her hand to assist her.

"Oh, and you, you a good girl too. I love you," Jacinda said, kissing Chase's cheek. "You are my other daughter."

Chase blushed. She did have ulterior motives in helping with the lemonade. She was secretly fascinated with Jacinda's kitchen. It was so authentic. She had a cast iron wood stove that she cooked on. Ristras and woven cloves of garlic hung from the rafters. The dishes were colorfully painted earthenware and the glasses were thick and handblown. Jacinda was an amazing cook—everything from scratch. Chase loved her food, except for the stuff with organs in it. Gitana had taught her the names of the icky stuff—the carne avocado and the menudo and something with brains in it with a name she couldn't pronounce.

Jacinda squeezed the lemons into the pitcher and set it and the glasses on a tray. She took some cookies that she always got from the patisserie and put them on a plate. "How long the baby?"

"Just over a two months. We didn't know until the other day."

Jacinda counted on her fingers. "Oh, my sweet, Lord Jesus. It will be a Christmas baby. What a sign, what a good sign." She raised her hands to the heavens. "You know, Graciela was born in the month of the Crucifixion. That was a bad sign." She narrowed her eyes.

Chase nodded her agreement.

"Why she not tell me sooner?"

"I think she was worried you wouldn't approve." Chase picked up the tray hoping this would end the discussion. She wanted Gitana to handle it.

"No, I'm not mad. It's a gift, a gift from God."

"Yes, it is." She took the tray to the living room with Jacinda in tow.

"I'm so happy," Jacinda said, sitting down next to Gitana on the couch. She touched her stomach again. "But how?"

"An accident by the doctor," Gitana started to explain.

Jacinda rolled her eyes heavenward. "There are no accidents with God."

"Yes, that's right," Gitana said. They both knew it was no use to explain the mishap. Jacinda would see it her own way.

Chase sipped her lemonade and wondered why Jacinda wasn't pissed off at them for being gay the way she was with Graciela. It appeared there were two sets of rules—granted they were polite and didn't use the Lord's name in vain. Gitana must have read her mind.

"So you're not angry about us being the parents?"

Jacinda looked puzzled.

Oh, no, Chase thought. She's going to make us say it. In all the time they'd been together, they never once spoke of being gay to Jacinda.

"You know, us," Gitana said, pointing at the two of them. "As two women together raising the child."

This time she got it. "I know the church thinks you two are bad, but I know in my heart that God makes everything. He made you, he made you love each other and he gave you a baby. You'll christen the baby?"

"Yes," they both said in unison.

Jacinda hugged and kissed them. "Such good girls. Do you have a name?"

"Angelica if it's a girl and Angel if it's a boy," Gitana replied.

She put her hand to her heart and smiled. "This is good, so

good." She kissed her rosary beads.

Graciela banged on her bedroom door. "Let me out of here, you crazy old woman."

Jacinda yelled something back in Spanish that didn't sound nice—something about pain and private parts from what Chase could tell with her limited knowledge of the language.

It suddenly occurred to her that she'd better learn Spanish because the baby would grow up to be bilingual. Maybe she should learn German and Italian while she was at it. She had studied French in college.

"I will make things for the baby. And here, take these." Jacinda got up and opened an enormous wooden hutch where she kept her special things. Chase leaned over and attempted to peer in. She half-expected to find the pinky bone of Jesus in there.

Jacinda pulled out a hand-carved wooden angel and two candles. "Put these in the baby's room. It will keep mija safe."

"I will, Mama." Gitana took the things gently.

Chase was still eyeing the hutch. Gitana poked her. "We have to go, Mama."

"Sí, take care." She hugged them both. "You take good care of mama and the baby," she told Chase.

"I will. I promise."

Graciela was yelling obscenities at the top of her lungs. Jacinda shook her head and then crossed herself.

Outside as they made their way to the car, they heard a pssst from the over grown purple sage growing on the side of the driveway.

"What on earth?" Chase said as she saw Graciela peering out of the bush.

"Be quiet, she'll hear you. Meet me around the corner," Graciela said. Her arms and legs were coated in black.

"What happened to you?" Gitana asked.

"I'll tell you later. You've got to get me out of here. I feel another exorcism coming on."

"All right, we'll meet you around the corner," Gitana said,

glancing at her mother's window.

Chase drove around the corner to Calle Delgado and waited for Graciela who hopped over the neighbor's short adobe wall.

Chase rolled down the window. "Hold on a minute. You're not getting in the car with all that black stuff on you. What is it anyway?"

"Soot. I had to climb out the chimney. It was the only escape route."

"How in the hell did you manage that?" Chase said, getting out of the car. She opened the trunk and pulled out a Tartar dog blanket and some doggie wipes.

"I used a rock climbing technique. It's called stemming. You use your hands and feet to counterbalance your body as you climb."

"Where'd you learn to do that?" Chase asked.

"I dated a rock climber."

"That figures," Chase replied, rolling her eyes.

Gitana lowered the window. "We better get going. Mama has spies everywhere."

"Right. I don't want her knowing we aided and abetted a fugitive. Here, clean up with these," Chase said, handing her the wipes. "They have lavender and chamomile in them. You'll smell nice."

Graciela scowled but wiped her arms and legs. Chase put the Tartar blanket on the backseat.

"What happened to your car?" Gitana said.

"That psycho bitch stole the battery, with her bad hip, no less."

"She probably had help," Gitana replied.

"Where to?" Chase said.

"Maloney's. I'm meeting Delia for drinks."

"So you're completely off Andrea now?" Chase asked. She hadn't planned on Graciela and Delia hitting it off at her dinner party but they had. Gitana's sister dating one of her writing buddies gave her a feeling of trepidation.

74

"She's too possessive." Graciela was using one of the wipes to get the soot off her white T-shirt, not very successfully. "Besides, Delia is hot and she's not into monogamy. She thinks it's archaic. Did you know she cleans house for people in the nude? She makes big bucks."

"I didn't know that," Gitana said, frowning at Chase.

"She doesn't clean our house. She writes porn. What do you expect? Nuns don't write porn."

"What about *Lesbian Nuns*? That was quite the book," Graciela said.

Chase glanced at Gitana. "This has been a very long weekend."

"Actually, I thought it was great. Hanging out with you guys was a lot of fun. I can't wait for Pride. Here, just drop me here," she said, pointing to the loading zone half a block from Maloney's. "Thanks, you guys." She hopped out of the car.

Chase took a deep breath, tuned into public radio and Garrison Keillor's *Prairie Home Companion*.

"Wow," Gitana said, leaning back in the seat.

Chapter Ten

Gitana came out of the greenhouse and said, "Where'd you get that?" pointing at the SUV.

"At the Hummer dealership." Chase opened the passenger door so Gitana could check out all the features.

"Are you test driving it? I thought we were going to Pride?"

"We are. In our new car—or SUV rather. I traded in the Passat. This thing is built like a tank. We'll get a baby on board sign and then if some moron hits us we won't even feel it. Do you like the color?"

"It's definitely yellow." Gitana peered inside.

"I thought it looked like a school bus—that way when Bud goes to school it won't be a shock."

Gitana nodded. Chase noticed she looked dubious.

"Let me go tell Nora I'm leaving," Gitana said.

"So she can keep on eye on the text-crazy employees."

"Yes, I feel bad leaving her on our busiest day of the week."

"That's one of the perks of being the boss." Chase wiped a fingerprint off the window with the sleeve of her T-shirt.

"I know."

"I think having Pride on Saturday is rather bourgeoisie. Lots of people work on Saturday excepting white-collar types." Chase got in the driver's seat and inspected the placement of the mirrors. She made a slight adjustment using the remote feature.

"Perhaps you could mention that to the Pride committee when we get there."

"I might just do that." Chase busied herself with the controls. She didn't have them completely mastered. There were so many. She grabbed the owner's manual.

"I'll be right back," Gitana said, staring at the massive machine.

"Okay." Chase didn't look up.

Gitana returned shortly. She opened the back door and slung her pack on the seat.

"Don't hit the teddy bear," Chase called out.

"Why is there a bear in a car seat?" She closed the door and got in the front seat.

Chase stared the car. "I'm practicing driving with a baby. I had the State Farm agent show me how to properly install it. He told me one of the common mistakes parents make is putting the car seat to one side instead of the middle. In the middle you can look in the mirror to observe the child's behavior instead of having to turn your head around and thus removing your eyes from the road."

"I see."

Chase pulled out of the parking lot. "This thing has balls."

They drove into town with Chase explaining all the different features of the new vehicle with the delight of ownership. Gitana mentioned something about greenhouse gases and fuel economy.

"Safety first," Chase replied. "As for doing my part to help the environment, I've changed all the lightbulbs in the house to fluorescent bulbs and ordered thirty trees from the Edgewood

Soil and Conservation Bureau to offset that. I thought the back acre looked a little sparse so I want to fill it in. There's still plenty of room."

"Oh no, not the trees again." Gitana leaned her head on the window and groaned.

"You don't have to plant this time. You're pregnant. I thought I'd hire Graciela. She needs a new battery and probably some other car parts by now."

The last time Chase ordered trees it had taken a week of solid digging to get them all planted. Then there was the watering which consumed every evening for an entire summer because the monsoons hadn't come. The ten poplars, ten chokecherry, ten green ash and ten plum trees had taken off and the property had become somewhat of a forest. Not all Chase's positioning had worked out though, and some of the trees had to be moved as they got bigger which meant their kindly neighbor with the tractor had to be enlisted to move them.

"You'll plan better this time?" Gitana said.

"Yes, now that I know what they're capable of. I have skills now."

"What does this get for gas mileage?" Gitana rummaged around for the paperwork.

"Not too bad." Chase had removed that part of the paperwork in anticipation of this discussion. "But I've got that figured out already. I've ordered a biodiesel conversion kit and there's a guy in town that can change it over. Then all you have to do is add a DSE alternative fuel additive to used frying oil and you have fuel. How cool is that? It's very economical after the initial investment." Chase didn't look at her.

"And how exactly are you going to pay for all this economy?"

"Don't worry, I've got it all worked out. I can write two moist mound sagas a year if I put my nose to the grindstone."

"What about your mystery novel?" Gitana inquired.

"I'll work on it."

Chase got on the freeway. She could feel Gitana studying her.

"Am I being obsessive?"

"Kind of, but in a sweet way. You're approaching this with your usual fervor." Gitana took her hand.

They picked up Delia and Graciela at Delia's rundown house in the University District. She lived with several other hot lesbians, according to Graciela. She had described the place like the Island of Lesbos. Chase imagined young nymphs in togas fucking on the seedy couch or on a bathroom floor in need of serious cleaning. Chase pondered her own dirty mind. Was this a by product of her moist-mound sagas? She should really concentrate more on her mystery novel, but she got stuck a lot. Perhaps, it was the mountain of research required to satisfy savvy forensic-type readers that was holding her back.

"Sweet ride," Graciela said as she slid in one side and Delia got in the other. They both stared at the teddy bear in the car seat. "What's with the bear?" Graciela asked.

"Training," Chase said as she pulled away from Delia's scary Victorian-style house. Chase bet it looked perfect at Halloween. Stick a pumpkin on the dilapidated porch and call it haunted.

"I dated a chick once with a bear. She took it everywhere including the bedroom, if you know what I mean. It was creepy," Delia said.

"Is the bear coming to Pride?" Graciela said.

"No, it stays in the car. I just want to learn to drive without snapping Bud's head off. All right?"

Gitana was reading the owner's manual. Chase was certain she was looking for the stats on gas mileage.

"That's cool," Graciela said.

Chase hoped she wasn't acting like her mother.

The parking lot at Pat Hurley Park was completely full. Chase had her first experience with the Hummer. She was reminded of some line from the movie *Costa Brava*, "Now, that you have it what to do with it."

"We're going to have to walk," Chase said.

"No, we're not. Do you still have all the stuff from the dealer?"

Graciela said.

"What kind of stuff?" Chase asked.

"The paperwork, that vanity plate, and the stuff on the window with the specs," Graciela said.

"It's in the glove box," Chase said.

"Let me have it," Graciela said. "Then pull it up on the grass over there."

"We're not doing what I think we're doing?" Gitana said.

Graciela ignored her. "Stop here. I'll be right back." She hopped out.

"I don't think this is a good idea," Gitana said, looking over at Chase.

"A burly all-man tow truck driver wouldn't set foot here, nor would anyone call one," Chase said.

"I think it's ingenious," Delia commented.

Graciela hopped back in the car carrying a short metal stake with a placard attached. She ripped off the "Please pick up your dog's refuse" part. "Got any gum?"

Gitana, seeing her protestations were for naught, dug around in her purse and pulled out a half consumed pack of Orbit sweet mint. "I'm still registering my protest."

"Your opinion has been noted and rendered moot," Graciela said. She popped several sticks of gum in her mouth and handed two more sticks to Delia who chewed rapidly.

Graciela stuck the vanity plate to the placard with her gum and took Delia's contribution to secure the manufacturer's information, including sticker price, to the window. "Perfect, let's go." She got out of the car and stuck the metal post firmly in the ground. She looked around to see if they'd been noticed. "All clear."

"Good work," Delia said, putting her arm around Graciela's shoulders.

Chase surveyed her handiwork. "It looks convincing."

Gitana rolled her eyes. They headed toward the blaring music, rainbow flags and the white tents of the vendors. Graciela snagged a brochure of events. Studied it briefly and handed it to Chase who perused it thoroughly.

"Drag queens in an hour. Got to see that," Graciela said.

Chase smiled wryly. She'd never understood the fascination with drag queens. To her, you were a guy or a girl and you did what you could with it. Drag queens still liked gay men but gay men liked men. So why would you fuck a guy that looked like a woman? Bo had dated a drag queen once. Chase had met him during one of the writer's meetings at Bo's house where he was camping out or rather leaching off Bo as they found out later. He plucked his eyebrows, wore a blond wig and had water balloons for tits. He served coffee wearing tight black slacks and a red turtleneck that hid his Adam's apple. His smooth crotch—was a mystery to Chase.

Bo did get a good short story out of his misfortune and it was published in the small gay magazine *Hung*. That was one of the good things about being a writer, you could exact your revenge with impunity using fictional wit and satire as long as you altered a few personal details. Chase found great satisfaction in this. She kept the knowledge to herself lest her prey became privy to her hunt for stories, details and diction.

"I see lots of eye candy," Graciela said. Both she and Delia turned around to check out a very well-endowed in the chest and scantily dressed woman in high heels and a black leather mini-skirt.

She did have nice legs, Chase thought. Gitana caught her looking and poked her. Chase made to look innocent until she noticed Gitana checking out the well-developed torso of a young black woman. They both laughed.

The roar of motorbikes filled the air and leather-clad women on Harleys rode across the grounds in an orderly procession.

"Dykes on Bikes, this doesn't get any better," Graciela said.

"Oh, baby, look at that one, tits for miles," Delia said.

"I love halters," Graciela said.

"Did it ever occur to you two that how you refer to women is derogatory?" Gitana said.

They passed the first vendor tent where they were selling rainbow bumper stickers, tank tops with pink triangles on the front, and various bracelets with rainbow beads and the occasional pewter-cast pot leaf.

"No, it never occurred to me. I'm just embracing my inner vagina," Graciela said. "My femaleness."

"You are so full of crap," Chase said. She picked up a hat with rainbow palm trees on the brim and set it back down again.

"Rainbow stuff is so old school," Delia said.

"I like the Human Rights Campaign stuff," Gitana said, picking up a tiny green tank top with the HRC logo of a blue rectangle with two yellow bands across it. She held it up.

Chase, suddenly understanding it was for Bud and not Gitana, although she had been wondering what she would look like in it, seized the moment. "I like that one. Let's get it." She pulled out her wallet and paid the stoic woman at the cash register who handed her an HRC brochure which Chase took with great enthusiasm. With this the woman smiled. Chase handed the tiny bag to Gitana and began reading the literature.

Their child would grow up in a gay household and they would need answers to the cultural issues of the day. She certainly didn't want Bud to turn into Anita Bryant or Pat Robinson because of an inadequate upbringing. This parenting thing was getting bigger by the minute. It was fortuitous that babies took so long to get built. She had seven months to get herself right. If she could write a novel in six, certainly she could master parenting in seven.

"Come on, this isn't a fucking library," Graciela said, pulling at Chase's elbow.

"I'm coming." Careful to fold it neatly, she shoved the brochure into her back pocket.

Gitana was already at the next booth signing them up for the Democratic Party.

"Is this a good idea? They're all conniving bastards," Chase said.

"We have a civic duty, now."

"We do?" Chase said.

"For the baby's future."

"Oh, I get it. Because the future really does matter. We can always run away to Canada if they start rounding up and putting us in camps. Let's be the smart early people when it comes to getting out," Chase said, eyeing the well-dressed woman in charge of the booth. People in blazers and trousers at a picnic were suspect.

"Camps, that's the least of it. They'll harvest us for organs before that," Delia said.

"You guys are paranoid," Graciela said. "Hey, let's get a beer," she said, noticing the beer tent.

"I can't. I'm driving and she's pregnant," Chase said, a little wistfully.

"Boring," Graciela muttered.

"Yeah, but that means we can get trashed and we'll have supervision. It can't get better than that," Delia replied.

"If you're obnoxious, you'll be taking the bus home," Gitana warned.

"Just make sure we don't hook up with some ugly chicks because our sense of judgment is impaired," Graciela said.

"Okay, Casanova," Gitana said.

"Hey, if I remember correctly, before Chase you were quite the Casanova yourself," Graciela said. Gitana blushed.

Graciela got in the beer line while the rest of them waited.

"She was?" Delia said. She appeared to examine Gitana in a whole new light. "I can see why."

"Mine—remember," Chase said.

"Of course." Delia went to help Graciela with the beer purchase.

"Casanova, huh," Chase said.

"I was young and unfettered." Gitana put her arm around Chase's waist. "And then I found you."

"Were you looking for me?"

"I was."

"Is that why the botanist was taking a women's studies class?" Chase inquired.

"It was a good place to start." Gitana kissed her cheek.

They had met in Professor Murphy's lesbian lit class—reading Adrienne Rich and Lillian Faderman. The class was divided into four groups of five. Gitana had traded with one of the other women so she could be in Chase's group. Chase figured it had nothing to do with her despite Gitana's ever-present proximity during each group study meeting.

Gitana asked her out for coffee. Even then Chase thought they were going to discuss their part of the group's project. Instead Gitana asked her what she planned to do with her life. Chase was an English major and most people, including her mother, assumed she'd go on to teach. She wrote intriguing and innovative term papers and had the support of her teachers. This was essential for grad school admission. Rather than skirting the question as she usually did, she told Gitana the truth. "I want to be a writer."

Gitana did not possess the defeatism of others. "What kind of stuff do you want to write?"

"I want to write lesbian novels." Chase put more cream in her coffee so she wouldn't have to meet Gitana's gaze.

"Do you have an idea for one?" Gitana took the cream away and touched her hand. "I'll share my dream if you share yours, completely."

"I've written two novels—both stunk."

"Who told you that?" Gitana asked.

"The editor who said I wrote like an eighth-grader with over-active hormones."

Gitana laughed.

Surprisingly, this did not upset Chase who was usually quite sensitive about her secret longing for a literary career. Gitana's laughter seemed to sparkle and Chase felt heartened by it rather than ashamed of her confession.

"So what did you do?"

"I took her advice and wrote another one. I sent it in and I'm waiting for another rejection notice, but this one is better than the last one. I took out a lot of the melodrama that I gravitated toward in my first novel."

"That's awesome."

Chase sipped her coffee and eyed her companion. "So what's your dream?"

"I'll show you."

They went to Gitana's studio apartment near the University. It seemed everyone Chase knew lived around the campus, except for her—she still lived at home in her mother's pretentious house. She avoided taking people there if she could.

Gitana's apartment had a futon bed in the middle of the room, a tiny kitchenette painted sky blue which Chase thought was an odd color for a kitchen, and large south facing windows covered with precariously constructed open-sided wooden shelves that contained weird plants that Chase had never seen before. The room looked like a jungle and smelled like paradise. Puzzled, she looked at Gitana.

"They're orchids. I want to have a nursery and grow orchids."

"They're beautiful." Chase gently stroked a petal. It was soft and looked so fragile like the slightest breeze would send the whole plant, pot and all, back to the jungles of the Amazon.

"So are you," Gitana said. She had her cornered.

"Well, you know I didn't really have anything to do with that—genetic punch bowl is more like it." Chase attempted to inch away without appearing rude.

Gitana put her arm up against the wall, effectively blocking Chase's escape. "Why are you making this so hard?"

"Making what hard?" Chase was thoroughly confused.

"This." Gitana kissed her. "I want you so bad it hurts."

Chase immediately broke all her rules of engagement. She kissed her back, ran her fingers through Gitana's long dark hair, let herself be pushed onto the bed, her T-shirt and shorts removed, her stomach kissed and her legs opened so Gitana could bite, suck and fuck her until she made animal noises and cried out for more. It was almost embarrassing thinking about it now. From that moment on Gitana coursed through her veins and nothing else mattered.

As they walked the grounds, Gitana tugged at her hand. "What were you thinking about?"

Chase promptly returned to the present moment. "I was remembering you as a Casanova the first time we were together."

"I wasn't being slick. I was so consumed with you I couldn't breathe. I thought I would die if you didn't let me touch you. You were tough to get."

"True love is never an easy target."

Gitana scooped her up and kissed her hard.

Chase suddenly wished they were at home so they could fall into each other's arms and make animal noises. Instead, she whispered, "I have never wanted anyone the way I want you."

Chase's moment of marital bliss was interrupted by a tap on the shoulder. She was certain it was Graciela and she thought her a bit rude for breaking up their moment. She turned around.

A large but decidedly handsome woman with dark cropped hair and buff arms, said, "I thought it was you."

Chase quickly realized who she was and blanched. This was the woman who'd been waiting for her the night she fell in love with Gitana. She'd come home late to find Tori sitting in her sleek black Saab outside the house. Chase sat in the front seat of the car smelling of orchids and sex trying to explain to Tori that she'd found the love of her life.

"Well, at least you two are still together. That counts for something, considering you broke my heart and caused severe psychological damage," Tori said.

"Who's she?" Gitana asked equally piqued.

"This is Tori." Chase studiously avoided Tori's angry glance and looked helplessly at Gitana. The thought crossed her mind that Tori had somehow discovered Gitana's identity because

Chase had never told Tori who she was. She found this disturbing.

"You know, for years I've been thinking about how you cheated on me."

"I can't see where I was worth all that," Chase said. Tori hadn't crossed her mind a day after they broke up. Obviously, there'd been a difference of opinion on the nature of their relationship. She did remember standing outside Tori's office—she was a TA in Chase's Jane Austen seminar—telling Tori that she'd get tired of her and Tori staring hard at her with the look of serious love. "No, I won't."

"My therapist says I need closure, so I got a little present for you."

Chase was horribly confused until Tori, a substantial butch, nailed Chase in the solar plexus. She fell to the ground and rolled on her side. This position rendered her vulnerable to another attack. She closed her eyes so she wouldn't see the size ten Doc Marten coming at her ribs. She'd heard broken ribs took a long time to heal and that the process was painful. She'd never actually had the shit kicked out of her although there'd been times she'd deserved it. She figured her past had found her and was exacting retribution.

She heard Graciela and Delia screaming and she opened her eyes to see a burly Hispanic woman, dressed in black commando gear and a security badge, pluck Tori up and prevent further damage. Graciela dashed out a quick right hook that would have decked Tori had the guard not grabbed her first.

"Hey, that's enough of that," the security guard said.

"What the fuck! She beat up my sister un-in-law."

"Yeah, and she's going to get charged with assault." She put cuffs on the infuriated Tori and marched her off, Tori glaring back at Chase. "First Aid," the security guard called out and pointed to Chase.

Gitana knelt beside her and peered anxiously at her. "Are you all right?"

"I think so." She'd caught her breath and got up on her knees.

A young woman with purple hair came running over toting a first-aid kit. "Are you bleeding?"

"No, just lost my wind. I'm fine, really."

Graciela and Delia helped her up. "Let's go to the first-aid tent and let them have a look at you," Gitana said.

"No," Chase protested. "I'm okay."

"Let me check for broken ribs," the young woman said, running her hands along Chase's sides. "Nope, you're good."

"Great. Well, thanks and we'll be on our way now," Chase said, trying to untangle herself from Graciela and Delia.

"Are you sure you're all right?" Gitana asked.

"I fine, really."

"Dude, you just got decked. I gotta show you some moves. I'm like, a green belt in Karate," Delia said.

"You never told me that," Graciela said. She let go of Chase.

"Well, you look like you have a pretty mean hook," Delia said.

"Nah, just schoolyard tactics." Graciela kicked the grass.

"Let's get her to a table," Gitana said.

"Maybe I do need a beer now," Chase said.

"I'm on it," Delia said, making for the beer tent.

The burly Hispanic security guard came back over. "No life threatening damage?"

"Aside from my pride, no." Chase dusted off her shirt.

"Sorry about that, usually I'm right there, but I didn't see that one coming. Normally, there's an argument first before punches fly. That was low. Who was she?"

"An ex-girlfriend."

"I can see why. I'd keep a lookout for any others." She adjusted her belt.

"I will and thank you," Chase said.

"No problem." She made off.

They found the nearest table with an umbrella and sat down. Delia returned with provisions, three Coors Light in plastic cups and a lemonade for Gitana. Graciela watched the security guard as she made her rounds.

"Man, she's tight. If I was a femme I'd be all over that," she said.

"Damn right," Delia said. She set everything down.

Chase took a big swig of beer. She was beginning to understand her mother and her martinis.

"What did you do to make her so mad?" Gitana asked. She brushed more dirt off Chase's shoulder. Her white T-shirt had an ochre tint to it.

"I slept with you."

"You didn't tell me you had a girlfriend."

"We broke up the minute you kissed me." Chase took another enormous swig. Her nerves were settling.

"Dude, who's the Casanova now," Graciela said.

Chase scowled at her. She could tell Gitana wasn't pleased that she'd left out this particular detail of her life.

"It's kind of like how I didn't know about Nora until she had me off the floor with her hands around my neck," Chase said.

"Oh, good, the story improves," Delia said.

"I'll say," Graciela said, as she and Delia toasted their paper beer cups.

"You do have a point there," Gitana said. She sipped her lemonade and seemed to ponder this.

"Remember what you told Nora, about how when you meet your soul mate it's a once in a lifetime event and if you pass it by it's lost forever?"

"Yes." Gitana stroked Chase's cheek.

"Wow, that's deep," Delia said. Her admiration and enlarged libido were evident.

Chase gave her a look.

"I know, she's yours."

Gitana took Chase's hand. "Are you sure you're all right? We could call it a day."

"What and miss meeting more of her ex-girlfriends," Graciela said.

89

Delia looked at Gitana. "Are any of your ex-girlfreinds as pissed off?"

"No, Nora is one of my best friends and she adores Chase."

Graciela yawned in mockery.

"What about the others?" Delia asked. She sipped her beer and peered at Gitana over the top of the cup.

"They were temporary liaisons without much emotional attachment."

"So pretty much one-night stands and fuck buddies," Graciela said.

"I wouldn't put it that way. It was more like young women exploring each other's bodies in a physical way," Gitana replied.

"Gag me," Graciela said. She turned to watch another exquisite example of womankind walk by.

"How about you, Chase?" Delia said.

"What is this, confession time?" Chase finished her beer.

"I'll get you another one," Graciela said, hopping up.

Chase glanced at Gitana.

"I'll drive home. I can still fit behind the steering wheel."

Graciela dashed off to the beer tent. "No telling stories until I get back."

Chase scanned the crowd looking for potential hazards. Gitana noticed. "How many others do we have to look out for?"

"At least three."

"That's the problem with Pride. Your past keeps popping up," Delia said.

Graciela came back with another round. Chase slipped a twenty in her pocket.

"Thanks, dude. So confess."

"Do I have to?" Chase sipped her beer and avoided the eyes fixed upon her.

A unanimous "Yes," was the response.

"All right, I guess I have to. I'll make it short. I was a freak magnet. I wasn't the pursuer."

"You were the fish," Graciela said. "Not a good position. So, sis put the moves on you."

"Pretty much."

"Nice work." She patted Gitana on the back.

"We know that part. Who was your first, second and third?" Delia said.

"You know, that's one of the pitfalls of hanging out with another writer, you probe."

"You were the one that brought up cannibalization which requires a lot of material." Delia reminded her.

"What the hell? Is that something kinky like in *The Hunger?*" Graciela asked, turning around yet again to check out a girl wearing a thong and pasties.

"You're going to throw out your neck if you keep doing that," Gitana said. She poured her leftover ice from her first lemonade into her second. The day had grown hot as summer slowly made its way forward.

"No, it's a writing term, smut-head," Chase informed her.

"Anyway, back to the subject at hand," Delia said.

"All right, back to my sordid past. It's comprised of three psychopaths. The first was Janet. She was on my soccer team when I was sixteen—up to that point I had no interest in boys and successfully avoided all school dances. Lacey had told me enough about blow jobs, sweaty humping and spooge that I was steering clear of sex."

"Okay, we got that part. Get to the juicy stuff," Graciela said. She took a quick peek at a tall black woman in a tight dress.

"Janet seduced me in my bedroom when we were supposed to be studying geometry. She pinned me down, kissed and banged me until I couldn't breathe or see straight."

"You weren't straight anymore," Gitana said.

"Good thing for you," Graciela said.

"We spent a lot of study time doing this which is probably why I suck at math." Chase sipped her beer and felt pensive. She was glad she was gay.

"She does suck at math," Gitana said.

"It was orgasms or equations."

"Enough math, go on," Delia said.

"Your impatience is why your writing lacks appropriate pacing. All you want to do is get to the end," Chase said.

"I know," Delia replied.

"Back to my story—my mother found us in a compromising position."

"Sucking face or booty?" Graciela said.

"That's disgusting," Gitana said, slapping Graciela on the shoulders, spilling her beer.

"Hey, watch it. This stuff is precious manna."

"Especially at four dollars a cup," Delia said.

"So which was it?" Graciela asked.

"The latter," Chase said.

"Rock on, dude," Delia said.

"My mother hauled us both into the living room. I was certain I was headed to military school and then I remembered there'd be lots of girls there. I was almost relieved because Janet entertained thoughts of us spending the rest of our lives together, right down to buying kitchen utensils."

"Then what happened?" Gitana asked, now seeming as eager as the others.

"My mother, in her usual cunning fashion, told us to keep our mouths shut and conduct ourselves discreetly."

"That was it?" Gitana seemed amazed.

"Stella is all about appearance and she's not horribly interested in adolescent sexuality."

"And then?" Graciela prodded.

"Enter liaison number two—not technically a girlfriend."

"A fuck buddy," Delia said, looking mournfully into her empty cup. Graciela took it and poured half of hers into it.

"I guess you could call it that," Chase said. She looked apologetically at Gitana.

"Don't worry. I had a few. You're supposed to do that so later on you can be a stable and monogamous partner," Gitana said.

The beer cart appeared.

"Hey, over here," Graciela called out.

The bare-chested, tight-jean-clad blond man smiled and came over. "Yes?"

"We need a round except for the fat lady." She indicated Gitana. "Do you have water?"

"Yes." He pulled a bottle of Dasani and handed it to her.

"I'm not fat yet," Gitana said, giving Graciela another good smack in the arm.

Chase waved off Delia and Graciela's attempt to pay. "I got it covered."

"Cool, thanks, man." Graciela sipped her fresh beer, leaving a trace of a foam mustache.

"Back to the story," Delia said.

Chase took a sip of beer and then resumed. She was feeling better by the moment. Beer—the true anesthetic. Tomorrow would be an entirely different affair.

"Janet caught me in my bedroom with the goalie. Stella had sworn Janet to secrecy about our affair and we had to do it in my room. So I figured that rule applied to all. Janet must have suspected something. She got past Stella easily enough and I was found out. It was horrible. Tears, screaming, and my first ugly breakup. I mean, I couldn't really be expected to be faithful, could I?"

"It's a bit late for remorse," Gitana said, opening her water. "I'm going to have to pee soon."

"Don't worry about it. It would be totally incomprehensible at that age. Hell, we're still sowing our wild oats," Graciela said.

"I couldn't conceive of it," Delia said. Now, she had the foam mustache. Graciela leaned over and licked it off.

"Thanks."

"And what about your next girlfriend?" Gitana asked.

"Now, you're interested," Chase said. She was getting more than she bargained for.

"This is all new to me," she said. She sipped her water and

stared intently at Chase.

"Great, Pride has become the confessional."

"Rock on," Delia said.

"It's good for your soul," Gitana said.

"My soul was doing just fine before this," Chase remarked.

"Get on with it," Graciela said. She took her sneakers and socks off and dug her toes into the grass.

She was such a contradiction, Chase thought—impatient yet perfectly relaxed. It was queer, but then she'd never understood Graciela.

"She was a sophomore in college and I was a freshman. She was a southern belle sorority girl and I was an anarchist." Chase envisioned her dark hair, long legs and a drawl that made you think of antebellum porches and wisteria. Now that was a good time.

"Like in *Rubyfruit Jungle*?" Graciela said.

"Something like that. She was a complete nymphomaniac and dangerously jealous. She cut my English Lit of the 1900s in half with a meat cleaver."

"Why?"Delia said, her eyes large with excitement.

"She thought I was sleeping with the TA."

"Were you?" Gitana said. She seemed to already know the answer.

"Well, kind of."

"Another brief liaison?" Delia said. She too took off her socks and shoes, sticking her feet in the grass. Graciela's foot stroked hers.

"She read me Anne Cameron's poetry. I couldn't help myself." Chase didn't exactly feel remorseful. It had been lovely in her attic room, the afternoon sun flitting across the bed and their naked bodies entwined.

"Dude, you did get around," Graciela said.

"I'm sorry," Chase said, looking at Gitana.

"Baby, I could tell you'd had a little experience."

"Really," Chase said. She finished her beer.

94

"There were just certain things a woman of experience knows." She took her hand.

"Oh." Chase wondered what these things might be, but she certainly wasn't going to inquire. At least not here.

"Aside from that there was Tori, whom you've had the pleasure of meeting."

"I feel like I know you so much better," Graciela said, putting her shoes back on.

"Gag me. Now, can we see about finding the parenting booth?"

"Sure. You guys check that out. We're going to peruse the sex toy booth. We can meet at the center stage for the drag queen show in twenty minutes. It'll be perfect," Graciela said, hopping up.

"I can hardly wait," Chase said. She picked up all their trash and dumped it.

Delia and Graciela dashed off like all the sex toys might be gone before they got there.

Chase rolled her eyes. "I hate Pride."

"Well, you'll just have to get used to it. We have to bring the baby. This is part of her life."

"Poor thing. I don't think not having seen a drag show is going to stunt her growth in any way."

Chapter Eleven

Chase stood in the middle of Hilda Hoftmeyer's living room with twelve screaming kids. This was the result of her foray at Pride into the realm of parenting. It was a playdate seminar run by a woman hardly able to run her own life let alone a class on the parenting of children. Chase had deduced this in the first fifteen minutes of class.

"Would you like some iced tea?" Hilda Hoftmeyer said. She was a stout woman in pale blue polyester slacks two sizes too small and a somewhat matching floral blouse. Her chubby face made her look like a blooming eleven-year-old in a forty-some-thing body. Chase found it disconcerting.

Chase was thinking more along the lines of a double martini. She was becoming her mother. Her silence must have informed Hilda.

"We have good German lager." Hilda's eyes twinkled.

"Sure." Her nerves got the better of her ethics.

"I make it myself in the basement. It's good stuff." Hilda went off.

Chase noticed that all the obviously new parents sat on one side of the room with glazed eyes as children screamed and tore about. Each held a plastic cup of the same kind Hilda handed her—the fortifier. It was Saturday morning and Gitana hadn't been able to come because she was at the Annual Orchid Event at the fairgrounds. Chase wished desperately that she were here. She sat down next to a sedate child who appeared to be older than the others. Suddenly, going to the Orchid Show seemed the better choice.

Chase looked around tentatively as if taking it all in at once would cause serious mental anguish. The playdate group was supposedly a mix of domestic partners, single mothers and the married, but it was difficult to tell who was who. Hilda was running the first session of exposure to children in their natural environment. Next week a kid shrink was to come. Chase bet there would only be iced tea that time.

Toddlers ran around and the older ones fought with each other or their parents. Bedlam seemed too tame a word. The scene reminded her of a movie she'd watched, *Daddy Day Care* with Eddie Murphy. She'd been renting movies with kids in them trying to get pointers. At least they'd been comedies so she could laugh off the impending dread she felt.

"My name's Addison," said the little girl next to her. She had dark hair in braids and wore tiny red spectacles. She looked like the kind of kid that got picked on. She held a notebook clutched to her breast and peered at Chase.

"I'm Chase."

"Where's your kid?" She put the notebook down on her lap as if she'd been using it for a shield and had now decided Chase was safe and could let down her guard.

"In my partner's belly."

Addison nodded. "I'm nine and I write stories."

"That's nice. I like stories."

"My dad says my stories are stupid."

"Where is he? I'll kill him." Deciding this was not a good thing to say to a child she amended her statement. "What I meant to say was he had bad manners and should be reprobated."

"He's at home with diarrhea. I put Metamucil and Ex-Lax in his Raisin Bran. He's been in the bathroom all morning."

"You're brilliant."

"I did score above the ninety-eighth percentile on the Stanford-Binet IQ test which allows me to become a Mensa member, but I don't believe in group mechanics although Mensa does have a healthy respect for individuality so I might join in the future," Addison said, her eyes shining behind her glasses.

"Wow." It just figured the first child she'd meet was genius. Why couldn't she find a nice simple kid who wanted her to play checkers and that she could let win. Well, she'd make the best of it. "Why don't you show me your stories. I'd like to read them."

Chase knew at that moment she would make a bad parent. She'd just praised a nine-year-old for poisoning her father. Gitana was going to have to police both of them.

Chase was about to take a sip of Hilda's fortifier when Addison grabbed her wrist.

"I wouldn't drink that. Remember my dad. Hilda's brew is worse. See, it's already started." Addison pointed to the line at the bathroom. She pulled out two Red Bulls from her over-stuffed red Lands' End backpack. She handed one to Chase.

"Should you be drinking that?"

"Is it any worse than the twelve cups of Kool-Aid and two brownies Hilda is dosing them with now? Do you want me to end up like that fat kid?" she said, tipping her head in the direction of the six-year-old porker who was sticking close to Hilda's ample thigh and grabbing at the brownie plate.

"He looks like that kid in the Willy Wonka movie," Chase said, thinking of fat kids and bratwurst. She took the Red Bull from Addison and stuck her cup of brew under her metal fold-up chair. They began to look at Addison's story book.

They were so engrossed in this pursuit that they missed the little boy who cut off several inches of a little blond girl's hair during the course of the collage-making session. There was much noise and screams of outrage from both parents and children.

"I hate kids," Addison said, looking up from her notebook and scowling.

"But you are one," Chase said, watching as the parents bustled their kids off.

Addison looked at her like she'd said the stupidest thing on the planet.

"I mean aren't you, kind of?"

"I consider myself a pre-adult, like a cocoon waiting for that glorious moment when I burst forth as a full grown person. This is a temporary condition."

"I got it." Chase smiled and nodded.

"Now can we get back to work?"

"Of course," Chase said.

Chase rationalized her avoidance of the group by spending time with Addison, which would still count toward her goal of child socialization. Besides she liked Addison. They went back to work until a pretty blond woman interrupted them. She wore a gray pin-striped suit. Her hair was pulled back and she looked like someone who tried too hard.

"There you are. I thought you'd be outside with the other big kids," she said.

Addison scowled at her. She was really good at scowling, Chase thought.

"I hardly think so. I wouldn't be caught dead playing tag or some other banal childhood game. I have more important things to do. Did you sell the house?"

"I did."

"Fantastic," Addison said, her voice laced with faux sweetness.

"What are you doing?" her mother asked.

"Chase is helping me edit my stories."

"Are you an editor?"

"No, she's a writer—a published writer," Addison said.

"I'm just teaching her a few tricks of the trade."

"How nice. I'm Addison's mother, Peggy McFarland."

"Nice to meet you." Chase stood up and shook her hand.

"I'm glad to see Addison has made a friend," Peggy said, patting her head.

"Don't touch me," Addison said, pulling away.

Peggy colored. "She has intimacy issues, according to her therapist."

"I don't like to be touched and the shrink is a dickhead and a waste of time and money."

"Addison!" Peggy reprimanded her unconvincingly.

"My shrink says the same thing about me." Chase poked Addison in the ribs. She looked startled. Chase smiled. "We could work on it."

Addison poked her back and laughed.

"See that wasn't so bad," Chase said.

"Says you."

"Uh, honey…"

"I know, we have to go and get the papers signed." Addison looked sullen. Then she glanced at Chase. "Are you coming next week?"

"I'm supposed to be working on my parenting skills," Penny said, looking apologetic.

"But usually, I sit in these stupid sessions while she's on the phone making deals." Addison hoisted her backpack up on her shoulder.

"Honey, don't be that way."

"I wasn't going to come again, but if you're going to I will," Chase said.

"Really?" Addison's face lit up.

"I'd like to talk to you and your mom again."

"Can I bring more stories?" Addison said, her face radiant.

"I was counting on it."

Addison smiled. Chase poked her again and Addison poked

100

her back.

Peggy gave Addison the car keys. "I'll be right out."

"Whatever. "Bye, Chase." She trudged off, swinging the car keys.

"I just wanted to thank you for being so nice to Addison."

"She's a great kid—or rather, pre-adult," Chase said.

This made Peggy smile. "You got caught."

"I did."

"Do you have children?" Peggy inquired.

"One on the way. I'm afraid I'm going to suck at parenting."

"You did fine with Addison."

"That's because she's just like me. What if I have some pansy kid?"

"You won't. See you next week."

Peggy walked away. She looked back over her shoulder at Chase in an odd way. Chase had no idea what it meant. She did realize one thing. Addison treated her mother the same way Chase treated Stella.

She took a covert look around and then slunk toward the door. Just in time, it appeared, as a piece of furniture was smoldering and several parents had their cell phones out. Chase breathed deeply and made a run for the Hummer.

"How'd it go?" Gitana said. She'd just come home from the orchid show and was maneuvering the dogs out of the kitchen by placating them with biscuits.

Chase was making a salad. "It was fine until a three-year-old got a hold of the barbeque lighter and torched the couch." She pulled out a purple onion and two beefsteak tomatoes.

Gitana sat at the kitchen bar. She looked pale and tired. "Are you sure you want to hang out with these people?"

"I am learning a lot and I met a new friend."

"That's a good thing," Gitana said, unloading the contents of her fair bag onto the kitchen island. She had an enormous amount of literature on orchids along with some fertilizer samples.

Chase chopped up a bunch of spinach. Spinach had a lot of iron in it. Gitana looked like she might need some iron. She had yet to notice the copious amounts of vegetables they were consuming, especially dark green leafy ones. Chase had grown an extra large crop of mixed greens in the garden for this purpose as well as twelve broccoli plants and three rows of spinach. All were abundantly generous. There was always trouble with tomatoes, regardless of variety, so several years ago she'd admitted defeat and bought them at the farmers market.

Gitana organized her literature and stuck it neatly into the cubbyhole box labeled for work materials. She put her arms around Chase's waist and kissed the back of her neck. Chase felt the outline of her body against her back. Pleasure coursed through her.

"What kind of friend?"

Chase turned around. "She's nine."

Gitana laughed. "I guess I don't have to worry."

Chase pulled her tight. "You never have to worry."

"You know this Saturday thing isn't going to work for me. I can't dump on Nora that way."

"It's all right. You're going to be a great mother. It's me we've got to worry about."

"You'll be fine." Gitana ran her hands under Chase's T-shirt. "Oh, my."

"I think it's my hormones. I've been thinking about you all day."

"At the orchid show?" Chase inquired, raising her eyebrows.

"Yes, it was a major distraction."

The next thing Chase actually registered was being seduced on the kitchen floor. Gitana was straddling her and they were both making animal noises.

As they lay together catching their breath, Chase noticed an excessive number of fur balls under the stove. She was going to have to clean better when Bud arrived.

Gitana looked into her eyes. "What are you thinking about?"

"Fur balls under the stove and improving my cleaning skills."

Gitana pinched her arm. "That's not very romantic."

"And after that unromantic thought I pondered putting dinner out for the dogs while you lit candles and ran a bath so I could love you more."

"Now, that's better. Meet you in five," Gitana said.

Gitana raced upstairs pretty fast for a pregnant lady, Chase observed. She filled up the dog bowls and got them a treat. They didn't seem to mind that dinner was an hour early because their parents were upstairs being naughty.

Chapter Twelve

"You've learned things. That's good. Writers are thinkers first—storytellers second," Alma said.

Chase sat with Alma under the veranda of Alma's house while the afternoon rain poured off the tin roof and splashed into the flower beds. The rhythmic pounding of the rain was like soft background noise. Chase had once read that if you were trying to get some sleep in a noisy hotel you should find an off-the-air channel and let the white noise lull you to sleep. Rain was like that for her.

The rest of the writing group hadn't shown up yet so Chase had Alma all to herself which she rather liked. Whenever the group meeting was at Alma's house she showed up early.

"I know," Chase answered Alma, "but it just seems so odd that I get stuck all the time. I can barely get a page out and I have to force myself. I look at that particular notebook with complete dread. I've never dreaded writing before. Now, I know why there are all those writing manuals. I never understood writer's block before."

"You love writing. You're the most prolific writer I've ever known." Alma poured them both an iced tea from the pitcher sitting on the white wicker table between them.

"I want to write more than moist-mound sagas. I've written so many and I'm sick of them."

"It would be nice to have a larger more diverse audience." Alma handed Chase her glass.

She drank her tea and frowned. "Yes, it's not like I don't appreciate my lesbian readers…"

"But there are only a finite number of them." Alma was good at finishing Chase's sentences. Picking up her train of thought effortlessly as if picking up a shiny penny off the blacktop—so evident that its presence couldn't be missed.

"Yes." Chase bit her lip and moved a stack of books on the white end table so she could set her glass down.

Alma leaned back in a wicker rocker with floral cushions. Looking at her, Chase imagined Margaret Mitchell sitting on her porch, the magnolias throwing off their scent while she contemplated writing *Gone with the Wind*.

"Just write the story line and follow your plot—you're good at that. Block out the places that require forensic details. Write the scenes, develop the characters, and fill in the details later—those nuggets of authenticity that readers are so adamant about can be inserted later. They aren't the story, they're the reality bites."

"That's what keeps holding me back." Chase flipped her mechanical pencil between her fingers like a baton.

"If you insert the forensic details later you can weed through your research and put in only the most crucial." Alma sipped her tea and stared at Chase.

"An overabundance of factual detail is the sign of a novice." This seemed to be the correct answer because Alma smiled at her and refilled her tea.

"You got it."

"Thanks, Alma." She flipped up her pencil and expertly caught it.

"Chase, can I ask you a personal question?"

"Does it have to do with my sex life?"

"No."

"Then, yes." Chase couldn't imagine what this would be. Writing conversations were as close as Chase ever got to baring her soul to anyone other than Gitana.

"How many of those mechanical pencils do you have?"

"Eighty-one. It's three times nine equaling twenty-seven added together seven plus two equals nine which is a multiple of three. Three is my magic number. Purple is my preferred color but blue or gray will work. I avoid red." Chase curled her lips in her best version of I-can't-help-it-if-I'm-crazy look.

"The trinity. The power of three. It makes perfect sense to me."

"Let's just keep this to ourselves."

"Of course. Always the same black and white marbled composition books as well?"

Chase nodded. "It has to be that way. It's how I write."

"Lots of writers have their little quirks. I'm not judging—just observing. You worry too much."

"I know."

Chase looked up unsurprised as Bo and Jasmine came out the back door. At Alma's house she expected you to let yourself in. She knew you were coming so it was kind of stupid to ring the bell. It seemed so relaxed to Chase whose house was rigged like a fortress—there was a gate at the bottom of the driveway, then there were the dogs and several more gates before you actually got to the front door. Bo had made mention of this fact once. Chase reminded him that she didn't like people.

"She was lost again." Indicating Jasmine, he flounced down on the wicker love seat. "I had to chase her down. She thought I was some kind of stalker."

Jasmine threw her hands up in total resignation. "I'm terrible with directions. The streets are so convoluted here. I can't keep it all straight. Chase's house is the only one I can find. I get on the freeway, take a left at exit one-forty, go straight, turn at the mountains. I can handle that."

Alma poured her a glass of iced tea. "Sit down and relax. We're still waiting on Delia."

Jasmine took her iced tea and made Bo move over. "Thank you."

"As a writer, you're supposed to be studying details. Next time someone is honking and flashing their lights you should recognize it means something." Bo said, taking the glass Alma offered him.

"Jasmine, he drives a green Pacer. How many Pacers are still around?" Chase said.

"It is an unusual car," Alma said. The rain had stopped and she eyed her saturated flower beds. She smiled.

"That car should never have been made," Jasmine said.

"It's ugly, but Laura-Lie has taken me any place I've ever wanted to go."

"Who names their car?" Jasmine said.

Chase and Alma both raised a hand. "What's yours?" Chase asked.

Alma drove a nineteen sixty-four faded red Volkswagon van. "Vaughn."

"Mine's Pauline the Passat or rather was. Now, it's Henrietta the Hummer."

"I give," Jasmine said.

"How's the story coming?" Chase said.

"It's progressing. I'm past page one hundred. I've never gtten that far." Jasmine flushed.

"That's fantastic," Chase said.

"I'm so excited. Maybe criticism is a good thing." Jasmine tuckd an errant hair behind her ear. She was attempting to grow her hair out again and this ear-tucking thing was becoming a nervous habit.

Like she had any room to talk, Chase thought as she flipped her pencil between her fingers. She caught Alma's eye and put the pencil back inside her notebook. She was obsessive. She knew it. This was another thing she'd have to curb if she didn't wasn't to raise a kid with weird lifelong habits.

"See, we need each other," Chase said, glancing at Bo who was scrutinizing her.

"Except you. Where's the mystery novel? You use us for beta-readers on novels that are safe for you. Don't get me wrong—I think they are well-written, funny and redemption bound—all admirable traits, but you already know how to do that," Bo said.

Chase got up to refill her already full glass. Alma put her hand over the top of the pitcher. "Avoidance tactic." Chase sat back down.

"We all suck. So what if your first mystery novel sucks? Isn't that the kind of stuff you tell us?" Bo said, refilling his empty glass.

"Point taken. When it's my turn I'll bring it. Deal?"

Delia came flying out the back door, letting the screen door slam behind her. Alma cringed. "Sorry I'm late. I had to drop Graciela at work. Jacinda removed the radiator on her car, with her bad hip no less."

"There's going to be nothing left of that car," Chase said. Graciela better start looking around for another clunker. The bus system in Albuquerque was not good. She needed to get around and Chase didn't want to be her emergency taxi service.

"I didn't know Jacinda had a bad hip. What's wrong with it?" Alma asked.

"We're not certain she does. It's more a sporadic sort of martyrdom. We added the phrase, with her bad hip no less, as a family joke of sorts," Chase said.

Delia passed out copies of a short porn story she was hoping to sell to an erotic anthology. They all began perusing it except Chase who was still concerned with family dynamics.

"Is Jacinda still mad about Graciela's jail stint?" Chase asked.

"Probably, but there's this other thing." Delia took a chair.

Jasmine was reading the story with a look of complete confusion on her face.

"What other thing?" Chase said.

"Jacinda caught us in her relic cupboard." Delia poured herself some tea and gulped half of it down.

"Did you find the pinky bone of Jesus?" Chase inquired.

"I don't think so. Why, did you lose it?"

"No, I've been waiting years to go in there. You got a free show and you didn't even care."

"A better question would be what were you two doing in there?" Alma asked.

"Graciela wanted some relic thing that Jacinda uses in her exorcisms. God, I've never been so scared in my life. Jacinda comes flying around the corner, carrying this religious candle so the shadow she projects is huge. I about jump right the fuck out of my skin. Graciela drops whatever she had and screams, 'Run!' and we hightailed it out of there."

"Ugh." Chase rolled her eyes and looking at Delia's story proceeded to circle the word "cunt" which ran through the first page four times.

"Delia, as part of the select sect of women of words, is it really necessary to use the F-word as a part of speech?" Alma asked.

"You do use it a lot," Bo said in confirmation.

"What's tribadism?" Jasmine asked. She tucked her hair behind her ear.

Chase coughed. These sessions reading Delia's work were always a bit of a shock for Jasmine. Alma, it appeared, was either more worldly or viewed the stories in an abstract way. She was interested in the quality of the writing rather than the subject matter. Alma had done wonders for the beauty of Delia's sentences to the extent that they were now almost literary porn.

"Did you realize you used the word cunt twenty-one times in ten pages?" Chase said.

"Really? I had no idea."

Chase handed Delia her copy with the circled words.

Bo had already set to work finding the word as if Delia's short story were some kind of word puzzle. "She's right."

"That might be a problem," Alma said.

"There's a lot of references to pink folds," Bo said, doing his own circles.

"What are pink folds?" Jasmine asked.

Jasmine's lack of knowledge of female parts astounded Chase. Maybe she'd never even masturbated and didn't know where anything was. Her clitoris could be a foreign land. It made her wonder about her husband Philip's ability in bed.

"Meat curtains," Bo said.

"In *Tristram Shandy*, I loved that scene," Chase said.

"What the fuck?" Delia said. She caught Alma's eye and rephrased. "I mean, I don't get it."

"Old book, funny, difficult to read but well worth it," Chase said.

"Meat curtains?" Jasmine said.

Delia sighed heavily. She'd obviously gotten the reference. "If you'd let me have an hour in bed with you you'd know every part of your body and some places you didn't even know existed." She drew a quick sketch on the back of the first page of her story and handed it to Jasmine. "There, all the parts including the meat curtains."

Jasmine studied the diagram. "I didn't realize you were so good at anatomy."

Chase noticed Jasmine stick the diagram in the back of her notebook. Delia noticed it as well. She smiled at Chase, who narrowed her eyes in warning. Delia ignored her. Had Delia been sitting closer Chase would have done bodily harm to get her point across.

"Back to the business at hand, the repetitive use of certain words is not good. There must be other words or euphemisms that could be utilized," Alma said.

"Unfortunately, my thesaurus doesn't include the word cunt

and vagina doesn't work for me," Delia said. "God, I really did use it twenty-two times—rock on. That's gotta be an f-ing record."

"Alma's right. There's got to be another way to describe this particular body part," Chase said. She had her own troubles with love scenes and was endlessly being advised by her editor to make them more graphic. As far as she was concerned, love scenes should be left to the reader's imagination. Everyone knew what went where and how it felt. But this was not a common sentiment for moist-mound sagas and so she relented to Ariana's suggestions with reluctance.

"What about nether regions?" Bo said. He poured his third glass of iced tea.

With tea containing only half the caffeine of coffee he was doubling up. Chase wondered how long it would be until he had to pee. Men's bladders amazed her. "It's too archaic," she replied.

"How about woo-woo," Jasmine said.

"Where'd you get that?" Delia said, giving her an intense gaze.

"On *The L Word*."

Delia raised an eyebrow.

"When I was clicking through the channels." Jasmine didn't look at her.

"Yeah, on your way to *Masterpiece Theatre*," Bo said.

"Or perhaps it was the *Antiques RoadsShow*," Chase said. She smiled in complicity with the others.

"Jasmine, you shouldn't be so defensive about your sense of curiosity," Alma said. "Writers need to be curious. It's what informs our writing."

"I know." Jasmine looked down.

In an effort to save her further embarrassment, Chase narrowed in on Delia. "I think sometimes you just put that word in there because you can. In several places you've told the reader about what's being done so the word is redundant."

"May the Pink Mafia never hear you say that," Delia said.

"Yes, let's perk up the description and you'll have a nice bit of porn here," Alma said, going back to the manuscript.

"May I use your bathroom?" Bo said, getting up rather abruptly.

"Of course. I expect after three rather large glasses of tea you should," Alma said.

"So who calls it a woo-woo on that show you don't watch?" Delia said.

Jasmine jumped in without a thought for the foil. "Dana Fairbanks. You know they kill her off in the third season." She blanched.

"Wow, even I didn't know that," Delia said.

Jasmine was trapped. "There's never anything else on."

"Yeah, sure," Delia said.

Chase looked on in pity. She was going to have to teach Jasmine some skill in taciturnity, and soon.

Chapter Thirteen

"Like I care if I get a fucking birthday cake from her," Graciela said. She shoved a tortilla chip in her mouth.

Chase and Gitana were having lunch at Gardenas with her and Delia. It was Graciela's birthday and Jacinda wasn't speaking to her. The luncheon was Chase's idea. She was trying to socialize and acclimate herself to holidays and family events. She didn't want Bud to adopt her hermit ways.

"We don't have to do this," Gitana had said before they left the house as Chase sorted through her clothes in search of a decent outfit.

"Does this look okay?" Chase held up a gray shirt and beige trousers.

"No." Gitana grabbed a white blouse off the hanger, held it up against them. She nodded. "When in doubt choose white. I think a pair of black jeans would do better. This is a little frumpy. When did you buy those hideous slacks?" she asked.

"The other day. I thought they'd be perfect for PTA meetings." Chase studied them. They were ugly, but they'd seemed like the beacon of respectability.

Gitana got the black jeans out and whisked away the offending garment. "Bud isn't even born yet. We'll get you proper outfits when the time comes."

Chase was humbled. Normally, she had good taste. The trousers were a sign that she was trying to be something she was not. She'd have to watch that.

"I mean it about not going. Graciela won't care. She's going to Delia's tonight where they will have a decadent party in her honor."

"But we're her family."

"I know," Gitana had said.

And now they were here and Chase thought Graciela looked pleased. The waitress came by with a pitcher of margaritas and spring water for Gitana. Chase ordered more chips and grabbed one of the few remaining ones before Graciela devoured them all.

"I slept with Jasmine the other day," Delia said. She took a sip of her margarita and sat back.

The tortilla chip headed straight for Chase's lungs. She gasped and turned red, coughing violently. Gitana patted her back. Delia offered to do the Heimlich maneuver and Graciela suggested a sip of margarita.

"How about some water," Gitana said, handing Chase her glass.

Chase took a sip and regained control of her breathing.

"Like I was saying, remember when we talked in group about sex and how I offered to show her the ropes, well, she took me up on my offer."

"Jasmine, your writer friend, the one who's married and obviously straight?" Gitana said.

"Yes," Chase said. She took several sips of her drink in order to drown the chip and to try and stave off her unease.

"Straight women are so hot. Rock on," Graciela said, giving Delia the high-five.

"Dude, this story is your birthday present from me to you with love." She smacked Graciela on the lips.

Their relationship completely confused Chase. Gitana had tried to explain it to her, but Chase still found it incomprehensible. Graciela had told Gitana that they'd slept together. Two butches getting together made no sense according to the rules of engagement set forth by the Pink Mafia.

"Onward, soldier," Graciela said.

Chase unraveled her silverware from the linen napkin and tried to catch the waitress's eye. Please let there be an interruption, she pleaded. She would never look at Jasmine the same way. She tried distraction. "Has everyone decided what they want?"

She looked around again. The restaurant wasn't busy and their table was offset as she'd requested. Who knew what Delia and Graciela were capable of saying or doing in a family establishment? She was glad of her choice.

"So," Delia continued, "the way it went down, Jasmine suggests we have lunch at the Sheraton in Old Town. I'm not thinking anything of it. I know the bar so I'm thinking lunch and a drink."

"Duh, hotel restaurant, hotel room," Graciela said. She poured another margarita.

Chase looked at Gitana in hopelessness. She took her hand. "It's her party."

Delia nodded. "Yeah, quick lunch, two drinks and we're at the front desk. Jasmine pays cash. The clerk is kind of funny about it until she pops him an extra twenty. He hands over the keys."

"Is this really a good family topic?" Chase eyed the margarita pitcher.

Gitana nodded. "I'll drive."

Chase topped off Delia's drink, hoping she might get sidetracked and not go into lurid details.

"Yes, then what happened?" Graciela asked. The huge slurp

115

she took off her drink reminded Chase of uncouth sailors sitting around a tavern waiting for the storm to subside so they could get on their rat-infested ship—something straight out of Melville.

"We get to the room and sit on the bed. Jasmine looks really scared so I say in my most compassionate and tender voice…"

"Gag me," Chase said. She made a show of studying her menu hoping this would be a clue to the others as well as the waitress.

"Ignore her," Graciela said, picking up her fork and pointing it at Chase. "She knows nothing of butch courting rituals."

It was true. She didn't. She was not a butch, but she wasn't exactly femme either. Gitana was pretty femme, but she was also responsible for most of the seductions.

Delia didn't miss a stroke. "I say I won't do anything she doesn't like and she can tell me to stop anytime."

"Straight women melt at this," Graciela informed them.

The waitress brought more chips. Chase was hoping they could order. The motherly looking Hispanic waitress got out her order pad, but Graciela waved her away.

Chase looked at Gitana. "Did you know about any of this stuff?"

"What stuff?" Gitana asked.

"Seduction methods."

Gitana shook her head. "It's news to me."

"You two need to get out more," Graciela said.

"What? So now you're the Dr. Ruth of lesbians," Chase said, snatching a chip and dunking it in the refilled salsa bowl.

"Then I sucked her fingers." Delia graphically demonstrated.

Finger-sucking was news to Chase. It had never occurred to her. What other things did she not know? It seemed that there were only so many ways to get laid but here was something else.

"Works every time it's tried," Graciela said.

"That's a blatant appropriation of the abstinence campaign," Chase said. She could hardly believe she was quoting Conservative rhetoric on the use of abstinence as a teen birth control method.

"Lovely, isn't it," Graciela said, helping herself to an enormous handful of chips.

"You aren't going to be hungry for lunch," Gitana said, pulling the chip basket away from her and in Chase's direction.

Chase, now extremely interested in the finger sucking, took Gitana's hand and put her index finger in her mouth. She ran her tongue around it and bit it softly. Gitana flushed.

"See, it works. She just creamed her pants," Graciela said.

Chase picked up her fork and poked her in the forearm. "Don't talk about your sister like that."

Graciela rubbed the sore spot and ignored her.

Delia, not distracted in the least, continued her narrative. "Then kissing. She can kiss."

The waitress came back. Thank God, Chase thought. A perfect diversion.

"Obviously more margaritas," Graciela said.

"And food would be nice," Chase said, pointing at the menus.

"Alas, to be continued," Delia said. She looked down quickly at the menu.

"Don't bother," Chase said.

When Graciela flipped her off Gitana touched her arm to prevent her from poking Graciela with her fork then smiled sweetly at the waitress and ordered spinach enchiladas. A choice Chase agreed with for the baby's sake. She ordered the same. Delia ordered some fish taco thing that Chase was certain was sick and perverted. Graciela ordered the grande nachos as if in defiance for being deprived of the chip bowl.

Delia continued with more lurid details of what went where while Chase and Gitana learned things they'd never thought of. Jasmine definitely got her education, Chase cogitated. The food arrived, which put an end to the birthday porn feast. The family birthday party couldn't be over soon enough as far as Chase was concerned.

On the drive home, Gitana took Chase's hand. "You did really well today. I'm proud of you."

"Not to mention I had to listen to sex stories the whole time."

Gitana hit the freeway and floored the Hummer. Chase looked over in astonishment. "You're right it does have balls," Gitana said, and smiled like a sixteen-year-old just discovering the utter thrill of speed.

"Just be careful—remember it's the safety corridor—double fine zone for speeding."

Gitana set the cruise control for five over. "You know what I don't understand?"

"What?" Chase stuck Gitana's finger in her mouth.

"That you can write moist-mound sagas, but you don't like to talk about it."

Chase let go of her finger. "I'm shy." She put Gitana's index finger back in her mouth, gently wrapping her tongue around it.

"Oh, my."

Chase let go. "You like?"

"Uh-huh."

Chase did it again. By the time Gitana got off at the Zuzak exit her face was flushed. "You've got to stop that or I'm going to have to pull over."

"Pull over."

The first dirt road they hit, Gitana pulled in. They tested the passenger's seat recline feature.

As Chase lifted Gitana's blouse, she said, "Good thing this thing has tinted windows."

"The Hummer is growing on me. It's very versatile," Gitana said, as she straddled Chase and undid her trousers, slipping her hand inside. "I think this finger-sucking thing is good for you too."

"Oh, yes. I like these stretchy pants too. They're very convenient," she said, reaching inside Gitana's maternity pants.

"Very."

Chapter Fourteen

Chase brought up Gitana's small cup of coffee. She was now allowed an espresso cup's worth. Chase referred to it as the weaning. Gitana considered it ruthless authoritarianism.

Gitana rolled over and opened one eye. "Is it time already?"

Usually the sun came through the adjoining sunroom door, lighting up the bedroom and indicating the break of day. It was mostly dark, the sun barely over the horizon.

"Where's the sun?" she asked.

"It's not exactly up yet." Chase looked around as if she noticed the lack of light just at that moment.

"Then what are you doing?" Gitana sat up, not looking happy.

"We need to get an early start." She handed Gitana the tiny cup of coffee.

Gitana studied Chase's outfit as she sat on the edge of the bed. She wore a green T-shirt and beige Carhartt shorts. "Why are you wearing a Blooming Orchids shirt?"

"It's my first day of work. Nora got it for me."

"Because?" Gitana gulped her tiny coffee.

"When Bud arrives you'll need to be home for a while so I need to know how to run the business, with Nora's help of course."

"Chase, you'll scare off the employees." She finished her coffee and sat up straighter.

"No, I won't. I've been reading Dale Carnegie's book, *How to Win Friends and Influence People*. I think I got it down. I've committed certain passages to memory." She got up and started making the bed around Gitana.

"What about your writing?"

"I got up early and already wrote my allotted number of pages. I'm more focused now that I don't have all day to piss around. Now, chop, chop. We've got work to do. I want to be there early so Nora can show me how to open."

Gitana groaned, grabbed her pillow, and put it over her head. "I don't think you're being very positive about this."

When they got to the nursery, Nora was waiting for them. "You look good."

"Thank you," Chase said, smoothing down the front of her shirt.

"And you're duplicitous," Gitana said.

It was a fine summer day, no clouds and perfect gardening weather. Chase looked contently around at the greenhouses and the tidy gravel paths that led to them. She'd wondered about a neon sign for the nursery but decided the nicely painted one did just fine. She must not institute too many changes immediately.

"It's a good idea," Nora told Gitana. "When Bud is able to travel and we set up a play area then work for you is feasible. In the meantime, Chase learning the ropes is a sound business decision." Nora adjusted her tool belt and looked slightly abashed.

Gitana eyed Nora suspiciously. "Did she pay you?"

"This is for Bud's sake." Nora didn't meet her gaze.

"Not you too," Gitana whined.

"What?" Nora said, digging around in her overall pockets.

"Calling the baby Bud."

"Well, if you'd use the ultrasound as medical science intended we'd know what sex Bud was and we wouldn't be calling him/her Bud," Nora replied.

"The ultrasound is used to detect problems. The baby's sex is a convenience. I want the baby to be a surprise—to know she or he is growing inside me without preconceptions so that the arrival will be as it should be," Gitana replied.

"Like in the caveman days," Nora said.

"And they tell me *I'm* the nut job," Chase said.

"This is your very own key." She handed it to Chase, then pulled out a pewter key fob in the shape of an orchid. "And this is your welcome aboard present."

"That's so nice." Chase gave her a hug.

Nora and Gitana stared at her.

"What?"

"You don't instigate hugs," Gitana said.

"This is the new me. Did you get the doughnuts and bagels as was prearranged?"

"Yes, they are in the truck."

"Orange juice, coffee and herbal tea for the freaky ones?"

"Of course," Nora said.

"Did you think of anything else they might like?" Chase had taken out a small notebook and was looking over her list, checking things off.

"A raise but that's not in the budget," Nora said.

Gitana peered over at Chase's notebook trying to get a closer look. Chase shut it and put it back in her pocket. "What are you two up to?" Gitana demanded.

"Employee breakfast. I want to show my appreciation for all their hard work," Chase said.

"It sounds more like bribery to me."

Chase unlocked the front door. "It is," Nora said, holding the door open for Gitana.

"You two need to read Dale Carnegie's book. It's all about presentation."

Both Nora and Gitana gave her a look of skepticism.

"I'm going to make this a fun place to work."

"Sure," Nora said. "Why don't we unload the goods? I told the employees to show up twenty minutes early for a staff meeting."

"So everyone is in on this except me," Gitana said.

"We knew you wouldn't agree," Nora said over her shoulder.

"Exactly," Chase said, following her to her truck.

At the staff meeting Gitana sat on one side of the break room as Nora introduced Chase. "Now we all know that Gitana is with child so we're bringing in her partner, Chase, to help run the business in her absence."

There was a strange quiet like a collective drawing in of breath.

Chase stood up. "Lighten up. This will be fun. I mean, I'm going to pick your brains for pertinent info. Nora will be guiding me through the day-to-day operations. Don't worry. I'm only crabby on Monday, Wednesday and Friday. I haven't water boarded anyone in at least two years and my only stipulation is that if I catch you texting while you're on the clock I'll break your fingers."

Nora and Gitana blanched. There was no response from the fifteen employees.

"Geez, you people really need to lighten up. Grab some chow and I'll be around later to see what it is you all do."

The employees still looked shell-shocked as they got breakfast. Chase joined Nora and Gitana.

"I thought that went well. Don't you?" she said. She bit into a bagel and felt serene.

Gitana rubbed her temples.

"Except for that bit about breaking fingers," Nora said, pouring a glass of orange juice and handing it to Gitana.

"I was just kidding. It's all about instruction through humor."

"According to the Mr. Carnegie," Nora said.

"You've got it," Chase said, slapping her good-naturedly. She looked at Gitana holding an empty plate. "Can I get you something?"

"No, suddenly I'm feeling a little ill."

"Ill at ease," Nora said quietly.

"I'll be in my office. Please show our new MOD around the place."

Chase looked puzzled. "MOD?"

"Manager on duty," Nora said, snagging a muffin.

Gitana looked pained and went to her office. Watching her go, Chase said, "Was I that bad? It was supposed to be funny."

"Don't worry. You're right about the texting and they know it. Seems to me it was the perfect way to let the employees know that you have the inside scoop."

"Gitana's worried I'll scare them off," Chase said, pouring another cup of coffee from the large silver decanter. She was glad Gitana wasn't there to see. Her downsizing on coffee in support of the cause was proving more difficult than she'd thought.

"Chase, this is a sweet job especially if you're studying botany or you like working with plants. Most of the employees have been here two years or more. The worst you'll do is call them on their bullshit. Besides, you're good at asking questions and being interested in new things. People like that. It makes them feel important."

"Thank you. I feel much better. Can I hug you again? I have to practice."

"Sure." Nora wrapped her big arms around Chase. "See, it's not so bad."

"No, it's really not."

"I'm proud of you," Nora said, stepping back and studying Chase.

"For what, exactly?"

"For realizing your full potential."

"You have read Dale Carnegie," Chase said, picking up her coffee cup with relish.

"No, I haven't, but I think I'll know most of it by the end of the week. Are you ready to get started?"

Chase gulped her coffee, straightened her shoulders and nodded. "Let's go."

Nora got Chase an apron and a set of clippers. Then she gave her cash register instructions. Technological advances such as bar codes and registers that indicated exact change made that part easy.

After that Nora sent her off with Eliza, the head nursery person, for lessons on orchids. Eliza looked at her tentatively. She was a small woman, with mousy brown hair, round black spectacles and thin lips which she endlessly applied ChapStick. Chase tried not to get caught up in studying her mannerisms for future writing projects and set herself to task for learning about orchids.

Soon Eliza seemingly forgot that she was teaching Gitana's psycho-wife about all the plants and their care. She methodically started from the beginning and went forward in a concise way. Chase liked this. It worked with her brain type.

"Orchids are of the orchidaceae family with eight-hundred described genera and twenty-five thousand species. They are the most advanced floral evolution ever known."

"Top of the plant chain, eh? What about the name? Is it Latin?" Word origins were always of particular interest to her. As a writer, she liked to know. Years of poring over the dictionary had only furthered this obsession.

"Actually, it's Greek for Orchi which means…" She stopped and blushed. She stroked the white petals of an orchid and avoided Chase's gaze.

"Yes," Chase said, now very interested.

"It means testicle," Eliza said quickly.

Chase laughed. "You're kidding, right?" She couldn't imagine Eliza making such a joke but maybe it was a long-standing practice of deceiving the newbies.

"It's because of the subterranean tuberoids. Theophrastos

first used the word, orchis in his book *De Historia Plantarum, the Natural History of Plants.*"

"He must have been a fag."

Eliza ignored this comment and proceeded with the tour.

Gitana came out of her office as they passed by. "How is it going?"

"I had no idea you liked testicles." Chase smiled smugly.

"Why did you give her the word origin?" she asked Eliza.

"She asked."

"All you need to know is care, feeding and type," Gitana said, pointedly looked at Eliza. She went back into her office.

"Ball queen," Chase called after her.

"I'm not listening," Gitana said as she sat down at her desk. "Carry on."

Eliza led her to the first greenhouse which was the potting house. "The orchids feed according to their natural habitat on air and other plants but not as parasites." She seemed adamant about that as if preserving the innocence of the orchid by stating that it would never do anything so loathsome. "On rocks in rocky soil, rain water, humus and their own dead tissue." In the greenhouse, she stuck a scooping shovel into a bucket of what looked like bark. "Ours are mostly terrestrial plants and grow in soil."

"I see." Chase fingered the soil. It looked like regular potting soil with big woody chunks in it. It must be magical to grow such beautiful and expensive plants. They didn't have orchids at the house. Gitana said she needed a break from them at home so she left the gardening to Chase and adored the cut flowers from the jewel garden. These plants that Eliza was gingerly examining were no tray of six from Home Depot for a dollar seventy-nine.

"All the orchids are marked. This one is a Calopogon, a bumblebee orchid. This one is a wild orchid from the Sumatran rain forest..."

"I like coffee from Sumatra with a lot of milk, of course."

Eliza nodded. Boy, these people are dry, Chase thought.

"This," Eliza said, pointing to one of the many orchids

perched on the tables, "is a Dactylorhiza Fuchsii or the common spotted orchid."

This made sense to Chase despite the overblown name as the orchid flower was indeed spotted.

"This one is a Gymnadenia Conopsea or the fragrant orchid."

Chase leaned in to smell it. This was the amazing scent that had filled Gitana's studio apartment the day of her seduction. She was about to relive that amorous moment when Eliza slapped a hardbound book with a dark green cover into her hands.

"This is the manual describing every orchid we feature. It is updated every time we get in a new orchid and is absolutely crucial to this job."

"Do I have to memorize the fancy name?" Chase felt the weight of the book and was alarmed.

"Only if you want to appear knowledgeable and thus credible to our discerning buyers." Eliza applied more ChapStick and adjusted her spectacles.

She suddenly reminded Chase of her Latin teacher in the ninth grade. The prim woman who'd been the physical incarnation of Miss Jean Brody but without her apparent disregard for convention. The girls had given her the moniker, "bitchi extremus."

"Got it."

"Good. The manual follows the nursery placement. I came up with its application so you can be assured that all is as it should be. You should begin there at the Anacamptis Pyramidalis. I will supervise and answer any questions you have. Shall we?"

By lunchtime Chase's head was pounding and she'd taken to counting the number of times Eliza had applied ChapStick which was fifty-eight. She now sat in the break room, poring over the orchid bible as Eliza put it, *The Kew World Checklist of Orchids*.

Gitana came in. "There you are. I've been looking everywhere. I thought we'd grab lunch."

"I don't think I have time for lunch," Chase said, looking morosely at the book. "I'm still learning about leaves and shit—

ovate, lanceolate or orbiculate, pseudobulbs and back bulbs and zygomorphic flowers. Damn, no wonder you studied botany. I thought you just liked flowers. The fucking customers are like walking orchid encyclopedias. Some lady asked me something about sepals, petals cattleyas and venus slippers and then something about concrescent sepals. I felt like I was on another fucking planet. Who are these people?" She slammed the book shut and rubbed her temples.

"They're orchid lovers." Gitana patted her back.

"No, they're evil aliens with a weird vocabulary."

Gitana laughed. "As your boss I order you to have lunch with me. Look, you don't have to learn everything about orchids in one day. I'll get you the orchid cheat sheet."

Chase lit up. "Like CliffNotes?"

"Yes, and then you do what Nora does, you guide the overly inquisitive, overly educated buyer to one of the botany students who are listed on the cheat sheet along with their special expertise and let them handle it. Besides, that woman who went on about the sepals should have known the difference between a cattleya and a venus lady slipper."

"That bitch. She saw my weakness and like a lioness went for the throat," Chase said, narrowing her eyes and suppressing the desire to water board the old hag.

"So take it easy."

"What's for lunch?" Chase said brightly.

"Nora went to Subway. I got you a club sandwich and sour cream potato chips."

"And cookies for dessert?" Food always cheered her up.

"Of course."

Chase fell asleep on the couch when they got home. In the background she remotely heard the phone ring. She was still comatose when Gitana brought her the phone.

"It's Lacey."

Chase opened her eyes. "Is it serious, otherwise I need to keep napping."

127

Gitana relayed this. "She says it's extremely important."

"It better be." Chase sat up and took the phone. Her whole body ached from standing, sorting and planting fucking orchids. She hated them already.

"What? One day in the workplace and you're a basket case," Lacey said.

"Oh, piss off. Now what's your emergency?"

"Well, it's not exactly an emergency," Lacey hedged.

"Ugh! I could still be napping."

"You won't sleep tonight if you nap too long."

"Somehow that doesn't console me." She nodded her thanks to Gitana who brought her a cup of red bush tea. She noticed the cup had an orchid lithograph print on both sides. They were everywhere. She'd never noticed. She was going to take a good look around the house. Gitana probably had orchid underwear that she didn't know about. "What's your gig?"

"Gig?" Lacey asked.

"It's text talk for what's up?" Chase was learning new words from the younger workers at the greenhouse. She took a sip of tea and studied the reproduction on the cup. It was a beautiful and quite accurate rendition of a fuschia-colored Calopogon orchid. Maybe she was getting it.

"It's about Jasmine. She asked me out on a date."

"Big deal. You two spend a lot of time at Pilates class or those other weird physical contortion exercise gigs." That was the conventional use of the word "gig." She wondered how it had morphed into a word about what was going on. "You socialized at Bo's Fourth of July barbeque. So what's so weird about girl time?"

"It's different."

"You're getting your nails done or something? Is that different?" Chase was really quite perplexed.

"It's lunch." Lacey was being incomprehensibly vague and this gave Chase trepidation as well as the desire to shake Lacey from her heels until all the facts fell out of her like change from her pockets.

"So? As long as it's not the Sheraton Hotel bar, you're cool."
Chase sipped her tea. Suddenly, images of Delia fucking Jasmine's
brains out popped into her mind.

"That's where she wants to go. How did you know that?"

"Really? She knows you're straight, right?" Chase sat at full
attention. Delia had created a Lothario.

"Well, yeah. We used to guy watch at Starbucks together after
Pilates. You know, it's just down the street from the classroom."

"She doesn't sound horribly committed to Philip. I mean,
he is her husband." She couldn't believe she was defending him.
Nervously she picked up the copy of *Orchid Monthly* from the
coffee table. She needed something to quiet her nerves. There
was an article on reproduction. She was scheduled for training
tomorrow in the reproductive room aka the nursery.

"Have you ever met him?" Lacey said.

"I can't say I have." Chase imagined him as a metro sexual go-
getter with a healthy dose of egocentrism.

"He's a dick, treats her crappy, and sucks in bed."

"Sounds like a beautiful relationship. Maybe you're reading
this wrong. She might just need a shoulder to cry on," Chase said.

"I don't think so. She told me about her enlightening
afternoon with Delia."

Chase could tell that Lacey was miffed that this particularly
juicy bit of information had not been passed her way. "I would
have told you, but I didn't want to blab in case Jasmine wasn't
comfortable with it. I mean, for all practical purposes Jasmine is
still straight aside from that slight detour." She underlined key
words like labellum, viscidium and pollinia so she could look
them up later. The magazine assumed the reader already knew a
lot about orchids.

"So what should I do?"

"Are you still straight?"

"Of course," Lacey said petulantly. This pleased Chase.

"Then tell her that. Make your date at Starbucks instead and behave as before."

"Avoidance tactics?"

"Exactly. Jasmine will get the point." Chase hoped. She would have a talk with Jasmine about choice, discretion and the dangers of bisexuality.

Chapter Fifteen

"I like the monkeys best," Addison said.

"Me too. They remind me of people I've known," Chase said.

Addison giggled.

It was Saturday and they were at the zoo with Hilda's parenting class. Addison laughed at the monkeys' antics as they climbed along the ropes in their cage. There was something magical about a child's laugh, Chase thought. She didn't remember laughing a lot as a child. She made other people laugh with her terse wit. She was a quipster. She would do her best to make Bud laugh a lot. "See that one over there—that's Mrs. Waine, my first grade teacher." She pointed to the monkey sitting in the corner with her arms crossed on her chest.

"She looks crabby."

"She was. If you were bad she made you sit in the corner with your back turned so everyone could make fun of you, but you couldn't see them."

"Like what kind of bad things?"

"Spit balls mostly," Chase said.

"What are those?" Addison licked her rapidly melting chocolate ice cream cone.

Chase did the same. That was the conundrum with ice cream. It was a summer dessert, but it didn't fare well in the sun. No one ate ice cream in the winter. Chase didn't know if it was a cultural thing or that it lowered your body temperature when the world was brilliant white and freezing and was thus unhealthy.

"Spit balls are tiny wadded up pieces of notebook paper that you spit on so they're tight and firm. Then you feed them into one of those Bic pens, the clear ones after you take out the ink cartridge. You load your arsenal and fire away."

"Sweet," Addison said, delight registering in her eyes.

"Yeah, we used to nail the teacher's butt."

"I'd get expelled for school violence if I did that. Under the zero-tolerance policy spit balls would be seen as an aggressive act." She bit into the cone and sent ice cream flying. A lady with a toddler in a stroller ran it over.

"Really?" Chase was mortified.

"Yes. Last winter my friend got suspended for a week for throwing a snowball at recess."

"That's a little over the top." Chase put that on her reminder list. Bud might be homeschooled after all. They'd have to hire a tutor for math.

"It's part of the slow but steady takeover by the government in its attempt to become the paternal entity that saves us from ourselves—which of course will backfire as historically it always does."

The man standing next to them watching the monkeys looked over at Addison. "Pretty sharp kid you got there."

"Actually, she's a pre-adult," Chase informed him.

"You mean like a midget or something?"

"I'm taking human growth hormone," Addison replied.

"You better go to college, little missy, with the smarts you got."

"Thank you, sir."

"Polite too." He walked off.

Chase and Addison burst out laughing. "You are too much," Chase said, wiping her eyes.

"No, I'm just like you."

"I think it would be better if you weren't. I'm weird and socially maladjusted."

"But you're improving." She dug a Wet-Wipe out of her backpack and wiped her hands. She pulled out another one for Chase and wiped Chase's sticky chin.

"Thanks," Chase said, using the rest of it to clean her hands.

"You want to go to the aquarium and see the jellyfish?"

"What about Hilda and the others?" Chase asked.

"I'll call her," Addison said, whipping out her cell phone. "And tell her you have a stomachache from eating all this processed food and we have to go home."

Chase was about to say wouldn't it seem more feasible if you were the one with the stomachache but thought better of it. "Isn't that lying?" The morals of this act concerned her more.

Addison sighed heavily. "Do you want me to tell her that we think the group is hideous, that we'd rather have our wisdom teeth removed than spend the rest of the day with them at the zoo?"

"No."

"This is politely rephrasing the truth. You could have a tummy ache. It could get better so we went to the aquarium because you didn't want to disappoint me."

"You don't have political ambitions do you?" Chase inquired.

"Of course not. Politicians are banal and corrupt." She pulled up Hilda on her cell phone, called, muttered platitudes and clicked off.

"All clear?"

"Affirmative." Addison hopped up, shouldered her backpack and looked inquisitively at Chase.

"I'm coming."

"Can I drive your car?"

"No!" Chase said.

"Just testing. I may be precocious, but you are still the official grown-up."

"I know and that's what scares me." Chase eyed the giraffes as they passed. She'd always thought they were the most amazing creatures.

"Don't worry, if you can handle me, Bud will be a cinch."

"I don't think I'm a good influence," Chase said as they passed through the exit gates.

"Why?"

"Because I thought it was funny when you poisoned your father," Chase said.

"Your best trait, the one that will make your child respect you the most, is honesty. That's all we want and parents hardly ever do it. My mom lies to me all the time and she has no idea that I know. That's almost worse than the lie. Lie to me and then underestimate my intelligence on top of it—now that is an insult."

Chase, having located the car with Addison's help, clicked the alarm and helped Addison get in the Hummer. "Gawd, I can't wait to get taller. This short stuff is really getting old," Addison said.

Chase got in the driver's seat and said, "SUV's are a little high even for height-challenged adults."

Addison smiled. "Thanks, for not underestimating me."

"Thank you for understanding me."

When Gitana got home, Chase and Addison were eating cherry Popsicles and perusing the *New York Times Book Review*. Both had blazing red lips.

"Well, hello there. Chase didn't tell me we had company. I'm Gitana."

"Addison." She offered her hand and firmly shook Gitana's.

"You're Chase's new friend from that class…"

"That stupid parenting class. You can say it. You don't go

and you're right not to. My mom bailed on me again so we're hanging out until she's done doing what she does."

"Got it." Gitana pulled up a stool at the kitchen island. "Whew, Saturdays are getting rough."

"Especially when you're pregnant," Addison said.

"Yes."

"You want some lemonade or water or something?" Chase said, getting up.

"Lemonade would be nice. So what are you two up to?"

"Well, Addison is also a writer, so we're going through the book reviews learning some dos and don'ts of the trade."

"And what's credible and what's professional jealousy," Addison said, circling a large passage and pursing her lips.

"I see," Gitana said.

Addison's cell phone rang. The tag ring was The Eagles, 'Witchy Woman.' "Excuse me, it's my mother."

Gitana frowned. "I hope you didn't teach her that."

Chase held up her hand, "I swear. See, there are others who use the phone in this way. I am not alone."

"Others? As in aliens from a parallel universe who despise their mothers."

"Exactly." Chase cleaned up the Popsicle wrappers. She kissed Gitana's cheek. "I missed you. We had the best time and I wished you were there."

Addison raised her voice. "No, I don't mind spending the rest of the evening with the housekeeper who only speaks Russian. Sure, hold on." She handed the phone to Chase. "She wants to talk to you." Addison scowled and went back to circling offensive phrases in the newspaper.

"Hi, Peggy. What's up?"

"I was wondering if you could drop Addison by the house. I'm going to be longer than I thought and Dickhead isn't around as usual."

Chase assumed Dickhead was Addison's father. "Sure, we're going out to dinner so we'll drop her by." She looked at Addison

135

studying the newspaper.

"Maybe if she liked, Addison could come to dinner with us," Gitana suggested.

"Is that all right with you?" Chase asked Addison as she put her hand over the minute hole that she'd always assumed was the mouthpiece.

"Let me check my appointment book. No, I'm not busy."

Chase smiled and mouthed the words, "smart-ass."

Addison smiled sweetly.

"Peggy, if it's all right with you we could take Addison out to dinner with us and then home. We won't be out late."

"That would be wonderful. Tell Addison to hit the ATM for dinner money."

"Addison has a debit card?" Chase said, somewhat taken aback.

"Of course. Thanks so much, Chase. I really owe you." She clicked off.

Addison rooted around in her backpack and pulled out a small black leather wallet and extracted her debit card. "It's how I get my allowance. Dinner, however, is not out of my stash. She'll be reimbursing me for this."

"Gotcha," Chase said. She glanced at Gitana.

"It's not like you can carry around a lot of cash," Addison said. "I mean, think of it—twenty dollars doesn't buy much. A twelve-pack of Red Bull at Costco is thirty-two dollars, a candy bar is a buck and a quarter, a composition book, three-ninety-nine and not to mention lead refills for these." She picked up her blue mechanical pencil and waved it around.

Gitana studied Addison's black and white marbled composition book and then the pencil. They were identical to Chase's.

"I had nothing to do with it. She came that way."

Addison nodded. "We have similar styles. It's less stressful writing in pencil and mechanical pencils are better because you don't have to sharpen them. I don't, however, twirl mine, or play catch with it."

"Okay," Gitana said.

"We'll feed the dogs while you get cleaned up. You could take a leisurely bath."

"That sounds lovely. Why are the dogs so tired? Both of them are passed out under the juniper tree." Gitana got up slowly. At four months she was really starting to show. Chase gave her a lift up.

"We played big ball for almost an hour," Chase said. Big ball was a game that used hard rubber balls with a handle so the dogs could pick them up and catch them. Jane was a master dribbler and if she were human would have made a great soccer player as she skirted and out-dodged her opponent, usually Chase, and got the ball to the net that Chase had installed. Annie was the catcher. Chase would throw the ball high and Annie would run and catch it by the handle. Addison had loved the game. They played until Chase begged off saying she was old and had to rest.

"Can I make their dinner?" Addison asked as Chase pulled out a bowl of boiled chicken, a pack of frozen chopped broccoli and two Russet potatoes.

"Sure."

"Why do they eat such weird food?" Addison said, as she poured the broccoli into their bowls.

"Because I have a dog cookbook and I don't like them to eat meat byproducts and wheat gluten."

"What exactly are meat byproducts?" Addison asked.

Chase started the potatoes to boil. "My point exactly, what are meat byproducts?"

Addison concurred and took the shredded chicken meat. "At least we know what this is."

* * *

Lacey watched as Gitana and Addison played skeet ball. "I thought we were going to the Artichoke Café."

"What's wrong with Peter Piper Pizza?" Chase asked.

Addison was cheering Gitana on as she attempted to throw

painted wooden balls into wooden rings.

"To Addison, fun is a foreign concept. I don't think sacrificing one evening to the betterment of a child's life is a horrid thing," Chase replied.

Jasmine came back with a large bowl of vanilla ice cream covered in yellow, blue and red sprinkles. "This place is great!"

Lacey sighed. "Well, at least someone likes it."

"Want a bite?" Jasmine asked.

"It does look good," Lacey said.

Instead of handing the spoon to Lacey, she fed her the ice cream. Chase watched at they gazed at each other and had something akin to spoon sex. Huh, she thought, maybe Lacey isn't as straight as she thinks. She claimed to be always on the lookout for Mr. Right but did very little to find him. Her best friend was a lesbian and her straight friends had bad partners. This was an interesting combo.

"I can't believe we ate all that pizza," Lacey said, pointing to the three large and now empty platters that still graced the red and white checkered plastic tablecloth.

"I'm going to have massive heartburn," Chase said, looking down at the empty platter of pizza.

"Oh, here, take one of these," Jasmine said, pulling out a bottle of Zantac. "This is good stuff."

"Thanks," Chase said, popping two pills with her enormous cup of Coke. She never had this kind of food, but then she had never actually been to this kind of place. Addison broadened her horizons and she felt fortunate.

Addison and Gitana returned to the table. Breathless, Gitana said, "She won."

"But you were really close," Addison said. Her eyes were shiny and Chase could tell she was tired.

"We'd better get you home," Chase said. She glanced outside. Night had finally come. She always found the lingering twilight of summer disturbing. She wanted night to come at a logical hour so she could begin her evening. With day clinging for so long, she ended up going to bed late which in turn screwed up her morning. This rigidity would have to be altered when Bud arrived.

"I had no idea places like this even existed," Addison said, gazing around in pure delight.

"Your parents never brought you here for your birthday or something?" Jasmine said.

Chase glanced pityingly at Jasmine and then looked at Addison. They nodded at each other in joint agreement that Jasmine was a complete airhead.

"Let me think about it. Uh, no. They wouldn't be caught dead in a place like this."

"That's why you're a pre-adult instead of a kid. You never got the chance to be one," Lacey said.

Chase kicked her under the table.

"Ouch," Lacey said, bending over to rub her shin.

"No, she's right. I've tried, but I can't seem to be like the other kids."

Addison stared morosely at her empty pizza plate. Gitana took her hand. "Addison, you can't turn off your brain just to fit in or be the way the other kids are. You're really smart and you should never want that to go away. Being a kid has more to do with having fun, with laughing and playing. You did that today."

Addison looked at her. "That's good spin, but I do like the concept."

Lacey laughed. "I still hold my opinion of you as a pre-adult. But I wouldn't worry about it—look at Chase—she was never a child either. She's been a weirdo since the day she was born and she turned out all right."

Everyone laughed and had there been proper cutlery at the table instead of plastic knives and forks Chase would have done Lacey bodily harm. Instead, she kicked her other shin.

"I guess you're right. I could put my jovial pre-adult photo smiling and having fun on my MySpace profile and see what that gets me. There must be others," Addison said.

"You don't do that do you?" Chase said. She'd heard horrid things about kids and the Internet.

"No, it's stupid narcissism. I only use the Internet for research purposes."

"Of course," Chase said, inwardly sighing.

Chase and Gitana drove Addison home. She lived in a massive house in the Foothills. The Sandia Mountains made up her backyard. Chase pulled up in the circular drive. "Here, let me walk you up so your mom will know you got in safe."

"Sure." Addison pulled her backpack up on her shoulders and led the way to the front door with its elaborate white stucco portico.

Addison plugged in the code that opened the front door. A tiny gray-haired woman with a face wrinkled everywhere and the tightest bun Chase had ever seen came rushing into the hallway. She definitely spoke a language Chase had never heard before except on television.

"That's fine. I'm off to bed," Addison told the woman. The woman nodded. She disappeared as quickly as she appeared. Apparently aware that Chase was confused Addison said, "She told me my mother isn't home yet. It's all right. I'll leave her a note. Thanks for a really nice day."

"But you understood what she said."

Addison smiled slyly. "That's our secret."

"So maybe I could see you next Saturday," Chase said, peering down the hall at a large painting of black and brown mustangs running wild on the prairie.

"Sure. Could we skip the Hilda-part and go solo?"

"Good plan but would your mom go for it?"

"She'd be delighted. After all, in her eyes I'd have a new babysitter but that's not what it is." She set her backpack down and didn't look at Chase like she feared the answer.

Grown people must have truly abused her sense of trust. "Of course not. I was hoping you considered me a compatriot despite my having exited pre-adulthood."

"But have you?"

Chase smiled. "Well, perhaps not. That's why I have you as one of my few mentors. It's an elite club."

"Do I get one of those double-breasted blazers with the coat of arms on the breast pocket?"

"I'll get my tailor right on it."

"You know how your friends hug one another…"

"Yes?"

"Could I have one?"

Chase squatted down thinking she'd had some short friends before but not this short and gave her a hug. Then she pinched her. "Don't let the bedbugs bite."

Addison squealed. "Uck!"

"My sentiments exactly. Think of what you want to do next week."

"Oh, I will," Addison said, looking cunning.

"Nothing overly dangerous or toxic."

"We'll see."

Chase watched Addison walk down the marble-tiled hallway with the gold-trimmed walls and an eighteen-foot ceiling. She looked so small. Chase let herself out.

When she got in the car, Gitana said, "You're going to make a great father."

"I hope so. Addison is so like me at her age it's almost freaky." She drove out of the driveway, glancing at the house again.

"It is. You know, they say you have two chances in your life for making good changes—once when you're a child and the other when you're a parent. Or surrogate parent in Addison's case."

"What are you saying? That we could work on becoming normal together?" She turned on Tramway and headed toward the freeway. The twinkling house lights seemed homey against the black mass of the Sandia Mountains.

"Not exactly normal but maybe eccentric without the savagery."

"How boring."

Gitana pinched her.

Chapter Sixteen

Chase hosed off the seldom-used covered patio with a barbeque station that had been built in when they bought the house. It appeared the previous owner liked to entertain. She and Gitana had never used it.

"You actually invited your fucking mother to your First Annual Labor Day Picnic," Graciela said. She was supposed to be helping Chase. Instead, she was drinking beer and being incredulous at every opportunity.

"You might refrain from calling her my fucking mother." She hosed off the tile bar that flanked either side of the gas grill. Dust turned to mud and ran off the countertops in great brown streams.

"That's what you always call her," Graciela retorted.

Chase pointed to the large sponge and bucket of soapy water. Graciela got the hint and put down her beer. "I'm turning over a new leaf."

"When will Gitana be here?" Graciela said, as if Gitana's arrival might get her out of chore duty. She made broad swaths with the sponge across the tabletop.

"She's going to Home Depot for the grill parts before she picks up Jacinda."

"That's great."

Chase waited for it to hit.

"*What!* You invited that crazy woman?"

"This is a friends and family affair. Gitana promised that she would make Jacinda leave the holy water at home and as a concession will return your car radiator."

"Really? Do you know how much a radiator costs?"

"No, I do not. No one has ever taken mine." Chase surveyed their handiwork. "Now, we have to go pick some flowers."

"Pick flowers? Like I know how to do that."

Chase handed her a pair of pruners. "Cut some of every kind and leave a lot of stem." She pointed to the height of cobalt-blue vases that she'd placed in the center of the table.

"Ugh! I can't believe I volunteered for this."

"You're working off your bail money if I remember correctly."

She tromped off. Chase followed her to what was Chase's magnum opus of gardening. It took up a quarter of an acre with a meandering path leading through it and it appealed to her sense of Jane Austenian strolls in the shrubbery. Despite the constraints of the desert climate she had succeeded in growing flowers in the desert. Flowers of all varieties, penstemons, purple sage, bachelor buttons, cosmos, sunflowers of many kinds from mundane to exotic, calla lilies, rudbeckia etc.

Graciela stopped pouting long enough to look around. "Holy shit, this has come a long way. Are you sure you want to cut them down?" She fingered a white zulu.

"That's what they're for. I pick from inconspicuous places." She handed Graciela a wicker basket to collect the flowers and said a silent prayer that she wouldn't butcher any of her precious

143

darlings.

She didn't. Graciela gingerly approached the flowers starting first with the purple asters and then moving to the calendulas, collecting almost with reverence. Boy, this is a new side, Chase thought. Graciela might be an atheist, but she was most certainly a natural pagan. Perhaps, we are all capable of change.

Gitana returned with the grill parts, her mother and two hot plates of tamales. Graciela sneaked a look in the back of the Hummer where her radiator sat propped up against the wheel well. Jacinda spotted her, clutched her rosary beads and mumbled a prayer. Graciela scowled at her.

"All I ask is that you two are polite to each other and for the sake of the other guests do not make a scene," Gitana said.

Jacinda nodded.

"For the sake of Bud, I will do this," Graciela said. She grabbed the grill and headed to the veranda.

Chase kissed her wife, complimented Jacinda on her tamales and then went to help Graciela with the grill. She relaxed and assured herself this was going to be all right. And for a moment it was—until her own mother arrived, followed by Addison and Peggy.

Stella was dressed to the hilt in a white linen dress and matching high heels which immediately sunk in the gravel driveway. Peggy grabbed her arm before Stella took a dive.

Regaining her composure, she introduced herself, "Stella Banter."

"I'm Peggy, Addison's mother. Addison is a friend of Chase's."

Addison stared at Stella like she might be an alien, a very tall alien.

Upon seeing her daughter, Stella said, "What's wrong with a little concrete?" She gingerly made her way to the front gate. She gained the steps only to discover that the front yard was a series of crushed rock paths lined by blue sage and maximillan sunflowers which opened up to the veranda that was brick rather than concrete. Her heels once again sank.

"Why are you wearing those stupid shoes?" Chase said. "Haven't you ever been to a... Addison cover your ears."

Addison did so obediently although she stared quite pointedly at Chase's mouth.

"A fucking barbeque?" She nodded to Addison who removed her hands from her ears. She was going to have to teach Bud that particular behavior as her anti-swearing campaign so far was a miserable failure.

"Not one that wasn't catered, in a normal yard with concrete, little tents and wait staff," Stella replied, looking around as if all that she wished for might appear.

"Chase, I've never been to a barbeque that wasn't catered," Addison said. In penitence she stared at the ground.

Peggy nodded and Stella pursed her lips in triumph.

"I guess we're all stuffed-shirt city folk," Peggy said.

"Good God, you people need to get out more." It suddenly occurred to her that she'd never been to a barbeque like this before she met Gitana. "Wait here and I'll get you a pair of proper shoes."

Gitana came out the door with a bowl of potato salad.

Addison rushed over. "Let me help you."

Gitana was delighted. "Well, hello there little darling." She handed her the bowl.

Chase brought back a pair of sage green Crocs.

"What are those?" Stella said, peering at them. "They're plastic."

"Sandals and they're very popular. Put them on before you break your ankle. I don't want you suing me."

"Speaking of which, Owen needs Gitana to sign the papers for the suit against the doctor."

"Slimy bastard," Chase said.

Peggy watched Addison help Gitana set up the table. "I can't get her to do a thing."

"Chase is exactly the same way. Gitana, on the other hand, is sweet as the day is long," Stella said.

"Grossly prosaic. One little Chase story and you're out of here," Chase said.

Stella pursed her lips again. "Do you at least have a decent bottle of wine and preferably a glass flute and not a plastic cup?"

"Yes, I raided your wine cellar and got a nice Pinot Noir."

"Thank goodness," Stella said.

"I wanted to thank you for the invite, but Dickhead couldn't come," Peggy said.

"And I was so looking forward to meeting him," Chase said. Peggy smiled at her. She might have been a little over the top on that one but curiosity was getting the best of her. Addison had a father and she wanted to see what he was like.

Stella gave her the look—she didn't appreciate being left out of the loop.

"Addison's father," Chase said.

"Oh. I had one of those as well but a timely staph infection took care of that. Imagine that," Stella said, "a gall bladder operation did him in before I got the chance to poison him myself."

Chase, having heard the story a million times, bade them sit down and she got them both a glass of wine.

Delia whisked by. "Hi, where's Graciela?"

"Unloading and, I imagine, stashing her radiator," Chase replied.

Jacinda, stroking her rosary beads, stared hard at Delia.

"She creeps me out," Delia whispered.

"Wait until she tries to exorcise you," Chase said.

"Never." Delia grabbed a beer from the cooler and went to find Graciela, looking quickly behind at Jacinda.

Chase laughed. "Where's Rosarita?" she asked Stella, who was engrossed with Peggy's tales of the evil husband.

"Unpacking the car. She brought some strange dish— something traditional. She insisted. She's been making tortillas all morning."

"You wouldn't want to help her or anything."

Rosarita trundled up the stairs and started across the yard.

Chase ran to help her. "Let me get that."

"Oh, mija, you're a good girl."

"Chase, you didn't tell me you got a housekeeper," Stella said, glancing at Jacinda.

"That's Gitana's mother, Jacinda. Mother, not every brown person in New Mexico is a servant. You two should have met years ago, but all of us have been remiss in our familial duties. That's going to change." Chase had never wanted to put Jacinda through the horror of meeting Stella but with the baby coming it could not be avoided.

Stella rolled her eyes and resumed her conversation with Peggy.

Like with like, Chase thought.

Jacinda and Rosarita however, hit if off. Chase didn't understand a word as they spoke in Spanish at a pace that even Chase's foreign language tapes couldn't beat. At this rate she and Bud would be learning Spanish together.

Gitana was getting everyone settled while Delia flipped burgers and chicken breasts while instructing Graciela on the procedure. According to Graciela, Delia was a master griller. "They have a raging grill fest at her house all the time."

Chase still imagined bacchanalian parties at Delia's place and now she was illustrating her prowess with propane at the family barbeque. Yikes!

Addison was on hand with the platter to receive the grilled meats. It all looked so *Leave it to Beaver* that Chase thought she'd captured picture-perfect suburbia. This was just what Bud needed. She walked over Addison. "You make a great helper."

"Uh, yeah, I'm on meat patrol," Addison said. She held up the platter. Her notebook fell on the patio. Her blush gave her away. She picked it up quickly.

"You were taking notes," Chase said.

"There were some good lines of dialogue."

Delia and Graciela stopped talking. They stared at Addison.

"Tell me you weren't talking about—you know what," Chase

147

said, glaring at them.

Graciela smiled, "Well, you little voyeur."

"I'm doing research," Addison said.

"Oh, crap, you're going to get me in trouble," Chase said, pointing at the two delinquents.

"I won't tell anyone Delia writes porn," Addison said.

"Hand them over," Chase put out her hand.

"This is censorship," Addison said, clutching her notebook to her chest.

"No, this is an unauthorized use of material."

"But—"

"I know more about publishing law than you do," Chase informed her.

"I am nine. It's not like I don't know things."

"Delia and Graciela know things I will never know," Chase said.

Addison carefully tore out the new pages she'd written and handed them to Chase.

Chase read them quickly, gasped and then rolled them up and smacked both Delia's and Graciela's heads. "This is disgusting."

"Thoroughly enlightening, I'm sure," Delia said, smirking.

"Just trying to help the kid out, sis," Graciela said. "It's time to pluck the meat anyway. Sorry Addison, the show's over."

"Maybe next time?" Addison said as she stuffed her notebook into her ever-present backpack.

"Sure," Graciela replied. She plucked off the hamburgers.

"Do it and I'll cut out…" Chase stopped and ordered Addison, "Ears."

Addison complied and covered her ears.

"As I was saying I'll cut out both your vaginas with a reciprocating saw."

"What's that?" Delia said.

"You don't want to know, but it would do a good job," Graciela said.

Chase nodded at Addison that it was safe to remove her hands.

148

"How long do I have to do this?"

"Until you're eighteen."

"That's a little extreme don't you think?" Addison said.

Graciela handed her a plate of hamburgers that were remarkably unburned.

"Those look fabulous," Chase said.

"I had a good teacher," Graciela said, looking fondly at Delia as Addison carried the plate to the table.

Graciela plucked the chicken breasts off next and looked around for Addison. She had been trapped by Jacinda and her face was very red from having her cheeks pinched.

Delia, it appeared, was still contemplating the reciprocating saw. "You know I saw this video on the Internet where they took power tools and put dildos and stuff on the ends and fucked each other. It was really amazing."

Chase grabbed the large barbeque fork out of Graciela's hand and poked Delia in the thigh.

"Ouch!" Delia said, rubbing the spot and then pulling up her shorts to look at it.

Addison returned with the platter. She set it down and rubbed her cheeks.

"You left a mark," Delia said.

"Poor baby," Chase said, taking a Wet-Wipe and cleaning the fork before she handed it back to Graciela who was smirking.

"Did she do something bad?" Addison asked.

"Yes. Now, let's go eat," Chase said.

As the guests got settled, Chase wished she had asked Jacinda to bring one of her religious candles, the patron saint of hospitality. There had to be one. What could really go wrong now? She tried to assure herself. They all eat and everyone goes home happy. There was a shifting about as people took their places. Addison insisted Peggy sit by Stella because she wanted to sit between Chase and Gitana in order to be out of Jacinda's reach. Chase wanted Addison as far away from Delia and Graciela who needed to be as far away from Jacinda as possible.

"I think this will work," Gitana said, as she surveyed the table. Stella was about to sit down at the end of the table. Despite her funny shoes she still looked regal. Chase saw the dogs in time to do absolutely nothing about it. Gitana followed her gaze.

"Oh, no, Stella watch out," Gitana yelled.

Annie and Jane came barreling through the back pasture in hot pursuit of a jack rabbit. The rabbit veered under the table and then made a sharp turn and headed toward Stella who was frozen. The dogs plowed right into her, knocking her flat. The jack rabbit hopped over her and took off, the pursuing dogs treating Stella's prone frame as simply another hurdle to cross.

Chase peered down at her mother. "You're lucky you didn't crack open your head."

The others stood around looking at Stella. Jacinda got down on her knees with a wet napkin. She made cooing noises as she put the cold press on Stella's forehead.

"So much for the bad hip," Graciela whispered in Chase's ear.

"For goodness sake's get me up," Stella said.

Chase and Peggy helped her up and into a chair.

"That was the biggest rabbit I've ever seen," Addison said.

Chase closed the gate that separated the front yard from the rest of the property. The dogs had failed Socialization 101.

Later that night, Chase had her head resting on Gitana's swollen belly. "I wanted today to be perfect for Bud, instead all we got was dysfunction."

"It wasn't so bad except your mother's high heels sinking in the driveway..."

"And Stella thinking your mother was our housekeeper."

"Then there was the jack rabbit incident," Gitana said. She frowned slightly. "Three is a good number. Things happen in threes."

"Is that why the pump went out, the leaking kitchen faucet flooded the floor and the dishwasher doesn't drain properly?" Chase said. *God, we need a good plumber*. She wondered if Delia or Graciela had slept with a plumber who might be contacted.

"Exactly," Gitana said. She kissed Chase's forehead.

"At least no one lit themselves on fire," Chase said, rubbing Gitana's belly. "I'm sorry, Bud. I strive for perfection or at least a modicum of sanity in our family life and all we get is fubars."

Gitana ran her fingers through Chase's hair. "What do you want for Bud—*Leave it to Beaver?*"

Chase looked up at her. She could lie and tell her that it wasn't so, that whatever came was all right—that they'd get through it, but that's not what she wanted. "Yes, I do."

"Chase!"

"I can't help it."

"Come up here—right this minute."

"You sound pretty authoritative. We might need that when Bud becomes a teen." Chase crawled up next to her and stroked her face. "I'm sorry."

"This is real life, not your world. It is what it is."

"I know that deep down I do. I'll just have to get the rest of me on board."

"Besides, we have an interesting life with interesting people in it. That's good. Bud wouldn't like a normal life. It would be stifling. Bud is in the right family." She kissed Chase.

Chase found it comforting. She hoped that she could do the same for Bud whenever circumstances overwhelmed the island that was to be Bud's life.

"By the way, what does fubar stand for?"

"Fucked up beyond all recognition," Chase replied, as she straightened up the covers. She tucked Bud in with the sheet.

"That's lovely and perfect. I'm thinking that's one word Bud is authorized to use."

Annie groaned which indicated it was time to stop talking and shut off the light.

"You've got a lot of nerve, missy, considering you floored my mother." Chase reached down and scratched her ears.

Chapter Seventeen

"What are you looking at?" Chase said, as the dogs watched her pacing back and forth. She had all her novels out and was perusing select parts.

Jane whined. Annie sat at attention, her head turned to one side in that quizzical way dogs have—that look of wanting to read your thoughts and ease your heart.

"I'm fine," she assured them. "I just thought I'd go through some of my old things. I'm looking for parts of myself in my novels. If I compile all these parts I might have a more accurate picture of myself. It's not easy finding oneself, you know."

Jane jumped up on her and tried to lick her face. "Let's just relax here. Mama still has most of her marbles." She knelt down so the dogs could lick her face. They acted like they could kiss away whatever plagued her. They ended up pushing her until she was flat on her back and Annie sat on her chest while Jane licked her face. "Hey, hey, that's enough," Chase cried, trying to push them off. She wasn't successful. Luckily, Lacey came up the stairs to the writing studio and the dogs were instantly distracted.

"I can't believe you let them do that." She was dressed in what Chase called "town clothes."

"It's a doggy facial."

"Yuck." Lacey pushed Annie away as she tried to sniff her cervix. "I see clicker training was a failure. Weren't their private lessons supposed to put an end to that?"

"I don't have the clicker with me."

"You should have it. Where is it?"

"In the junk drawer," Chase said, getting up.

"Good place for it." Lacey flounced down on the couch.

Lacey and Bo were the only two people Chase knew that flounced. It was as if their bodies collapsed like a balloon when they were in the presence of furniture.

"Clicker training was designed to help Jane with her self-esteem training not Annie's crotch sniffing."

"She doesn't look like she has a self-esteem problem."

Jane had hopped on Chase's faux leather office chair and looked at them inquisitively as if to say in dog speak, "So what's on the agenda?"

Annie spotted the much-sought-after jack rabbit and bolted out the door. Jane spun off the chair leaving it rocking in her wake as she followed her sister.

Chase ignored their antics as commonplace. "Jane is taking an online course at the Carnegie Institute."

"Yeah, right." Lacey looked around. "Why is it so neat and organized in here? I can actually find the couch."

"Your perceptive abilities are outstanding." Chase gathered up her books and put them back in the cupboard. She didn't want the writers group to think she'd gone off to self-aggrandizement land. "It's my turn to host the writer's group." She remembered she hadn't washed out the coffeepot. Bo would be horrified if he so much as sniffed a less than sanitary decanter. She filled the sink in the kitchenette with soapy water. She pulled some cups from the overhead cabinet. They could use a washing as well, she decided.

Lacey came over to dry them. They stood in companionable silence. Then, it occurred to Chase that Lacey was doing a drive-by. She ventured out of the city only under unusual circumstances. The hinterland had no appeal despite the beauties of New Mexico. "Why are you here?" Chase asked.

Lacey dried a cup and avoided Chase's gaze. "What? Can't a friend drop by?"

"No one drops by where we live unless it's a neighbor in need of something like a shovel or a chainsaw." She handed Lacey another cup.

"All right, I came for a little chat."

"What's wrong?" Chase always imagined the worst—a brain tumor, death in the family, horrible car crash or strange diseases. She scrubbed out the coffee decanter more furiously than was necessary. The soapy water resembled a Jacuzzi.

"It's nothing terrible." She knew Chase too well. "I just have a question. You know, I got to thinking how in high school you always thought boys were gross and all they wanted was to stick it in you—that they had a boy smell and it made you sick."

"I don't get where this is leading." She rinsed the sparkling decanter. Lacey dried it. Between the two of them it looked brand-new. She stuck it in its cradle.

"Well, I met this guy. We've kind of been seeing each other." Lacey went to sit in Chase's computer chair, first wiping the dog hair from the seat.

Chase leaned up against the kitchen counter. "And?"

"We had dinner at his apartment. I mean it was nice and all but something was different." Lacey turned around in the chair. She was either looking out at the mountains or pretending to.

This was like trimming the dog's toenails, a combination of pleading and wrestling. "Different how? He decorated weird, he was wearing a toga when he answered the door, he had a tank full of piranhas and he wanted you to stick your hand in the tank,

154

that kind of different?"

"No, it wasn't like that."

"Good God, Lacey, fucking spit it out."

Lacey turned to face her. "We started making out after dinner and well, it grossed me out. I mean, normally I'd be screwing him by now, but I didn't like what he was doing or trying to do."

"Maybe he just wasn't the right guy. He wasn't forceful or anything?" Chase didn't want to have to threaten to cut off his balls with her orchid pruners because he'd manhandled her best friend.

"No, nothing like that. I think he thought it was kind of sweet—like I was a virgin or something. I got all flustered and left."

Now Chase was really confused. She had some idea where this might be leading, but she preferred not to go in that direction. "Sometimes, even the best candidates don't float your boat."

"He is a nice guy, but I just didn't feel anything, you know, down there."

"Lacey, don't worry about it. You're not a spinster yet."

"You're a pillar of compassion."

"Thanks. Now you better hightail it before the writers group gets here unless you want to join."

"I can't even write a decent postcard."

Chase reached out and gave her a hug.

"I like the new you. You're much more user-friendly," Lacey said.

"Watch out for the jack rabbit on your way out."

"Stella told me what happened at the party."

"Why does she talk to you?" Chase inquired ruefully.

"Because I'm nice to her like you should be."

"I invited her to the barbeque didn't I?" Chase said defensively.

"Yeah, and then look at what you did," Lacey said, pointing at the computer screen saver. Chase had taken the photo of Stella wearing the sage green Crocs and through the miracle of Photoshop enlarged and stretched Stella's feet so they resembled large clown shoes. "I couldn't help myself."

"I'm sure. Okay, I'm off. Tell Jasmine hi for me."

"You two are still hanging out?" Chase asked as Lacey headed down the stairs.

"From time to time," Lacey said over her shoulder.

"Uh-huh."

Since Chase hadn't finished her mystery novel, she begged off critique. "I've got to get it all down and then we can spend hours, weeks and months poring over it, but I don't want to stop now and think about it yet. Does that make sense?"

Alma reached over and touched her hand. "Yes, it does. Finish it and then we'll help."

Bo put his coffee cup down rather forcefully, probably more forcefully than he intended. "Honestly, you're not dogging us?"

"No, I swear. Even with the moist-mound sagas I finish them completely unless I'm having trouble with the ending before I edit."

"Dude, that's cool," Delia said. "Some writers are like that."

"Precisely," Alma said. She refilled her black tar coffee from the decanter.

Chase winced. Her cup was closer to café-au-lait, the kind French parents give to their children in training to become true café dwellers.

"Some writers edit along the way like Kurt Vonnegut who writes and rewrites the same page over and over again until he gets it absolutely perfect and then he moves on. It's like fucking insane. I couldn't do it if God-on-High instructed me. I would've sucked as Moses," Delia said.

Chase laughed. "You've been hanging out at the Ortega house too much."

"I know. Jacinda's got little plaques and shit everywhere. It's like osmosis or something. Next thing I know I'll be spouting proverbs."

"That might be a good thing," Alma said.

"Oh, no, Delia as the next money-grubbing TV evangelist.

156

Horrors," Bo said.

"That's a great racket. I wish I could pull it off. It certainly pays better than writing porn."

Jasmine pored over her manuscript. She was next for group critique. Her manuscript was never far from her person. Chase suspected that she was afraid her husband Philip would snatch it. Jasmine was as superstitious as the rest of them when it came to manuscripts. Even though they were all supposed to have innumerable backup copies—they didn't. It was endless secretarial business to keep it all updated so they usually had a working copy that they periodically backed up. Chase was the worst. She had her composition book and that was all until she typed it into her laptop.

So far she'd been lucky. Others had not been so fortunate. The French writer Collette had lost a manuscript in a taxi—never to be found. Someone probably threw it away without ever bothering to open it and see what it contained. Or Garrison Keillor who had lost the best story he'd ever written in a train station lavatory. It still haunted him.

"We could do mine if no one else is ready. I've added a character and I'd like to know what you all think," Jasmine said.

"Works for me," Bo said. "I'm still trying to make the deadline on that snippet for *Hung Magazine*."

"Can we pass on critiquing that one?" Alma said. She took one of the Danish cookies from the tray on the coffee table.

"Please. That dick stuff doesn't work for me," Delia said. She got up and retrieved a Dasani from the fridge. "Anyone else?"

"I'll take one," Chase said. Bo's special blend of coffee was eating a hole in her stomach.

"Listen, girl, I read your dyke porn," Bo said.

"Children, let's play nice," Alma said.

"I'll run copies," Jasmine said. She located the section she wanted them to critique. "If that's all right with you."

"Mi Xerox is su Xerox," Chase said.

"It's erotica not porn, by the way," Delia said, handing Chase the bottle of Dasani.

"Same difference," Bo replied, crossing his arms and his legs simultaneously like a Venus Fly Trap on the defensive.

"Actually, it's not," Alma said. "The sole purpose of porn is the graphic display of sex whereas erotica is about the language and subsequent movements that culminate in sex."

"She's got you there," Chase said. The copy machine was whirling away in the background. It must be quite the section Jasmine wanted them to peruse.

"All right, my story is porn," Bo said.

"It's cool, dude. I wish I could write the pure porn, but chicks aren't like that. It's all the stuff before that turns them on," Delia said.

Jasmine returned all flushed. "Sorry, that took so long." She handed out the copies and then she sat down and got up again. "Maybe I do need a water. My throat is a little dry."

Something was up, Chase thought. Usually, Jasmine dreaded critique, but she seemed more excited than afraid. They'd find out soon enough.

Jasmine sat back down. "So take a few minutes to read through and then we can see if it works."

They bowed their heads practically in unison except for Chase who looked on in amusement. Looks like we're in the church of the written word she thought, accolytes of parsing, hunters of adverbs and adjectives. Some to kill, some to keep. Chase was still pondering this when she came upon the part where Jasmine's protagonist now had a lesbian partner. She looked up. "What the hell is this? You've got a dyke in the story."

"I thought he needed a partner." Jasmine avoided Chase's gaze.

"So make her a lesbian? I don't get it," Delia said.

"I just thought it was a nice twist. It's not like I don't know enough lesbians to create a realistic lesbian," Jasmine retorted.

"This is hilarious," Bo said. He poured more coffee. "We've got a dyke writing straight fiction and a straight woman writing lesbian fiction. Will wonders never cease?"

"Bo's right. You'll narrow your market," Chase said.

"Don't we know," Delia said, giving Chase a high-five.

"I don't care," Jasmine said.

"My only concern is that you've written a hundred pages without her. You've got to bring her in earlier. Her sudden appearance is very disconcerting to the reader," Alma said.

"At least I have Alma's support," Jasmine said, sniffling.

Chase twirled her pencil. This latest development concerned her. Jasmine didn't pull a dyke out of her ass. This meant she'd thought about it. Chase learned long ago that coincidences were often a cheat. Lacey stopping by with her gross-out boy experience and Jasmine's sudden interest in lesbians were not random events. They were connected and Chase aimed at finding out how.

"Do they fuck?" Delia asked.

Alma gave her the look.

"I mean does the dyke have a meaningful and intimate relationship with another woman?"

"I don't know yet," Jasmine said, glancing away.

"Let's run a pool on who pulls off the better lesbian versus the straight character. Five bucks a pop," Bo suggested, a glint in his eye.

"I'm in," Delia said, reaching into her back pocket and digging out her Harley-Davidson leather wallet complete with silver chain.

"For purposes of expanding characterization I'll do it," Alma said, reaching for her black canvas messenger bag.

Jasmine and Chase eyed each other.

"Deal," Chase said.

"I'm up for the challenge," Jasmine said, rolling up her manuscript and smacking her leg with it.

"Ready, set, go," Bo said.

Chapter Eighteen

"Did you find one?" Chase asked.

"Do we really have to do this?" Addison said, clutching her cell phone to her chest.

They were sitting in the waiting room of the gynecologist's office. Chase had been barred from taking part in the office visits after she'd been belligerent with Dr. Bertine about his qualifications and his ability to give appropriate prenatal care to her beloved wife and child. She had told him that since he and his staff had ultimately caused the initial screw-up, but now fortuitous gift of life, she had reservations about his credentials. She went so far as to inquire whether his medical degree wasn't some sort of correspondence course. Chase had wanted Gitana to get a new doctor, but Gitana liked Dr. Bertine and had insisted on keeping him.

"I think it's a good idea. It's part of the new 'us'."

"I liked the old 'us' better," Addison said, swinging her legs and crinkling up her face.

"Change is often painful." Chase scrolled through her iPod searching for the song she'd chosen.

"Very." Addison pulled out her iPod from her backpack and downloaded her song for her mother's name tag.

"So what did you choose?" Chase asked as she inputted her song.

"'Wrapped Around Your Finger,' by The Police."

"How'd you decide on that one? The Police were around years before you were born."

"I did a keyword search for songs of slavery and bondage," Addison replied.

"I don't think that is necessarily an improvement on your last one," Chase said, referring to Addison's choice of 'Witchy Woman.'

"What did you pick?"

"A better song," Chase said, picking up a magazine and thumbing through it. There were a zillion ads for diapers and formula.

"Such as?" Addison asked, pulling the magazine out of Chase's hands.

An older woman sitting across the waiting room stared at Chase as if she were an over indulgent parent, not Addison's cohort.

"I chose Sarah McLachlan's song 'Fallen.'" Chase didn't look at her.

"Oh, that's a much better choice," Addison said smugly. "Isn't that the song with the line, 'I've sunk so low, in it?"

"Well, yeah. At least I'm putting the blame on myself," Chase retorted.

"Gag me." Addison stuck a finger toward her open mouth.

"Okay, we'll keep trying," Chase said. "Each week we'll move forward."

"Like a twelve-step program."

"Precisely. How do you know about twelve-step programs?"

Chase asked, suddenly alarmed that her nine-year-old cohort might have been a heavy drinker or a heroin addict.

"My mom made me do it for cuticle biting. It worked. See, look." Addison held out her hands for inspection.

Chase admired her little hands. They did look good.

"I've noticed you might need a little help there." Addison pointed to Chase's hands. She had three Band-Aids on the really bad ones and her other fingers were marginal.

"I know. I can't stop it and this baby thing isn't helping." As if to substantiate her addiction she gnawed on her index finger. "It's a horrible habit."

Addison grabbed her hand. "Then take control and stop it."

The older woman sitting across from them now looked confused. Perhaps she thought Chase was mentally disabled and Addison was her midget caretaker.

"I can help you."

"How?" Chase looked longingly at her pinky which still had potential. Now that she was about to lose the habit, she craved it more.

"One finger at a time. We'll start with your thumb because those are the hardest. Here give it to me." Addison dug through her pack until she found a black permanent marker. Taking Chase's right thumb she drew a line around it. "Okay, this one is off limits. You can assault the other nine, which in your case since you're down three already, leaves you six. We'll do one finger a week."

"Wow, this is going to be a lengthy process."

"How long have you done it?" Addison asked, putting the black marker back into the pack.

"All my life."

"I don't think ten weeks to unlearn a lifelong habit is excessive."

"You've got a point there," Chase admitted.

Luckily, she was spared further analytical ruminations by Gitana who returned to the waiting area positively beaming.

"Everything okay?" Chase asked.

Gitana handed her a note from the doctor—a synopsis of her current condition. Chase read it quickly. The note mostly pertained to keeping up the prenatal vitamins, avoid heavy lifting and that Gitana's pregnancy was progressing satisfactorily. "How much longer is he going to be angry with me?" Chase said. "And don't you think his note is a little vague? What does progressing satisfactorily mean exactly?"

Ignoring her questions, Gitana said, "Dr. Bertine gave you this." She handed her the Lamaze class video.

"Great," Chase said, turning it over and reading the back cover.

"Let me guess, she got thrown out of Lamaze class as well," Addison said.

"You guessed right," Gitana said.

"That guy was a total homophobe. You couldn't expect me not to stick up for 'our' people."

"I'm thinking a twelve-step anger management program might not be a bad idea," Addison said as they exited the waiting room and headed to the parking lot.

"Twelve steps?" Gitana asked.

"Addison has me on a ten-step program for my cuticle biting," Chase said, holding up her thumb with the black line around it.

"You're a good influence on her," Gitana said.

"I'll talk to Robicheck about my problem with my angry mouth."

They parted ways. Addison and Gitana were headed for the Albuquerque Art Museum and Chase was off to Dr. Robicheck's office.

Dr. Robicheck's office was five minutes from Dr. Bertine's office. Seeing as she still had fifteen minutes to spare, she hit the Starbucks on the way.

"Hey there," Chase said, as she picked up her Chai. Lacey and Jasmine were sitting at a table by the window in a secluded corner.

"Hi," Lacey said. "Sit down. Jasmine and I were just catching up on old news." She said this quickly and patted the seat next to her equally quickly like she was afraid of slipping up, so that if she got the preliminaries over quickly all would be well.

"I can't. I've got to see the shrink in ten minutes."

"How is that working out?" Jasmine asked.

"Okay, I guess." Chase sipped her Chai and stared at them. This wasn't a polite lie. She honestly couldn't decide if she was a saner person. It hadn't been that long. Maybe sanity was like a twelve-step program.

"I think you're much better," Lacey said.

"Thanks for the endorsement."

"And you are more user-friendly." Lacey held her arms out for a hug.

Chase obliged. It was painful in front of a crowd, but she did it.

"Just testing," Lacey said, releasing her.

"Right, well, off to crazy-land. See you at group, Jasmine."

"I won't make you hug me," Jasmine said. She did touch Chase's hand.

As Chase made her way to the door she caught the reflection of Jasmine and Lacey at their table. Jasmine was playing footsy with Lacey who didn't appear to mind.

Chase wondered if she was already in crazy-land. Why had her life taken this sudden rollercoaster ride once she decided that she could change?

Sitting on Dr. Robicheck's couch, Chase shifted positions several times.

"You seem a little agitated," Dr. Robicheck said, making an annotation on her yellow legal pad.

Chase had noticed when she went to OfficeMax to pick up her composition books that she had developed an aversion to yellow legal pads.

"Me? I'm fine."

"Chase, these sessions do not prove useful if you don't relay what is going on in your life. My asking you how you are is not a polite convention." She crossed her legs and stared hard at Chase.

"A complete waste of my co-pay." Chase crossed her legs at the ankles and leaned back trying to appear comfortable.

"Was there a lot of carnage?" she asked, referring to Chase's habit of burying roadkill.

"Only one prairie dog."

"And?"

"I think Lacey might be gay and dating one of my writing group friends who now has a lesbian character in her novel," Chase blurted.

The doctor did not change expression, not even a raised eyebrow. "And you find this disconcerting?"

"Yes." Chase abandoned her ruse of relaxation and sat upright.

"Do you feel that you are changing?"

"A little." Chase uncrossed her legs. Her foot had fallen asleep. The good doctor had purchased a new print of a white calla lily. It was almost erotic.

"Isn't it possible that your friends might do the same thing?"

Dr. Robicheck wore a white linen suit with a light green shirt. Chase stared at it.

"How come you're not wearing brown?"

"Excuse me?" She looked down at her outfit as if seeing it for the first time.

"You always wear brown—all brown, today you have white on and you have a new print and two new books on your bookcase and you're using a different pen." Chase's voice had gotten high and squeaky, like she was on the verge of a panic attack.

"Are you taking your medication?" Dr. Robicheck looked alarmed.

"Religiously." Chase stood up and got a cup of water from the watercooler. At least that was in the same place in the corner. "Next thing you'll be rearranging the furniture."

"Chase, calm down. Change is inevitable."

Chase sat back down. She studied the Dixie cup. The pattern

was different. It was a leaf motif. Last week it had been multi-colored stars.

Dr. Robicheck noticed. "Yes, they're a different pattern. It's fine. Did it occur to you that you're suddenly noticing that things change when in actuality things change all the time?"

"I don't like change. It makes me nervous. I thought my medication was supposed to make me sane."

"It's not a miracle drug. It won't make you a perfect human being, but it will keep you from having episodes."

"Like the one I just had?" Chase said anxiously.

"Perhaps we should up the dose."

"That might be a good idea."

After the horrid session, Chase managed to locate Gitana and Addison in the gift shop of the museum.

"How'd it go?" Gitana asked.

Addison was leafing through a book on Frida Kahlo.

"Robicheck is increasing my dosage." Chase didn't look at her. Instead, she picked up a boxed set of postcards of Georgia O'Keeffe's flower series. Chase preferred these to the bone series which she thought morbid.

"Why?"

"I had a little episode in her office. I think I scared her."

"What happened?" Gitana calmly took the postcards away and set them back on the shelf.

"She changed some of the things in her office and her clothes were a different color. It upset me."

"Maybe it upset you because we're going through so many changes," Gitana said, pointing to her stomach.

"I don't know, but you'd think a shrink would know better than to go modifying things without informing her patients."

"You're right. She should have sent out cards or a memo or something."

"It would show good manners," Chase said.

Addison came over with her purchases. It still freaked Chase out that a nine-year-old had a debit card and was so proficient at using it. She herself had trouble with the keypad at the grocery store checkout counter. It seemed they were endlessly moving the "enter" key.

"What'd you get?" Gitana asked.

"A Frida Kahlo book. Look at all the creepy paintings. I love it." Addison showed them a particularly gruesome one titled *Self Portrait 1940*.

"Look at the detail," Gitana said, pointing to the crown of thorns around her neck.

"I just like the blood part," Addison replied.

"Her paintings give me nightmares," Chase said.

"Wuss. And then I got this print of Edvard Munch to put over my bed."

"That's interesting," Gitana said.

"Don't you think *The Scream* is an odd choice for a bedroom?" Chase said.

"No. I feel like that a lot. It's a manifestation of my inner self," Addison replied.

"Of course," Chase said. She contemplated what her manifestation of her inner self would be—probably a Salvador Dali, either *The Persistence of Memory or the Metamorphosis of Narcissus*.

"Can we go to the Atomic Museum?"

"Sure," Chase said.

"I might have to beg off," Gitana said.

"Are you tired?" Chase asked, alarmed that they had taxed her.

"A little. I told Mama I'd stop by. She's got some unusual relic she wants to give us for the baby. She's been on eBay a lot since we gave her your old laptop."

"She got Internet access?" Chase said.

"Mr. Griego, her next-door neighbor, set her up. He took her to Best Buy and they got a router so she can use his ISP. She makes him fresh tortillas in exchange."

"So now she's bidding on Jesus' pinky bone?" Chase asked.

"Something like that." Gitana bent down and gave Addison a

hug. "Watch her," she said, indicating Chase.

"I know. She'd get lost trying to get out of a paper bag," Addison said.

Chase kissed Gitana's cheek. "Be careful. The canyon construction makes me nervous. Take the Hummer."

They watched her go and then Chase asked, "Why do you want to go to the Atomic Museum?"

"I want to see how they blow things up."

"You're not looking up bomb-making on the Internet?"

"Not yet," Addison said as she led them out to the parking lot.

It was early evening when Chase drove Addison home. There was a car in the drive. Usually Peggy never got home until nine or ten. She knew Addison was spending her in service day off from school with Chase. They looked at each other puzzled.

Addison said, "My mom's home. How odd is that?"

"Maybe she made a great sale and wanted to be home with you to celebrate," Chase said as she parked behind Peggy's four-door black Lexus.

"Gag me. It's more like a slow day and everyone else is busy. Walk me up?"

"Of course." It was now standard procedure that Chase would come in to say hi to the Russian housekeeper, Olga, and hug Addison goodbye.

"There you are," Peggy said as they entered the front hall.

"Sorry. We didn't think you'd be home," Chase said.

"Slow day."

Addison smirked.

"We went to Jacinda's for dinner. Once she found out we had Addison with us there was no putting her off," Chase said.

Addison smiled sweetly. They both knew that Addison wanted to see Jesus' pinky bone. Jacinda had given her and Addison a tour of the relic hutch. Not only that but a burnished cherry rosary. It was amusing to see Addison smiling and joking with a group of people who were quickly becoming her new family. Chase wondered if Peggy saw this.

"That's great," Peggy said. She looked tired and distracted.

"I'm off to bed," Addison said. She looked at Chase as if daring her not to perform their ritual. Chase knelt down and gave her a hug.

"Good night and don't let the bedbugs bite." She pinched Addison who went squealing down the hall.

Addison stopped and turned, "What exactly are bedbugs?"

"I don't really know. So what do we do?"

"Wikipedia!" they both screamed.

"I'll text you tomorrow with the answer," Addison said.

Peggy and Chase watched her walk down the long marble hall, her runners making squishy sounds with her enormous backpack hiked up on her shoulder like a soldier off to war.

"What does she have in that thing do you suppose?" Peggy asked.

"Her life from what I can tell. I've never been privy to its complete contents."

"You're so good with her," Peggy said.

Chase could almost feel Peggy's longing like a tug at her coattails. "Ah, it's just the newness factor," Chase replied. "I'll be on the old hat list before you know it."

"I don't think so. I really need to spend more time with her. The problem with real estate is that it's so spur of the moment. One minute we're going to the museum and next I've got to go sell a house. It's been very frustrating for Addison." Peggy pursed her lips like she might honestly be considering the point.

No wonder Addison wanted to go to the museum. She's never been, Chase thought.

"But there's the money thing—her schooling, this house, the tennis lessons—it all takes money," Peggy said.

"I suppose it does." Chase awkwardly shifted from one foot to the other.

"Then there's clothes, shoes, entertainment."

"The debit card allowance," Chase added.

"Exactly."

Chase refrained from asking how much a child of nine needed in her account. When she got home she'd grill Gitana about their expenses. She had absolutely no idea what it cost to run their lives. She hadn't thought about schools either. She should send for brochures. Good God, she was horribly behind and she hadn't even known it. "Well, I better get going."

"Thanks again, Chase." Peggy touched her arm and smiled placidly.

She wanted to tell Peggy to go sit with Addison and listen to her tell about her day, but Chase knew it was already too late. Both of them were past that. Chase wondered when the disconnect had occurred between herself and Stella.

Later as she lay in bed stroking Gitana's belly all her worries resurfaced—money, schools, quality time and Bud's future.

"I hope Bud grows up to be just like Addison," Gitana said, staring at the ceiling.

"Except that Addison despises her mother," Chase said. She put her ear on Gitana's belly to listen to Bud's heart beat.

"Bud won't hate us until she's thirteen. Then, we'll send her to boarding school," Gitana said.

"Or him."

"Or him. You want a girl."

"Not necessarily," Chase said, not meeting her gaze.

Gitana gave her the look.

"All right. I'm just worried about the peeing thing."

"What?"

Chase crawled up next to her. "You know, how you hold it."

"Chase, it's not that hard. Besides I've got lots of cousins and uncles. I think they could help."

"I guess you're right. Do we have a lot of money?"

"What do you mean?"

"Peggy says she has to work a lot to pay for all Addison's expenses," Chase said.

"I think we can fit Bud into the household budget. Besides, by the time Stella and Owen get done with the suit Bud will be

170

a millionaire."

"Still, I think we should set a budget and see if we can trim anything. I stopped by Office Max and got the Quicken program. I want you to save every receipt. I got a basket for that purpose—so even if it's an ice cream cone, get a receipt."

Gitana groaned.

"I don't think you're approaching this in a positive manner."

Gitana sat up and whacked her with a pillow.

Chapter Nineteen

"What's with the black marks?" Nora asked, referring to the Magic Marker rings around Chase's fingers.

"It's part of my ten-step program," Chase replied as she was reviewing the order to the supplier for orchids that Gitana had given her. She was doing a lot of reviewing lately.

"For?"

"Cuticle biting." Chase chewed on her pinky, one of her last remaining fingers that wasn't blacklisted or bandaged. "Do we really need all of these?" She pointed to the order.

"Yes. We sell orchids—hence we must have orchids in stock. You don't seem to be doing well with your cuticle program," Nora said, taking the order form away from Chase.

"This one is still available. Give me a break. I've given up the other four."

"Oh, I get it. A black ring around the digit means it's been freed from the savagery of your teeth."

"Willy couldn't have said it better."

Chase left off the orchid order and moved on to logging the household receipts into her Quicken program. She'd taken to lugging her laptop around. Her rewrite was getting behind and her editor kept asking for progress reports. She took advantage of down times at the nursery to do a little catch-up. She pined for one of the new smaller and lighter laptops, but it wasn't in the budget and this one was only two years old and it appeared light compared to the one she'd given Jacinda. She was currently stockpiling diapers instead. She had enough to make an igloo so far. It wouldn't be fair to Bud to sit in poopy diapers because she desired a new laptop when she had a perfectly good one.

"Willy?" Nora inquired.

"Shakespeare."

"I hated Shakespeare," Nora said. She got them both more coffee. Chase poured hers into a Java Juice cup she kept for that purpose.

Nora smirked. Chase conceded, "I know, but it's a small deception. I can't do without it."

Gitana waddled in. She added two more orchid types to the order list that Nora was inputting. Without looking up she said, "Yes, we need them." She reached over and grabbed Chase's Java Juice cup.

"You don't want that," Chase said.

"I do. I'm parched. I think this heat is making Bud thirsty. Between the two of us I need to haul a couple of gallons of liquid around with me."

"You could wear the Hydro Pack we use for hiking," Chase suggested.

"I'm not wandering around with that on my back." She took a sip while continuing to peruse the order.

Nora and Chase looked at each other.

"This isn't Java Juice."

"It isn't?" Chase said, doing her best to feign surprise.

"You little sneak." Gitana took another sip.

"Hey, hey, that's enough," Chase said, grabbing the cup.

"You've been cheating behind my back," Gitana said, putting her hands on her hips.

"A little coffee on the side—that's not so bad."

"Maybe not, but there's this other thing," Gitana said, going to the office door and opening it. She whistled and the dogs came rushing in.

Chase looked at Nora and read the panic in her face. "Oh, shit, I mean shoot," Chase said.

"How long have they been coming to work?"

The dogs leapt up on Chase's leg and kissed her. Then they went about exploring her and Nora's shared office space. The trash can was of special interest. Chase watched them closely and hoped they wouldn't do anything horrid.

"Well?" Gitana said.

"Since before Labor Day. I wanted them to be more socialized. Everyone loves them and they haven't destroyed one single orchid." Chase refrained from mentioning their other minor misdemeanors.

"How can I trust you anymore?" Gitana said.

"I did it for Bud."

"Bud doesn't want Scooter Libby for a father."

Nora laughed, caught herself and faked a cough.

Chase glared at her. "No more minor indiscretions," she said.

"Lies," Gitana said.

"All right, lies. Can the girls stay?" Chase said, doing her best to look penitent.

"No customer contact. I don't want a lawsuit. Work areas only. Okay?"

"Gotcha."

"I'll place the order," Gitana said, taking the form from Nora.

"What, now you don't trust me?" Nora asked.

"Does duplicitous sound familiar?"

"Not really. Look, from now on I'll be your snitch," Nora declared.

"That's better."

"Thanks a lot," Chase said, going back to her receipts. At least this made her look busy. She put her trash can up on her desk as the dogs' interest in it had gone from curiosity to search and seizure.

"You get what you give," Gitana said, going to her office door.

"That sounds hostile," Chase said.

Gitana smiled and went into her office.

"Well, that went well considering," Chase said, giving the dogs a biscuit from the can she kept in her top drawer.

"We were lucky," Nora said, going over next week's schedule and making minor changes—one of the cashiers had a dentist appointment.

"I'll say. You could've been fired and I could have been thrown out of the house."

Nora laughed.

"Okay, out you go," Chase said to the dogs. "Mama's got work to do." They cruised out the door in search of perpetrators who could have infiltrated the perimeter while they were away from their post.

Eliza came in. "Hi there," Chase said. She liked Eliza now. She had been very patient with Chase while she learned about orchids. Thanks to her Chase had grown quite knowledgeable.

"Hello," Eliza said. She looked at Nora who smiled at her and then Eliza burst into tears.

"What did you do to her?" Chase said, leaping up, getting Eliza a chair and a box of Kleenex.

"I didn't do anything," Nora replied, gaping at Eliza.

Eliza blew her nose. "It's not her. It's my life. I just can't take it anymore. I give up." She raised her hands overhead.

Chase wasn't sure if this was a sign to God that like Job his test was ruthless or unlike Job, Eliza wasn't up to the task.

"What's wrong?" Chase asked, hoping none of this had anything to do with her. She was fairly certain she hadn't stepped on Eliza's toes in her dealings with the staff. She was taking a positive attitude toward discipline and no one had been fired yet.

"Oh, nothing," Eliza said tearfully.

Chase had read in her *Guide to Women's Health* book that some menopausal women had crying jags. Eliza didn't look old enough to be menopausal—but sometimes it started early. Chase was learning everything about girl-parts. Gitana had threatened to take the book away several times. Chase was now hiding it in the bathroom cabinet.

"It must be something," Nora prodded.

"Well, I'm having a bad patch. I guess. I keeping hoping things will get better but then another bad thing happens." She grabbed another wad of Kleenex.

Chase braced herself. "Like what kind of things?"

"My dishwasher flooded the kitchen floor this morning. The faucet keeps leaking into the cabinet under the sink so the whole room stinks of mildew. I sat on a melted candy bar during lunch and totally ruined my pants—now I look like I have poop on my pants. My check engine light came on and my gyno says I have to have my uterus cauterized to stop my abnormal bleeding cycles."

Chase winced at this last one. "Okay let's break it down. There's the plumbing issues, the car issues and the laundry issue. But first, turn around and let's see the pants."

Eliza did so.

"Yep, that looks like poop all right," Chase said.

"That's helpful," Nora said.

It seemed to Chase that Nora was intently staring at Eliza's ass in more than a professional manner. But she said, "I know— we've got coveralls for the cleaning crew. You could wear those."

"Now, there's a fashion statement," Eliza said. "But it is better than poop-looking stuff on your butt." Her eyes met Nora's.

Nora smiled.

"Okay, next." Chase looked at her list—plumbing. She picked up her cell phone and scanned through her call record until she found Ricardo's number. They had used him to fix their plumbing issues. "One of Gitana's cousins is a plumber." She dialed the number. "Ricardo, it's Chase. I need a big favor. I have a friend with a bad plumbing problem."

Chase listened and pursed her lips. "Yes, okay I'll edit your science fiction story if you fix her sink and do not say or do anything perverted. Understand? And just a heads-up, her girlfriend is six feet tall and built like a truck so I highly recommend you behave yourself." She gave him the address and clicked off.

"Do I really want this guy at my house?" Eliza asked, sitting on the corner of Nora's desk and looking more relaxed.

"He's all talk. Besides he's a midget and a coward. Your well-built girlfriend is a deterrent."

"I don't have a girlfriend," Eliza said.

"Yeah, right." Chase drew a heart on a piece of scratch paper with Eliza's and Nora's names in the center. She held it up to show them.

Nora tried to grab it, but Chase held it away from her.

"Look, I've been watching you two. It's so obvious. Just get it over with."

Nora blushed and then seemed to summon up all her inner butchness. "Eliza, will you go out with me?"

An endless silence.

"I'd love to."

"How about dinner?" Nora said shyly.

"Wonderful."

"Now, to continue the problem solving, the check engine light, we can utilize the mobile auto service that keeps up our trucks. They're scheduled up here tomorrow to do oil changes anyway." She consulted her list again. It was the uterus cauterization. "Well, that last one might prove difficult."

"It's all right, Chase. I think you've done enough," Eliza said.

"Whew," Chase said, taking the list and wadding it up.

"I've got to see about the seedlings," Eliza said, making for the door. She turned around. "I'll see you later, Nora."

Nora did this wave thing and Chase thought that love was fucking weird. It could turn the biggest butch into a sappy ball of emotional mush.

Chase rolled over in her chair to the door to make sure Eliza was out of earshot. "So where are you going to take her?"

Nora seemed dumbstruck. "I don't know. Do you have any ideas?" Nora appeared to have jumped into panicmode.

"I'm not very good with romance."

"But you're a romance writer," Nora said, her voice rising.

"That's different. I don't know how exactly but it is," Chase said, pondering the question and just as promptly dropping it. Creation had never made sense to her. It happened and she was thankful. One does not question the Muse.

Gitana came in and sat on the corner of Chase's desk and casually reached for the Java Juice cup. Chase snatched it up.

"Nora asked Eliza out on a date. We're trying to figure out a romantic place for dinner," Chase told her.

"The Melting Pot," Gitana said.

"It's fondue. You have to cook all your food in that stupid pot of oil. You could starve," Chase said, remembering the episode vividly. She'd come home and made two peanut butter sandwiches.

"And while you wait you can talk," Gitana said.

"How do you know when it's done?" Nora asked.

"You will. The wait staff tells you everything you need to know. It's very educational," Gitana said.

"Educational is good. Eliza likes to learn things," Nora said gratefully.

"Don't forget to carbo load before you go," Chase advised.

"Problem solved." Gitana reached over and hit the enter key on Chase's laptop.

"What are you doing?" Chase said as the black screen came to life.

"Seeing what you're working on."

"It's a paper on orchids." She moved the laptop closer.

Gitana moved over. "I don't think so." She read it aloud. "She took the wet pink folds in her mouth, waiting for the thrust of

178

her lover's hips."

"Will you stop," Chase said, covering her face.

"Boy, is that hot. Can I read the rest?" Nora asked.

"No." Chase snapped her laptop shut.

"You're behind," Gitana said.

"Just a little." Chase didn't meet her gaze.

"You need to be finishing your book. I'm sure little Miss-Snotty-Editor has been calling."

Chase scowled. Gitana despised Ariana who treated writers like minions of the monarchy. When Ariana called and Gitana answered the phone she would yell across the house, "Your snot nose editor is on the line." This pissed Ariana off to no end.

"Why does she call me that?" she'd demand.

"Because you're a bitch," Chase would respond, and Ariana would snort, "That's what it takes to get you on deadline."

"All she wants is progress reports," Chase told Gitana.

"Chase, go home and power-edit and get it over with it," Gitana said.

"But I need to be here."

"How about the morning shift? That's the most crucial time. Help Nora set up and edit in the afternoons."

"Is that all right with you?" Chase asked Nora.

"Nothing should stand in the way of completely sexy literature," Nora said.

"Yeah, right."

"Off you go then," Gitana said.

"Do you want me to take the dogs?" Chase said.

Gitana looked out the office window onto the greenhouse grounds. "No, they appear to be quite busy. When did they learn to become sled dogs?"

Annie and Jane both had their harnesses attached to a small garden cart and hauled it around as Eliza and Heather, her assistant worked the pots.

"The other day. It's hard on your back and they love it."

"Only you," Gitana said. "Now, go."

Chase packed up her laptop and wistfully looked around.
"We'll be fine," Nora said.

Chapter Twenty

"I'm telling you it's almost done. It'll be perfect and yes, I did fix the ending. Now, go away. I know, next Tuesday—like I could forget." Chase threw her cell phone on the couch after she clicked off, and accidently nailed her writing mascot, Curious George, in the forehead.

"Sorry about that George," she said, turning around to stare at her computer. "I need to write better so I have less work at the end. Remember Kurt Vonnegut—every page perfect before he moved on. Ugh! I could never do that. I wouldn't get anything done."

"Who are to talking to?" Lacey asked. She stood in the doorway of the writing studio.

"Curious George." Chase swung around in her chair and pointed at the stuffed monkey. She attempted to look peevish to convey that she was busy. Lacey did not take the hint but took a seat on the couch next to George.

Seeing that Lacey was not going away Chase got up and poured them both an iced tea. "Now, what brings you up here on such a pleasant day?" she asked in an effort to accelerate the visit.

"Thanks. I'm parched," Lacey said, taking the glass. "It is a nice day and when one sees the world shining bright and full of promise it makes your inner self brim with unblocked Chi." Lacey took a sip and leaned back on the couch.

"Have you been going to Jasmine's meditation class?" Chase scooted George over and sat on the couch next to Lacey.

"How'd you know?"

"Because Jasmine always talks like that after her class. You're acting guilty. What's up?"

"Philip doesn't want her to go to meditation. He says she gets all weird."

"That guy is a total prick. Does she tell him that he can't go golfing because his testicles sweat and he might get ringworm?" Chase finished her iced tea. She needed about three more if she was going to get through the afternoon.

"What's that?"

"I don't really know. It's something guys get. Now, what do you want?"

"Can I kiss you?" Lacey sipped her iced tea and stared unblinking at Chase. She acted like she'd asked for a ride to the airport or if Chase would feed her cat and water the plants while she went away for the weekend.

"Excuse me?"

"I need to kiss a woman and you're my best friend and I trust you more than anyone in the whole world—so I figured you should be the one. Can I have some more tea?"

"Sure," Chase said. Lacey had the uncanny ability to drop big piles of doo-doo and then walk away with no concern for the consequences.

Lacey was looking at her. "I don't know why you're making such a big deal about it." She poured the tea.

"Oh, I don't know. I'm married with a kid on the way and

you're straight—just to name a few."

"Will you just do it?" Lacey said.

"Not until you tell me why. Is this some diversity training class where everyone has to kiss a lesbian? It's not normal behavior except for lesbians." Chase's voice had become high and squeaky.

"I want you to kiss me because I really like Jasmine, but I don't want to kiss her and discover that I don't like it. I wouldn't want to do that to her." Lacey sat down next to Chase and put her hands in her lap.

"That almost sounds altruistic for you," Chase said. Lacey did look pensive.

"Chase, please will you just do it?"

"I've got to call Gitana first and get her feedback. She is part of the equation."

"All right. I just hope she's open-minded about this. It really is more like a public service than anything else."

Chase rolled her eyes and grabbed her cell phone from Curious George. She dialed.

"What's up, babe?"

That was the nice thing about cell phones—you no longer had to introduce yourself. Name tags did it for you. This always made Chase smile. Whenever Ariana, her editor called, it came up as a private number so Chase knew it was her. She'd answer, "Hi, Ariana," but Ariana would always say, "Hi, Chase, it's Ariana," and get all flustered. It shifted the balance of power. "Lacey wants to kiss me. I called to get your permission."

She laughed. "Do you guys have something going on I need to know about?"

"Lacey might be attracted to Jasmine who is trying to seduce her. Lacey doesn't want to be freaked out or hurt Jasmine's feelings if she doesn't like it. That's my best summation."

"All right then, but save some for me and if Lacey converts we get a new toaster oven since ours committed an act of self-immolation the other day."

"I hate when they do that. I'll let you know how it goes,"

Chase said. She clicked off and gave the phone back to Curious George.

"So it's all right?" Lacey said.

"Yes, but if you convert we get a toaster oven."

"It's a deal." Lacey was sitting on the edge of the couch like a cat ready for the pounce.

"Let's relax for a minute." Chase found she was actually nervous. For Lacey's sake she would pretend not to be. They both took a couple deep breaths. "Ready?"

"I think so. I mean, yes," Lacey said.

Chase moved over next to Lacey and leaned over and touched Lacey's face. She moved closer and kissed her. Lacey kissed back—their tongues circling each other. Lacey let out a little moan and they opened their eyes.

"You're a great kisser," Lacey said.

"How'd it make you feel?"

"That if you weren't married I'd be taking your clothes off right now."

"Wonderful. Now go tell Jasmine. I've got to get back to work."

Lacey gave her a bone-crushing hug. "I love you. You're a true friend. Got to go." Lacey jumped up and flew out of the room.

Chase went back to her computer and her editing deadline. She never really understood later-in-life converts. Had Lacey awakened this morning and decided she might be a lesbian? It made no sense, but then she had a hard time figuring herself out. How the hell was she supposed to figure anyone else out? Therapists were supposed to do that, but, her view therapists fell into the same category as the weatherman. They both produced guesses masquerading as science.

She got some work done, completing the find and replace of a set of names beginning with the same letter. How did shit like that still escape her? Cynthia, Carol and Chris. They were minor characters, but it was a gross oversight. She hated giving Ariana ammunition. Chase's entire improvement as a writer was tied to thwarting Ariana's list of writing faux pas.

While Chase muttered obscenities at her manuscript Gitana slipped into the studio and kissed Chase's neck.

"Hey, baby. Where are the dogs?"

Chase always knew when Gitana got home because the dogs were the alarm system. "They're having an ice cream cone with Nora and Eliza."

"Why didn't they come home with you? What's the occasion?"

"Alone time with my wife."

Chase swung around in the chair to face Gitana who held two cords that looked suspiciously like they belonged to their bathrobes. Gitana smiled at her.

The phone rang. It was Lacey. "What's wrong now?"

"The WiFi isn't working at Starbucks and I want to look up you know, that c-word."

"What's that?" Chase said.

"The thing you gals do… down there," Lacey said.

"Got it. Straight people do it too."

"I know, but I've never done it. I wanted to look it up on Wikipedia," Lacey said.

"They have stuff like that on there?"

Gitana was taking her clothes off in a striptease fashion—slow and deliberate. Chase was sure pregnant women doing stripteases was against the law somewhere on the planet.

"I thought it was a good place to start and then there's this thing Jasmine told me the other day about practicing on mangos."

"Excuse me?" Chase said.

"You cut it in half and sort of suck on it," Lacey explained.

"I don't want to hear any more."

"Can't you look it up for me?"

"I can't. Gitana is tying me to a chair right now."

It was true—the now naked Gitana had taken the bath robe cords and tied Chase's free hand to the chair.

"Is that something I should learn?" Lacey inquired.

"You might want to wait a bit—look, you know what you like

down there. Do that to Jasmine and you'll be fine."

"I can do that. I'll be fine. Won't I?" Lacey said with obvious trepidation.

"You've had a lot of practice."

"I should be insulted."

"Don't be. Remember the deal." Chase clicked off. Gitana grabbed the phone and chucked it on the couch. It hit Curious George in the head. The poor bastard has had a hard day, Chase thought as Gitana tied her other hand to the chair.

She pulled off Chase's shorts and flicked her tongue up her inner thigh. Chase moaned and struggled for a moment before letting go. Oh, she thought if Lacey gets this her life will be heaven.

"I missed you," Gitana said as she straddled Chase and slipped her fingers inside. Chase moved against her. Gitana kept kissing her until Chase came.

"Oh, God," Chase said. It was odd not being in control of part of your body while your lover brought you there. She contemplated asking if she could do the same, but decided that tying up your pregnant wife might be out of line.

Instead, she let Gitana untie her and then Chase sucked her fingers while her hand played elsewhere. It was perfectly lovely and then they went to the couch and did the mango thing until they heard the horn honk in the driveway and the dogs came flying across the yard and up to the studio.

Chapter Twenty-One

Tuesday afternoon, Chase sat on the deck having a beer. She'd sent her finished manuscript to Ariana. The wave of relief that finishing a book produced was like floodwaters seeping into her house of creation and washing it clean, leaving only clear space.

The dogs napped at her feet. Life felt calm. Gitana was at an orchid show in Santa Fe. Late September had arrived bringing its fine colors. The poplars that lined the driveway crackled with their brilliant yellow leaves. Chase planned to take the dogs and Addison up to Fourth of July canyon for a hike to see the changing of the leaves. Gitana was past hiking. She had trouble getting up the stairs.

Now that she had finished her moist-mound saga, her mystery novel popped up in her head like a bagel in a toaster. She'd realized that she needed to do more research on straight people. This turning out a viable straight character had proved more difficult than she'd anticipated and something still wasn't right.

Her ruminations were broken by the rumblings of a large truck and the dogs barking their brains out. Chase paid no attention. The propane trucks, the garbage truck and the UPS guy all came up the rutted dirt road, their engines and shocks making horrible noises and the dogs always barked.

A white truck with Lowe's in huge blue letters on the side panel pulled up in their drive. The dogs were beside themselves. Chase shooed them into the gated side yard. They could still see but not attack the driver. This was important. Annie had almost bitten the county sheriff when he was making inquiries about a neighbor's wife gone missing.

The driver was a large Hispanic man. "Hola, are you Chase Banter?"

"Yes. I don't remember ordering anything."

He frowned and studied his clipboard. "I'm making an appliance drop. You need to sign here indicating you received the delivery."

"Is this about the toaster oven?" Chase said.

"Yes, ma'am."

"Seems like an awfully long way for a toaster oven. Couldn't you have just shipped it?"

He dropped down the lift and swung open the back door. "I don't think so. The invoice says a toaster oven, a stainless steel fridge, a dishwasher and a glass top stove. You remodeling?"

"Not that I was aware of. Who bought all this stuff?" Chase hoped Gitana hadn't slipped over the edge about the state of the appliances because the dishwasher still leaked and the fridge had developed an odd buzz. This was not in the budget.

"All the note says is "Love Lacey, don't even think about returning it." There's a lot of exclamation points."

"I see."

"You've got to sign for it." He handed Chase the clipboard.

"What happened to your fingers?" he inquired.

Chase had two Band-Aids on her fingers and black electrical tape around the rest, giving her no access to her cuticles. Her ten-step program was going badly. "I'm supposed to stop biting my cuticles," she said as she signed her name. She hoped this wasn't going to turn into a speech on weakness—how she needed to harness her inner strength. She'd had enough of those. Non-cuticle biters just didn't understand the complexity of the issue.

"I know what you mean. I can't stop." The driver held up his hands. They looked like a war zone. "Does that tape thing work?"

Chase handed the clipboard back. "Kind of. Pulling off the tape to chew makes you feel guilty, but it doesn't always stop you."

"Guilt is a powerful motivator."

"Went to Catholic school, did you?"

He smiled. "Yep. I better get this out of the truck or the boss will have my ass."

Chase had him put the stuff in the sunroom until they sorted out the kitchen. When he finished Chase got him an iced tea. "Here sit down and take a rest, that was hard work."

"Thanks."

"It's beautiful out here," Raul said, for he had introduced himself.

The mountains still clung to the greenery of summer, but the aspen groves were starting to turn.

"Yes, it is." Chase looked at scenery she forgot to see until a stranger mentioned it.

"What do you do?" Raul asked. He sipped his iced tea with the gratitude of the truly thirsty.

Chase topped it off with the glass pitcher she'd brought out. "I'm a writer."

"Really? That's great. I'm a reader. I love to read. I know that seems kind of strange for a delivery driver—antithetical. I've never met a writer."

"You're not your job, Raul. Raul is intelligent, gregarious and a reader." Chase finished her iced tea and refilled it. They were sitting on the loading gate which Raul had lifted to the perfect height.

"You're right. You know why I like this job? It pays well and I get out and about. I'm not stuck in an office. I talk to people that I want to and not to people I have to."

"That's how to look at life," Chase said.

"What about you? Do you love to write?"

"I do. I can't imagine my life without it." Chase topped off his glass. A beautiful rufus hummingbird buzzed in at them and then off to the feeder in the front yard.

"So what do you write?"

"Lesbian romance novels." Chase cringed every time she was asked. Somehow, romance coupled with lesbian was the ghetto of all ghettos, genre-hell where the world scorned her efforts.

"What's wrong with that? My wife's a lesbian. I'm sure she'd love your work. How many books have you written?"

"Eleven."

"Hell, that's something to be proud of."

"Did you mean your ex-wife's a lesbian?"

"No. We're still married. Going on fifteen years now. She was a lesbian when I married her." Raul leaned down and tightened the laces of his work boots.

"I'm missing something. I have to be."

Raul laughed. "Yeah, it's kind of weird but it works."

"But how?" Chase asked, her brow wrinkled in confusion.

Raul picked at his thumb. Chase dug the roll of black electrical tape out of her pant's pocket. "Here use some of this."

He pulled off a piece and wrapped it around his thumb.

"The arrangement," Chase prodded. Her curiosity piqued, propriety couldn't stop her.

"Oh, yeah, well, Marisa's a little different."

"Obviously."

"She pretends I'm a woman."

Had Chase been drinking her tea she would have spewed it all over at this revelation. "This is the weirdest fucking story I've ever heard."

Raul chuckled. "I don't tell it to many people." He wrapped

some more electrical tape around the pinky and ring finger of his left hand.

Chase noticed he was wearing a simple gold wedding ring. "No, I suppose not. So it works in the sack? I mean that's got to be the testing ground." She found it difficult to ask this question, but it was the most crucial one.

"Sure, I let my hair down, shave my legs, wear a silk robe and you know." He demonstrated by taking his hair out of the rubber band. He shook it out.

He was a handsome man with his long black hair and his smooth olive skin and dark, almost black almond-shaped eyes.

"You're a lesbian with a real strap-on?"

"Exactly."

Chase studied his features. He could pass in a darkened room like a bar or bedroom. She supposed it was no different than her being a father. Oh, hell, the world was a strange place. At least it's not boring. "You know, Raul, you're all right."

"I was wondering…" He stopped and blushed. "If I sent you one of your books, would you autograph it for Marisa? She'd be so excited."

"I've got promo copies. Let me get one and you can take it home."

"That'd be great. She's going to be flabbergasted that I met you. She's very proud of our community."

Chase ran up to the studio and rummaged in her closet for the box of books. She knew she should be more reverent with her novels, but once the editing was complete she was so sick of it that she never wanted to see the book again. It was only times like this—making Raul's—day that those copies had meaning.

Chase autographed the title page using her best most legible scrawl.

"I'm going to read it to her tonight. She loves me to read to her. She says I have a sonorous voice."

"You two sound perfect for each other."

"I better get going. I might be considered tardy."

He pulled out a small black notebook from his front pocket and studied it. "Perfect. I haven't used that one in six months. The old flat tire routine."

"Especially on our road. So you keep notes."

"We call it the The Black Book of Excuses." He winked at her.

"That's a great idea. Maybe I could make up one for my editor."

"You could call it The Writer's Book of Editorial Excuses," he suggested.

Chase laughed. "I like that."

Raul dug in his front pocket again. This time he pulled out a business card. "Here's my number. You need anything—or want to go out to dinner sometime just give me a call."

"I will," she said, and actually meant it.

Raul started the diesel. The dogs barked and Gitana came up the drive. She pulled the Land Rover off into the wild grasses so the delivery truck could pass.

She drove up to the house, honking at the dogs in the daily ritual of "Mama's home" and they danced gleefully at the gate on their hind legs like furry can-can dancers.

No one except a fur kid could make you feel so loved and needed, Chase thought, probably not even Bud.

"So what was that about?" Gitana asked as she walked up the drive from the garage.

"It was the toaster oven."

"They sent out a truck for that?" She opened the front gate and gave Chase a peck on her cheek.

Chase wanted to see her reaction to Lacey's surprise gift to see if it differed from her own.

Gitana walked into the sunroom, which now resembled an appliance warehouse. "What on earth?"

"Lacey."

"We can't take this. What all is it?" Gitana said, peering at the boxes.

"Stove, fridge, dishwasher and a toaster oven. All stainless steel."

"Must have been quite the conversion," Gitana said, stroking the fridge box.

"I tried. She won't take it back. She said something about saving her life."

"Still." Gitana bent over and studied the picture of the dishwasher on the front of the box.

"Enjoy it. It's pocket change for Lacey. Besides we should get a payoff for putting up with her ass."

Gitana smiled. "She'd say the same thing about you."

Chase flicked open the silver box cutter. "Sticks and stones and a new stove."

Chapter Twenty-Two

Chase stood in the middle of her mother's living room. Lacey and Stella cocked their heads in unison and peered at her from where they sat on the sofa. "I feel utterly and completely ridiculous," Chase grumbled.

"That's two adverbs in one sentence," Lacey said.

"So?" Chase straightened the dark blue blazer.

"You're the one who harps on Jasmine about killing adverbs and adjectives if possible."

"I don't know if this relationship is a good thing for you," Chase said.

"*What's that supposed to mean?*"

Chase could see the panic on Lacey's face.

"Don't let her get to you," Stella remarked. "You and Jasmine make a fine lesbian couple—and you make a fine lesbian." Stella studied Chase's brown penny loafers. She scowled. "They look too new. Hand them over."

Chase sat on the couch and took off her shoes. "That's the fourth time in your life you've actually said the word lesbian."

"Lacey is opening my eyes to a completely new culture."

"Wow, you act like you never had a lesbian daughter for the last twenty years. Next you'll be using the word dyke."

"You've always been hostile about sharing your domain. Lacey isn't." Stella raised her eyebrows and lowered the right corner of her mouth, studying the shoes. "Besides, I thought the word dyke was politically incorrect." She took out an emery board from her purse.

"Only if you're straight. Gay people can use it," Lacey said. She was lounging on the white couch looking like a bored movie star.

"I see," Stella said. She sanded the toes of Chase's brand-new penny loafers.

"Something's wrong with new shoes?" Chase asked, looking mournfully as her recent purchase was being destroyed. She glanced down at her socks. "Do these work?" They were navy dress socks but didn't seem the right hue.

"Top drawer, right side," Stella said to Lacey, who dashed from the room. She didn't look up from her destruction of Chase's shoes.

Lacey returned to the living room. "Here, these are much better." She gave her a pair of cream colored dress socks.

"Now, back to the matter we were discussing before we got into shoes and socks. What are we going to use for a career for you?" Stella said, referring to Chase.

Lacey flounced on the couch. "I know," and said nothing more.

Stella raised her eyebrows and tapped her fingers on the arm of the couch. "Ready."

"Proust," Lacey replied.

Lacey's favorite dramatic tactic was being cryptic. One-word answers designed to amp up the conversation.

Stella rubbed her hands together impatiently. "And?"

"The guy in the movie *Little Miss Sunshine* was a Proust scholar. Few people know about Proust other than he's a French writer. No one reads him. We'll get her some particulars on Proust and that's her occupation."

"I have read Proust," Chase said.

"Really?" Lacey said.

"In French, no less."

Stella smiled, which was rarity. "You really are smart. I'm glad to see that expensive education of yours wasn't wasted." She picked up her purse and dug out her car keys. Then as if to make up for that slip of affection she said, "How is your therapy going by the way?"

"Fine. Can't you tell? We're hanging out. Resolution with your mother is straight out of Freud," Chase replied petulantly. Why did she have to bring that up now? Chase thought.

"I always thought Freud was a pervert." Lacey picked up her purse and rooted around for her sunglasses.

"Am I going to need one of those?" Chase said, pointing to the purses.

Stella and Lacey stared at her and burst out laughing making such comments as "Now, I'd like to see that," and "Wait let me get my camera."

"Forget I said anything. Let's go," Chase said. Checking out straight people was losing its appeal.

Stella and Lacey regained their composure. They got in the black Bentley parked in the drive.

Chase sat in the backseat and Lacey rode shotgun. Stella started the car. She put it in reverse and floored the gas pedal. They flew through the stone gate. She hit the brakes and the car spun sideways. "How was that?"

"More like what was that?" Lacey said. "I almost peed my pants."

"I'd give it a nine." Chase nodded.

"A nine?" Stella knitted her brows.

"You were a little close on the right side."

Stella studied the mirror.

"Why are we doing this?" Lacey said.

"I used to do it until Gitana got pregnant," Chase said.

"I missed her doing it. So I took it up. It's actually quite fun," Stella said.

As they drove up the oak-lined entrance to the country club, Chase thought how easy it would be to describe it in a novel—old, moldy and verbose fit the cliché of money and snobbery. She hadn't been there since she was sixteen for a dance—thrown out later for illicit copulation in the women's powder room with her tennis pro.

The valet came out to greet them. "Thank you, James," Stella said, handing him the keys and a twenty-dollar bill.

Her mother did have class, Chase thought. She was never cheap.

"James, do you remember my daughter, Chase?"

James studied Chase. "No, ma'am, but she certainly has your lovely countenance."

"Thank you," Stella said.

Then James stuck out his hand to Chase. "But I would like to make your acquaintance."

Chase shook his hand. "It's nice to meet you." He looked to be about her age. His hair was dark and pulled back in a neat ponytail and he had a well-trimmed goatee.

They walked off and Chase whispered to her mother, "Was he here then?"

"Yes. He was at University the same time you were. He's a writer as well." They walked up the stairs and into the massive mahogany hall of the club.

"What does he write?" Chase asked her interest piqued.

"Sci-Fi," Lacey said.

"He told me the average book sells approximately two thousand copies and the rest end up on the remainder table. Most authors do not make money. So it is a labor of love," Stella said as she waved at various people in the dining room. "His appraisal of the situation has given me insight into your career. I didn't realize it was so difficult and I commend your efforts."

Lacey and Chase stared at her open-mouthed. Stella sighed heavily as if disappointed with their predictable response of shock at a compliment aimed at Chase. She pointed to a table.

They moved to a corner table, a vantage point that allowed a view of the rest of the room. They sat at the thick wood table with hard chairs. This is stiff business, Chase thought, envisioning a comfortable chair that ought to have gone with the luxury of the place. "So you have a better perspective on writing."

"No, I expect better of you."

"You expect me to buck the current publishing trend."

"Yes," Stella replied.

"Sit over here," Lacey said, pointing to the middle chair. "So we can talk trash and can't be seen while you observe the person we're backstabbing."

Stella flicked out her white linen napkin and studied her dinnerware. "It's not backstabbing. It's human nature being observed."

"Nice repackaging job," Lacey said.

A waiter in full tails who looked like a penguin came for their drink order. He looked at Lacey.

"I'll have a gin martini," Lacey announced.

"I'll have a beer," Chase said.

Lacey kicked her under the table. "She'll have a glass of Chardonnay."

"Ma'am?" He looked at Chase inquiringly.

"Yes, that's a much better idea." Chase rubbed her shin.

"I'll have iced tea, please," Stella said.

"Very good." He left.

Chase had never known her mother to turn down a martini. "You're not having a drink?"

"I'm on call."

"On call? You have a job?" Lacey stopped gawking at the other diners and turned her gaze firmly on Stella.

"It's more like volunteer work." Stella opened her menu with a snap.

Stella was equally good at dramatics. Lacey leaned forward. Then she looked at Chase who shrugged. They both knew that Stella wouldn't volunteer to pick up a paper clip for a crippled blind person.

"For?" Lacey said.

Chase picked up her menu and pretended not to be interested. This was a proven antidote for dramatics.

"A little PI work for Peggy," Stella replied.

Chase looked over the top of her menu. "As in Addison's mother?"

"This is news," Lacey said.

"New friend?" Chase said.

"As a matter of fact we have a lot in common."

The waiter returned with their drinks.

Lacey sipped her martini. Chase looked at her wineglass. "I don't like wine."

"It's an acquired taste. Just try it," Lacey said.

Chase sipped it. "Ick."

Lacey picked it up and took a drink. "It's fine."

Stella went back to her menu. She furrowed her brow.

Lacey hadn't opened hers. She must know what she wants, Chase thought.

"Addison didn't mention anything." Chase sipped her wine again and puckered up.

"She wasn't supposed to," Stella said.

"And why was that?"

Stella put her menu down. "I thought it would make you angry."

"Why?" Chase felt her face grow red as if in anticipation.

"Turf war." Stella didn't look at her.

Chase watched her mother's face. Her mother didn't like many people—women in particular. Chase didn't blame her. Women in her mother's possible circle of friends sucked. They were egotistical, jealous and petty snobs. Peggy had her issues, but she was real.

"I'm just surprised Addison didn't tell me."

"We threatened to take her backpack away." Stella glanced back down at her menu, thus successfully avoiding Chase's hot gaze.

"Am I that bad?" Chase asked. She took another sip of the odious wine to fortify herself for the answer.

"You can be," Lacey and Stella said in unison.

Chase furrowed her brow and let out a heavy sigh. They waited for her response. "I suppose you're right. Anger was my first emotion; however, I'm glad you found a friend with some good traits—it's beats the icky ones you're forced to hang with."

Stella smiled. "Lacey, please pick your chin up off the table. Chase is becoming a decent human being and we should support that."

"Thanks and ditto," Chase said, giving Lacey a good poke in the ribs.

Stella pursed her lips but then smiled.

The penguin waiter returned to inquire about their order. "Are you ready?"

"Yes, thank you," Stella replied. "You may begin, Lacey."

"I'll have the lobster bisque," Lacey said, her eyes gleaming.

Chase, who had not had a chance to look at the menu properly, chose the same, thinking if Lacey was drooling over it the stuff couldn't be half bad.

"I'll have a Caesar salad and the grilled tuna," Stella said.

The penguin picked up the menus that Stella had slid in his direction. "Very good."

After he trundled off, Stella commenced with Chase's education on upperclass straight people. She cocked her head toward the large paned windows that lined one wall of the grand eating hall. "Those people over there are poor as church mice, but they never let on."

Chase attempted discretion and glanced at them as she sipped or pretended to sip her wine. The man was impeccably dressed in a white linen suit with a burgundy ascot. He looked like the writer Tom Wolfe, Chase thought, remembering his photo on the back cover of *The Bonfire of Vanities*. His wife was frumpy. She wore a simple floral print sundress making her look almost Amish excepting the low cut front that exposed the tops of her large fleshy breasts.

When she'd finished her inspection, she said, "How does that work?" Wealthy people always confused her despite her privileged background. Her life before she met Gitana had become a blur of patchy memories, which explained her apparent lack of knowledge when it came to straight people's ways. She'd been hanging out with mostly gay people for so long that she'd forgotten the old ways. She realized her comfort zone and it wasn't in this world, but perhaps this would make her a keener observer.

Stella sipped her tea and then pontificated on the woes of the pretenders. "Her wealthy father regularly bails them out. Richard, the husband, resents this but is too inert to change his behavior."

"What does he do, sit on the couch, fingers poised on a calculator that he never turns on?" Chase knitted her brow and studied the portrait of inertia.

"They charge everything and when it gets bad, Daddy settles it all up to avoid an embarrassing bankruptcy," Stella replied.

"Would you do that for me?" Chase asked.

Her mother sipped her tea. "No, I would not."

"I didn't think so." Chase remembered asking for what she needed and getting it when she was growing up. Money was never mentioned. She knew that Lacey paid for everything with a credit card that her accountant took care of. Lacey's father had left her mother for another woman when she was six. Her mother moved to Italy to lick her wounds and sent Lacey to boarding school. Lacey had been on her own since she was sixteen. Stella was the most mother Lacey ever had and Lacey was the daughter

Stella really wanted.

"Now that couple over there positively hates each other but to part company means dividing up the assets and admitting failure which neither will assent to."

Chase looked over at the attractive well-dressed couple on her right. They looked straight out of *Town and Country*. "Are straight people all miserable money-grubbers?"

"I wouldn't say that, but money doesn't necessarily make for happy, loving couples," Stella said.

"Poor people are the opposite. They bicker about money, thinking that if they had money life would immediately right itself." Lacey kept glancing at the paneled door which led to the kitchen.

"How do you know that?" Chase said.

"The lottery."

"What?" Chase often felt the urge to cure Lacey of her cryptic speech pattern by beating it out of her. Instead, she pinched her thigh.

"Ouch! Why'd you do that?"

Stella smiled at Chase in apparent approval. "We'd like you to elaborate. Lacey, you have the annoying habit of replying in incomplete sentences, which your audience finds annoying as it creates a seeming endless set of questions in order to make sense of your enigmatic statement. It's tedious as well as rude," Stella said.

"I couldn't have said it better myself," Chase said. "Thank you, Mother."

Lacey looked hurt for a moment and then seemed to cast the criticism aside as so much linguistic trash. "I see people waiting in line at the convenience store buying lottery tickets on Saturday night for the big Powerball. They're always talking about how they'd spend the money. They seem so certain that money would make them happy. Is that thorough enough for you people?" She snapped open her napkin as if abusing it would dispel her anger.

"Well done," Chase said, neatly unfolding her own napkin.

The penguin brought their order on a rolling cart topped with silver covers set on white linen. He lifted the covers and set the plates down with much ceremony as if the lobster bisque and tuna would object if they were mistreated. "Anything else, ladies?"

Stella looked around the table and then replied. "We're quite well."

Lacey dove into her lobster bisque.

Chase choked down more wine and thought wistfully of a taquito. She tried the bisque. It was saucy with lumps in it. She was not impressed.

Her mother's cell phone beeped. She quickly retrieved it from her purse. It was a text message. She texted back. Her fingers flew over the keypad.

Chase was impressed. She had difficulty navigating her phone and had a tendency to leave it at home, behavior motivated by her lack of technical skills and her anti-social behavior. With Gitana's pregnancy she did carry the phone now but still maintained her animosity, agreeing with Garrison Keillor who once remarked that it was amazing how we went to the moon and back without a cell phone but wouldn't dream of going through the produce department without one.

"We have to go," Stella said.

"Why? Where are we going?" Chase asked.

"To spy on Dickhead. Peggy wants photos of his infidelity so she can file for divorce on grounds of adultery. She's afraid he will fight for custody of Addison just to spite her. As you know, Addison despises him."

"Let's go," Chase said, getting up abruptly.

"What about my bisque?" Lacey said, looking down mournfully at her bowl.

Chase threw a napkin on top of it. "Take it with you."

Lacey was mortified. "I can't do that."

"Why not?" Chase said.

"Etiquette."

"Have some balls, Lacey," Stella said. She picked up the supporting plate under the soup bowl and grabbed a spoon. "There, now let's go."

Chase was actually liking her mother which freaked her out. She remembered an old Civil Rights ditty, "The times, they are a changin'." Maybe her animosity for her mother had taken a sudden holiday without giving notice.

Lacey set her shoulders back and walked out of the dining hall with the plate. No one said a word.

Once outside, Stella commanded James to retrieve the car. "An express lunch, ma'am?" He eyed Lacey's plate.

"Yes. A certain important appointment came up."

James nodded and went for the car.

Her mother pulled out her cell phone and texted Peggy again.

"How does she know where he's going?" Chase asked.

"She put a GPS on his car," Stella replied.

"Wow, she's good," Lacey said. She took a bite of her lobster bisque. "Want some?" she said, holding out a spoonful.

"Uh, no thanks," Chase said, looking at the creamy sauce with distaste. Maybe when they were through with the escapade they could swing by Taco Bell and she could have a seven layer burrito and a taquito.

James pulled up with the car. Stella popped him another twenty and got in, waiting impatiently for the two others and then floored it once everyone was inside.

Lacey held onto her bisque for dear life. "What's with the driving lately?"

"We are on a mission," Stella said. The tires of the Bentley squealed as she pulled out of the parking lot onto the adjacent street. "Now, Chase will you reach under your seat and pull out the camera bag."

"A couple of incriminating photos and Peggy and Addison are free," Chase said.

"You got it." Stella got off the freeway and pulled into the parking lot of a hotel.

"Isn't that him?" Chase said. She'd only met Dickhead once when she was picking up Addison. He'd sort of grunted at her as they passed in the hallway.

Stella looked at her GPS screen. "That sneaky bastard. He parked at the Hyatt and crossed over to the Marriott." She raced the car through the parking lot to the other hotel. Lacey barely kept the plate from slamming into her chest. Bisque soaked the napkin and would soon soak Lacey. "I really wish you'd stop doing that."

"To reiterate, we're on a mission," Chase said. She pointed at the entrance of the Marriott. "There he is again."

"Well, doesn't he think he's smart," Stella said, smirking. "Parking across the street but still in a hotel parking lot isn't an Einsteinian move when there's no reason he should be at a hotel in the first place." Stella grabbed the camera bag and pulled out two straw cowboy hats and tacky cheap black sunglasses. "Here put these on and go take pictures of each other in the lobby." She shoved the camera at Chase.

"I thought you wanted pictures of *him*," Chase said.

"I want you to get a picture of him going into the hotel then I want you to get his hotel room number." She slapped the straw hat on Chase's head and handed Lacey the other one.

"I'm not wearing that," Lacey said. She was still holding the plate.

"Give me that," Chase said. She opened the car door and set the plate down on the pavement. She pulled Lacey out of the car.

"I don't understand why you're so gung-ho," Lacey complained.

"He's Addison's father. He is fucking some cheap whore and I want him hung up so he can't get at Addison. Is that a good enough reason?" Chase stared hard at Lacey who looked taken aback.

Stella observed her. "You'll make a fine parent."

"Thank you." Chase smiled as if her mouth, unaccustomed to doing that around her mother, were relearning a gesture from when she was an infant and hadn't know any better. She shouldered the camera, adjusted her silly hat and slapped the glasses on. "Operation Ball-Slammer, ready for action." She looked back at Lacey again.

"All right, I'm in. I just hope he's not an NRA member."

"He's not," Stella said.

Chase didn't want to know how she knew this. She grabbed Lacey's hand and made for the door.

Once inside Chase said, "Stand over by the fountain and I'll take your picture. Do you have your phone?"

"Duh," Lacey said, pulling it out of her blazer pocket.

"Good, I'll photograph you and you set your phone to video mode."

"Why?" Lacey asked.

Chase watched as he came through the door. "Just do it."

The urgency in her voice made an instant impression on Lacey. She opened her phone set it up and waited for the cue. "Now," Chase said. She began snapping photos of Lacey by the fountain with Dickhead in the background at the front desk. She looked over at him once. Their ruse must be working because he didn't notice them. Her mother was right. They looked like stupid tourists.

He got the key and went to the bank of elevators. "Shouldn't we follow him?" Lacey asked.

"Too obvious. Let's see your phone."

Lacey handed it to her. "Over here." Chase took them to the far corner of the plant-strewn atrium. Behind the ficus tree she replayed the video making sure to turn up the sound. "That's room five-twenty, Mr. Smith."

"You're brilliant," Lacey said as they headed back to the car.

"Did you get it?" Stella asked as they slid into the car.

"Sure did." Chase hit play and showed her mother.

"Oh, this is much better." She wrote down the room number in a slim black leather notebook, putting in the date and time.

Chase leaned over to observe this. "You're taking this pretty seriously."

"I think I may have found my calling," Stella said, her eyes gleaming

Chase remembered how she felt when she completed the first chapter of her first novel—complete euphoria. She had found her purpose. What had been foreign was now familiar.

"So now what?" Lacey said.

"Now we do some serious spying," Stella said.

Stella grabbed another black duffel bag from the trunk and they headed to the lobby of the hotel.

Chase watched as her mother schmoozed the desk clerk. The well-groomed desk clerk happily supplied her with a chart of the hotel and allowed her to choose a room of her pleasing.

"That was slick," Chase said as she punched the five button.

"It's all about presentation," Stella said, handing Chase the duffel bag. Chase handed it to Lacey who looked miffed but said nothing.

Once inside Room 518, Stella pulled the heavy emerald green curtains open. She drew her eyebrows together.

"Can you see him?" Lacey said, looking over Stella's shoulder.

"Not yet but I will." She pulled various equipment from the black duffel bag—a Nikon D700 digital camera with a high-powered lens, a set of enormous binoculars, a tripod and some kind of goggle-looking things.

"What are those?" Chase said.

"Night vision goggles," Stella said, laying out the equipment on the bed, careful not to get the fuzz from the amber brocade bedspread on any of it.

"Let me try them," Lacey said, carefully picking them up and examining them.

"It's light in here," Chase said.

"It's not in the bathroom," Lacey said. She tromped off.

"She's not all there, but she does have moments," Stella said, looking through the camera and adjusting the lens.

"Are the curtains open over there?"

"You betcha," Stella said, as she began rapidly snapping shots. "We got you, you slimy bastard." She turned around. "High-five, baby." She held out her hands.

Chase slapped them. The world was definitely off-kilter and she felt like a sailor canted on the deck of the wrong boat.

Chapter Twenty-Three

"I'm sorry I didn't tell you about my backpack," Addison said, avoiding Chase's gaze.

They were on their way to an Isotopes baseball game. Chase had no idea why Addison had expressed a sudden interest in the sport. She thought kids were into soccer these days.

"You were under pressure," Chase said. She hoped she wasn't condoning behavior that would one day turn Addison into some corporate monster that enslaved the masses in a third-world country with her "don't tell" philosophy. The Congo came to mind.

"No, it was wrong. I succumbed to blackmail, thinking only of myself and abusing your trust," Addison said, studying her hands as they gripped her backpack.

Chase's vision of the Congo popped like a soap bubble. Addison had morals and a conscience. "Well, if I behaved better toward my own mother it wouldn't have happened in the first place—a cause and effect thing."

The old ballpark had undergone a serious makeover—modern architecture of steel frame and a groovy color scheme of adobe sand and sage green with some red thrown in to make it fun. The grounds were xeriscaped. Chase noticed the yuccas with their red blooms and the wild grasses. She was always interested in the horticulture of the city in an effort to see what would grow in the hot dry climate of New Mexico so she could add it to her garden with a fifty-fifty chance of species survival.

Addison pulled two tickets from her backpack.

"Where'd you get those?" Chase put her wallet away. She never ceased to be amazed by Addison's organizational skills.

"My mom gets them free at work—for her real estate clients."

Addison handed them to the large man wearing a red vest and white baseball cap with the Isotope logo of swirling atoms. Chase thought the logo was stupid. Before the city had lost the team due to lack of financing in the eighties the baseball team had been called the Dukes—named for the Duke of Albuquerque who had colonized the place by killing off and subduing the indigenous people. Not that she thought this was a good name either, but the name Isotopes was in reference to the bombs made at the two labs in New Mexico, Sandia and Los Alamos.

"Can you buy those hats at the concession stands?" Addison inquired.

"Sure can—take a left and you'll see the souvenir shop."

"Thank you."

"Well-mannered kid," the man remarked.

"Yes, she is," Addison said.

Chase smirked. "I'm going to make a terrible parent," she said as they walked off.

"Why?"

"Because I'm not very mature. If I was a normal parent I would chastise you for being a smart-ass with that man. Instead, I thought it was funny. That's not good role model material."

"Ha! That'll be the day. He got what he deserved. Grown-ups

210

shouldn't use the third person when the kid is perfectly aware of what is going on." She led them toward the souvenir shop.

Chase made a mental note: Don't treat Bud as if she weren't present by using the third person.

At the souvenir shop Addison picked out a khaki-colored hat with the Isotopes logo stitched in reds and yellows, then a huge yellow foam hand giving the number one sign and a small wooden bat.

"Are you sure you want all that stuff?" Chase asked as she tried on a black visor.

"I want to look authentic."

"Does that mean we get a hot dog?" Chase placed the visor back on the hook and turned her attention to the hot dog stand located in the walkway behind them.

"Of course," Addison said picking up the visor Chase had been looking at and tucking it under her arm with her other purchases. She went to the checkout counter and pulled out her debit card. When she had finished she handed Chase the visor. "Here, you'll need this. It's really bright out there."

Chase put it back on. "Thanks. Now, what do you want on your hot dog?"

"The works," Addison said, as she clipped the sales tag from their purchases with a small pair of scissors she'd fished out of her backpack.

Carrying the hot dogs, Chase followed Addison to their seats, happily musing about taking Bud to these kinds of events. She hoped Addison would help her at least in the beginning until she got good at maneuvering these activities. Bud was to have as normal a childhood as possible.

They went up two flights of stairs and were behind home plate.

"Wow, these are great seats," Chase said as they sat down. She started in on her hot dog. "These are really good," she said, after taking a large bite.

Chase had read about baseball games, saw photographs and

the blurbs on the television when a big game was on, but she'd never sat in the stands, smelled food that everyone knew was bad for your HDL or heard the fresh roasted peanut vendors as they made their way up the stands hawking their wares. She thought she might give those a try as well. The murmur of the crowd and the hum of the grandstand music all made her feel like she was on another planet. It was fantastic.

Addison took out a pair of enormous binoculars that looked a lot like the pair Stella had used for surveillance. She scanned the crowd.

"Don't you want your hot dog?"

"In a minute," she said, and then, appearing satisfied, she set the binoculars on her lap and ate her hot dog.

Chase sipped her Dr. Pepper and watched as the players did some practice throws. They wore white uniforms with red piping. The other team wore blue uniforms and yellow piping. She didn't know who they were, but it didn't matter. All she had to remember was who wore what color. She could handle that.

Addison put down her half-eaten hot dog and resumed her watch.

Something was wrong. She studied Addison. "Why don't you tell me what's really going on? We agreed no secrets."

Addison sighed and pursed her lips as if to demonstrate the difficulty of her confession. "My dad is dating this woman who has a kid. I wanted to see for myself."

"How do you know they're here?"

"I overhead my mom talking to him. Something about settling up this afternoon and he said he was going to the ballgame and she said you never took Addison to a ballgame. I raided my mom's stash of tickets. I wanted to see what they look like."

"I'll be right back." Chase raced back to the souvenir shop and grabbed a pair of binoculars. "These the best you got?" she asked the vendor.

"Lady, this is a souvenir shop. They'll get you a good look at home plate."

Chase paid and went back to the stands.

Addison was scanning the crowd. She looked up as Chase squeezed past her. She sat down. "All right, let's find the bastard. I mean your father."

"He is a bastard," Addison said.

"Okay, you scan that side and I'll get this side. We'll do it in quadrants."

"I found him," Addison said. She pointed. "Down there."

Chase pointed her binoculars in that direction. "He's by himself." She was hopeful.

"For the moment," Addison replied. She slurped at her Dr. Pepper as if retribution might be lurking in the recesses of the crushed ice.

"Want another one?" Chase asked.

"No, I'm fine." She pulled a Red Bull from her pack and poured it in the plastic cup with the red and orange Isotope logo like she was mixing a drink.

Chase was worried. A smart hopped-up kid with a grudge could do ugly things. "What are you planning on doing... exactly?"

"I haven't quite decided." She went back to her binoculars.

This added to Chase's anxiety. The announcer read the line-up for each team as the players ran out on the field. Chase couldn't concentrate. She didn't know a lot about baseball, but there was always Wikipedia if Bud had questions. She wondered what parents did before the Internet. They probably made shit up. Parenting wasn't so simple anymore. Kids could check facts now.

Addison went back to staring at her father long-distance.

The Isotope batter whacked the ball. He made it to first base and kept going as the ball sailed upward toward the centerfield fence.

Chase tapped Addison's shoulder. "Hey, look, something is actually happening. He might get a home run." Chase jumped around in her seat like all the others—she almost felt at one with

213

the rest of the world. Maybe that's what sports were about—a sense of unity. The batter made it home. The crowd, including Chase went mad. "That was exciting." She looked over at Addison. "Did you see it?"

"It's a boy with red hair and freckles. He looks like Ron Howard when he played Opie in *Mayberry RFD*."

"You've seen that show?"

"Nickelodeon."

"Who are we talking about?" Chase asked.

"My father's new kid."

"Really?" Chase grabbed her binoculars and honed in. Addison was right. Daddy was playing it up big. A chunky blonde appeared to be the boy's mother. That's who Dickhead is doing, Chase thought with disgust.

"See him?"

"Yep. His mother's nothing but a fat tart." Chase put the binoculars down on her lap. She looked over at Addison.

Addison was sitting back in her seat, looking over the program and eating her hot dog. "Let's have another one of these. They're really good. Should get the spicy brown mustard this time."

"I thought you'd be upset." Chase eyed her warily. She didn't want to set her off but absolute denial wasn't a good thing either. It could surface years later and cost a fortune in shrink fees.

"He's a boy. I can't compete with a boy and it all makes sense now. My father is as I suspected him to be. He's very insecure. He feels more comfortable with those people for whatever reason. It's perfectly understandable that he's more comfortable with a boy. I'm not able to grow a penis and if I had a little brother I'd be jealous and feel slighted. This way I don't have to deal with it. I always knew my mother was too sophisticated for him hence his attraction to the frumpy blonde—case closed, moving on."

"It's that easy?"

"I never really liked him in the first place."

"I'll go get us more hot dogs," Chase said, quite relieved. She could deal with her own neurosis but other people's frightened her.

"Better hurry. Looks like we stand a chance of winning," Addison said. The crowd roared as another batter hit a home run.

Chapter Twenty-Four

There was entirely too much change for Chase. First, there was Nora and Eliza and now Lacey. It was like she was in the fun house and everyone, once familiar, had gone weird.

"I just don't understand why you're not more militant," Lacey accused her.

"I don't know what you mean," Chase said.

She and Lacey were having coffee at Starbucks. Chase had an appointment with Dr. Robicheck later that day.

"Yes, you do." Lacey slurped her latte.

Chase wasn't ready for this kind of discussion. In the back of her mind, squarely filed under things to be fearful of, was gay parenting—specifically rights and how Bud would fit into a world where most kids had a mom and a dad. It was going to be awkward and she didn't like it.

Lacey stared at Chase. Before she was a militant lesbian, Lacey had always been distracted by scoping the crowd, thus Chase was free from scrutiny. She had found that most restful, but now Lacey was focused and seemingly always asking questions about being gay.

"You know, there are whole days when I don't have a lesbian thought. It's quite refreshing to be liberated from the apron strings of my vagina," Chase replied. This would shut Lacey up.

Lacey's eyes grew wide and she positively gaped. Chase knew she had the advantage. A lesbian couple walked by. The one with the buzz cut took an appraising look at Chase. Her girlfriend with the curled back hair doused heavily with hair spray grabbed her girlfriend's hand in a proprietary manner.

Lacey watched them closely as they walked from the door to the counter. "Is there a chart?"

"Of what?"

"Lesbian hairstyles," Lacey replied.

"I don't think so. Why?" This was definitely a curve ball, Chase thought. She'd been using a lot of baseball lingo since her foray into professional sports.

"I heard there are seven. I want to know what they are."

"Why? Do you want one?" Chase asked, studying Lacey's well-coiffed hair.

"I want to be close to my people." Lacey finished her latte and wiped her mouth.

"We need to go to the bookstore," Chase said.

"To find my people?"

"No, to get a book. We might see some hairstyles, though."

"I'm in," Lacey said, hopping up.

They strolled by the lesbian couple with the two of seven lesbian hairstyles. Lacey apparently couldn't restrain herself. She stopped. "I just love your hair. I was wondering where you get it cut."

Chase was mortified. The one with the flattop, smiled. "New to the fold?" she asked Chase.

Chase nodded. "We need to come up with a handbook."

"I wish," Lacey said petulantly.

"We get it cut at Supercuts," the woman replied, her girlfriend eyeing Chase and Lacey suspiciously.

"Thank you," Lacey said. She gave Chase her I-told-you-so look.

"Whatever," Chase responded as they left. When they got in the car, Chase glanced at Lacey. She did look different—more sure of herself. Still, there were hurdles. "Have you told your parents?"

Lacey turned on Cutler and toward San Mateo. Chase hated this intersection. It was the most accident prone in the entire city.

Lacey breezed through it. "No, but I told my accountant. He said that's great. He won't have to worry about a prenup."

"Why'd you tell him?"

"Because he's a bigger part of my life than my parents. Besides, I don't think my parents would care and it doesn't matter if they do. It's a little late to impose any sort of moral parenting on me now."

"That's true. Where is Jasmine living?"

"At her condo. She's thrown him out."

"Good," Chase said.

Lacey pulled into the Uptown District. "Have you been here yet?"

"No."

"It's fabulous. It's like real big city stuff—a Pottery Barn and a Williams-Sonoma." Lacey pointed as they looked for a parking spot.

Chase noticed the modern architecture, the chrome and bright colors of purples, reds and oranges. It was like a PeeWee Herman mall. Lacey pulled into a spot.

"So Jasmine and you are both serious about this relationship?"

Lacey put the car in park and looked at her. "Of course. I love Jasmine and I intend to spend my life with her."

Chase was taken aback. "Don't you think you're moving a little fast?"

"Like you have room to talk. Who went home with Gitana

one night and never left? What was it, a four-hour courtship?"

She had a point. Chase would talk to Jasmine—tell her if she hurt Lacey she'd kill her. That might be a little extreme. Maim, perhaps. "That's different."

"How?" Lacey pouted.

"We were already gay."

"What? So I'm not gay enough to have a partner," Lacey said.

Lacey looked really pissed off. This alarmed Chase. "No, I didn't mean it that way. You're my best friend and I love you. I don't want you to get hurt."

Lacey stared at her. She gave her a big hug. "You're such a better person now. I love the new you. Come on, let's go get your book."

Chase was startled. They got out of the car. Lacey linked her arm in Chase's. She tried not to freak out.

"What book are you getting?" Lacey said as they walked toward the bookstore.

"*Heather has Two Mommies*." She didn't look at her.

"Aha! You are worried."

"Maybe just a little," Chase admitted.

Lacey opened the door of Borders for Chase who smugly thought, we know who favors the trousers. Lacey said, "I think we should start a whole new method of total confidence—of utterly confiding in each other as an embracing of our gayness."

"Have you been to meditation class again?" Chase asked.

"Yes, why?"

"It's your good vibes-speak," Chase replied, eyeing the aisle placards for the right section.

"No, I mean it," Lacey said.

"All right. No more secrets, but it has to be a gradual progression. This new life of mine is getting a bit overwhelming." Chase headed toward the gay and lesbian section.

"I can accept that. We'll nurture each other."

Chase automatically cringed at the word "nurture."

Lacey noticed. "Say it."

"Say what?" Chase scoured the lesbian section.

"Nurture," Lacey said. She stood looking at the "B" section. She counted. "They have ten of your books. I hadn't realized you had so many." She picked one up off the shelf and studied the cover. It was a half-naked woman walking through a cornfield.

"All those autographed copies I gave you, you never read one of them." Chase found the book and snatched it from the shelf. There was only one copy and she needed it. She felt like one of those ladies at the sale table finding the only jewel in a stack of unwanted cast-offs.

Lacey defended herself. "I wasn't a lesbian then. I'm going to read every last one of them."

This gave Chase an uneasy feeling. "You don't have to." She didn't like people she knew reading her stuff—other than the writers group, but they were looking at craft not for stolen details whittled from her friends' and acquaintances' lives. She was a spy and a thief who did not wish to be revealed.

"I want to." Lacey scooped up all ten books.

"But you already have copies."

"Royalties, dummy," Lacey said.

"You shouldn't do that."

"I love you and now I can appreciate all your hard work." She kissed Chase on the cheek.

"You're really freaking me out," Chase told her.

"I know and I like it."

Chase stood in Dr. Robicheck's office. She was ten minutes late. Lacey had dropped her off—they hadn't had time to retrieve Chase's car from Starbucks. Lacey would pick her up after her appointment and take her back to her car.

"Was there a lot of roadkill?" Dr. Robicheck said, picking up her yellow legal pad and crossing her legs.

"No, I was in town actually. I lost track of time while I was at the bookstore." Chase sat down in her usual spot on the soft brown leather couch. Today Dr. Robicheck was wearing a red

220

business suit with a cream blouse. She resembled a raspberry swirl.

"Doing a book signing?" Dr. Robicheck raised her left eyebrow as if expressing her interest by using this gesture.

"Oh no, I never do those."

Chase noticed the cobalt blue glass vase filled with sunflowers. Her wildflower garden, which included sunflowers, was going to seed. These somewhat unnaturally perfect sunflowers must be from a florist.

"Going out tonight?" Chase said, using her interrogation technique of startle and sneak that she'd learned from her mystery writing.

Dr. Robicheck stared at her. "That's a little personal, don't you think?"

"You ask me personal questions all the time." Chase shifted on the couch and tried to get comfortable.

"But you're the patient."

"And you're the doctor. Where does it say that I can't ask a personal question?"

Dr. Robicheck furrowed her brow. She wasn't used to being cornered, Chase thought. She told the doctor, "I know all about me and frankly I'm bored with it. I think I'm doing much better, but I still have to come here so I thought we could talk about you. I know nothing about your life and right now I think you're in love—the new kind, not the repackaged, rekindled kind."

Dr. Robicheck looked completely taken aback. Chase wondered if she'd get thrown out. Can one get thrown out of therapy? Did a therapy bouncer come and escort you away? What about the Hippocratic Oath? Surely that stood for something.

Then Dr. Robicheck smiled. "I suppose you're right. I am a perfect stranger to you."

Sensing her advantage, Chase said, "So are you in love?" She suppressed an urge to get out her mechanical pencil and her notebook. She crossed her legs and looked intuitive or what she thought might pass for intuitive. She wondered if they might switch chairs. "You know what would make this complete?"

Dr. Robicheck raised an eyebrow. "No, what?"

"If we switch places."

"Excuse me?"

Chase stared at her. Maybe that's where she got her own annoying habit. "My mother told me that using the phrase, 'excuse me' was a cop-out."

"How do you figure?"

Chase got up. She patted the couch. Her escapades with Delaney, her mystery novel's detective, had taught her that you had to force the issue. She had sufficiently distracted her subject—now it was time get the doctor to do her bidding.

"Because, the phrase 'excuse me' should be used as a way to get past someone, say on a busy train or bus, or trying to get a frozen pizza out of the cooler at the grocery store when some dumb fuck is standing in the way oblivious to your needs." She was now standing beside Dr. Robicheck's rolling office chair. "Up, Up."

The doctor appeared so frazzled by Chase's diatribe that she actually did it. Chase continued. 'Excuse me' is a prelude to asking a stranger a question or if you're slightly deaf and didn't hear what the other person said. It is not to be used as a tactic for avoiding a question by pretending you don't understand what the other person was saying." She whirled around in the black leather chair with its ergonomic side panels and finished, "When you did understand what the other person said."

Dr. Robicheck glanced at Chase with the look people gave her when she'd completely bamboozled them. "Are you taking your medication?" she asked.

"Yes. Now, let's talk about this love affair. Were you married before?"

"I don't think I like this."

Chase noted that the doctor's calm calculating demeanor had rapidly dissipated.

"I hope he's not looking for a sugar-momma. You've got to watch people like that. First your pants, then your wallet."

Dr. Robicheck stared at Chase like she was speaking a foreign language.

Chase rephrased. "Meaning that he is interested in seducing you and then spending your capital instead of his own if he has any."

"It's not like that, I assure you."

"I'm just watching out for you." Chase pushed up and down on the chair lever adjusting the height for the hell of it.

"I appreciate your concern." Dr. Robicheck squirmed on the couch like she was trying to get comfortable.

Chase looked up at the clock. "Oops, time's up." She got up. "One more question, are you divorced?"

"Yes. Why do you ask?"

"Because this relationship scares you. Just remember good love is redemptive. Until next time then."

Later that evening Chase was making a spinach and feta quesadilla in her new bright red quesadilla maker from Bed Bath and Beyond that she'd purchased after her appointment with Dr. Robicheck. She'd taken a sudden interest in kitchen gadgets as if the clutches of domesticity had caught her haunches and she'd rolled over and was letting her belly be stroked. She relayed the details of her exchange with Dr. Robicheck to Gitana who was setting the table.

"You'll probably find yourself in a case study in one of those shrink journals," Gitana commented.

"Yeah, with a title like Role Reversal teaches Empathy—a Theory of Sharing."

Gitana laughed. "I think it was brilliant. It makes people grow. You've grown a lot."

Chase looked up from chopping olives with a new stainless steel meat cleaver. "Really?"

"Really. Dinner smells fabulous. Your cooking skills have improved as well."

Chase slipped Annie a piece of feta which the dog adored. Annie must have been a Greek sheep herder in a previous life. "I hope so."

Chapter Twenty-Five

"What the hell are you two supposed to be?" Chase said, standing in the living room staring at Nora and Eliza.

Nora was dressed in all black with numerous brightly colored socks of purple and orange and yellow stuck all over her. Eliza was dressed completely in pink with what looked like a white plastic pot as a hat.

"She's static cling and I'm the fabric softener," Eliza said.

Chase didn't have to wonder whose idea this was. Nora smiled at her sheepishly.

Gitana came around the corner. She'd been getting dressed in the den. They'd moved a futon bed in there because the stairs were too steep for Gitana who couldn't see her feet on the way down because of her protruding belly and had almost fallen. Now they lived downstairs and Chase did all the running upstairs for things they needed. She was getting quite fit.

"Oh, you guys look so cute—fabric softener and static cling.

How inventive is that," Gitana said.

Chase frowned. How the hell did she know that? Nora gave her a smug look. Halloween was a stupid holiday anyway—candy and weird outfits. The only thing she really liked about it was the pumpkins. She grew pumpkins in her garden. She grew them in their own special patch. They fascinated her. She had Howdens that by fall were simply enormous, Jack-o-Lites and Small Sugars that could be used for baking or as carving pumpkins, and the decorative Rouge Vif'd'Etampes. From a fluted yellow flower and a vine came this hard plump thing. It never ceased to amaze and delight her.

She usually managed to find homes for all of them. She kept two of each kind for next year's seeds. Addison had chosen one of the Howden pumpkins. It was the largest pumpkin either of them had seen. Addison had been tentative about taking it. "I mean, it is the biggest one."

"So?" Chase had said, snapping the vine carefully with the hoe. She loaded it into the bright red wheelbarrow—like that one poem by who—she couldn't remember, a guy with a weird name. She remembered exactly how the type fit on the page—short lines in a neat rectangle. She'd have to scour her English Lit books until she found it. It was twentieth century, at least that would narrow the search.

"Well, what if someone else wants it?" Addison said, touching the smooth skin. "It's so perfect."

"You got here first and you want it. Have you been listening to that Evangelical radio show again?" Chase thought Addison sounded like Lacey after yoga practice—all full of my brother, my sister, my planet speak that they all spouted. She eyed Addison suspiciously.

"No," Addison said. She didn't look at Chase. "All right. Yes. I find their dogma interesting."

"You're not going to become a Jesus freak are you?"

"Or course not. It's research." Addison stroked the pumpkin again.

"So why are you worried about your fellow man or woman wanting your pumpkin?" Chase positioned the pumpkin in the wheelbarrow so it wouldn't roll when they took it down the slight incline from the garden to the driveway. They'd have to use the dog ramp to roll it up into the Hummer.

"I'm not."

"You know, being a writer is a selfish-grab-what's-out-there kind of profession. If you want the pumpkin you got to take it."

"I want the pumpkin. I am a real writer and I'm giving you my radio until I'm cured."

"Good. Now lead on." Chase hoisted up the wheelbarrow handles and started toward the driveway.

Addison picked up the hoe and carried it over her shoulder looking a bit like a small Russian peasant of the kind Chase imagined in a Tolstoy novel.

"Chase, will you help me get my face on," Gitana said, yanking Chase abruptly from her musings in pumpkin-land. Gitana had dyed her hair green and was wearing an all orange suit. Chase was to attach the black triangle-shaped things to the Velcro patches on Gitana's stomach to make a jack-o-lantern face. Chase wanted a sinister mouth. Gitana opted for a smile. A pumpkin was the only thing they could figure out for a very pregnant lady. It was either that or Twiddle-Dee and Twiddle-Dum, but Chase refused to be Dum, it was a matter of pride. Besides, Delia and Graciela would never let her live it down. Instead, she was an Oompa Loompa.

"That looks good," Nora said, coming over to straighten out the nose.

Chase, Nora and Eliza stepped back and surveyed Gitana's stomach.

"You make a great jack-o-lantern," Nora said, giving Gitana a hug.

"What about me?" Chase said, donning her yellow rubberized wig. She had white pants puffed out at the hips by taking the pockets out, stuffing them with batten, and then sewing them on

227

the outside of the pants and a blue T-shirt. She had thought it quite ingenious.

"Well, of course you look fine," Nora said, diplomatically. Eliza smiled and nodded.

Chase had the distinct impression she was being humored and she didn't like it.

"We better get going," Gitana said, taking Chase's arm.

"I'm not going to like the party. Delia probably has some repulsive ideas for party games, like butt darts or bobbing for cow eyeballs," Chase said as they all got in the Hummer.

She'd removed the bear and the car seat so they'd have more room. Her Oompa Loompa pants caught on the gearshift. She wrestled with it. Looking over at Gitana she could see that she was doing her best not to laugh. Nora leaned forward to see what the holdup was. Chase caught her eye. "Not a fucking word," she said.

Nora glanced at Gitana. It was too much. They laughed until tears started.

Eliza leaned forward and pulled Chase free. "Minor wardrobe malfunction."

This statement got everyone going including Eliza.

"We'll just call her Chase Jackson," Nora said, between gasps.

"This is not the least bit funny," Chase said, starting the car. She tucked her protruding pants beneath the seat belt so there wouldn't be anymore "malfunctions."

Then as a payback, she shoved the Willy Wonka CD into the player, thinking that'll teach you all to fuck with an Oompa Loompa.

In preparation for this, Gitana opened the glove box, almost hitting her head on the dash as they bumped down the dirt road from their house to the county road. She pulled out a box of twelve neon orange earplugs and handed four of them to Nora and Eliza like she was passing out gum drops.

Chase was indignant. "That's not fair."

"To use a cliché, life's not fair." Gitana inserted her earplugs

228

and looked out the window.

"Much better," Nora said, easing back in her seat.

Chase turned it up.

Eliza leaned forward. "I don't mind it. It's kind of fun."

"Thank you, Eliza. Nora doesn't deserve you."

"What was that?" Nora screamed over the music.

"Nothing," Chase said smugly.

They pulled up in front of Delia's run-down Victorian house, which was completely out of place with the rest of the squat, square adobe houses with their neatly xeriscaped yards full of red salvia, purple sage and Spanish broom—all drought resistant plants and thus politically correct. Delia's yard was horribly overgrown with orange trumpet vines, Hawthorn and Sweet Briar Rose crawling up one side of the porch. A wisteria, unsupported so it leaned over like an old woman with osteoporosis, killed the grass beneath it. Untrimmed cypress lined one side of the yard and neglected pink, yellow and white rose bushes lined the other side. A moss-covered birdbath sat in the center of the yard with bird poop covering every inch of it.

"This place is disgusting," Chase said as they pulled up front.

Eliza looked mortified. Nora squeezed her hand.

"It's a great place for a Halloween party. Look, they even have pumpkins on the front porch," Gitana said brightly.

"This place looks like the Bate's Motel," Nora said as they got out of the car.

"All it needs is the sputtering neon sign," Chase said. Why the hell her mother had let her watch those Alfred Hitchcock movies was a mystery. Even now, she didn't like taking showers when no one was home, didn't feel safe around chef's knives and was scared shitless by large flocks of birds.

"Do not sit down on the toilet seat," Chase said.

Eliza's eyes got big. She was a neat freak.

Nora put her arm around her shoulder. "We'll go together."

As they walked up the front steps, the ruckus inside was definitely not above OSHA standards. Chase found this reassuring—maybe it wouldn't be so bad after all. Then, she got her Oompa Loompa pants caught on the door knob.

"Those pants are a hazard," Nora said.

"You actually came," Delia said. She gave her a big hug.

"They made me," Chase said, looking around for items of perversion and health hazards. There didn't appear to be any.

A young woman dressed as Dorothy of the Wizard of Oz hopped up and dashed toward Chase. "Is it really you?"

Chase stood puzzled.

"Number one fan," Delia said. "This is Donna."

"Nice to meet you," Chase said.

"You two have a chat and I'll bring you a beer," Delia said. She led the rest of them off.

"I've read absolutely everything you've written. I just love it all," Donna gushed.

"Thanks." Chase always felt uncomfortable meeting fans. One of her writing manuals had elucidated at great length about dealing with readers. How readers often created literary personas on their own and were horribly disappointed when the creators of their favorite works didn't live up to their fantasies. Not to mention, Chase was meeting an adoring fan while dressed as an Oompa Loompa. Delia better hurry up with that beer. If she'd set her up, Chase would kill her.

"Are you always that funny?" Donna dressed as Dorothy asked.

Chase stared at her dark hair in ponytails, pale skin with drawn on freckles and thought she did kind of look like Judy Garland. She could be nice and funny. It wouldn't hurt her and she'd make this woman happy. "Only on Mondays, Wednesdays and Fridays."

Donna laughed. "You are funny."

Chase had passed the test. "Now, that I've got you here, why don't you tell me what parts of the books you thought were funny."

"Oh, I'd love to. I was hoping you might ask me so I brought notes." She pulled out a set of typewritten notes including page numbers from the basket that usually held Toto. She gave them to Chase.

"Wow." Chase perused the notes.

"Some of the novels really require sequels. The characters are so compelling. I've made lists of all the character attributes so you wouldn't have to go back searching."

Chase quickly read through the research section. This woman was amazing. "You've done a lot of work here."

"Oh, I love it. Most people think I'm creepy."

"Are you creepy?"

Donna laughed. "No! I'm just thorough. I'm not a writer, but I love novels. I like to be part of the process. These notes are my way of doing that."

"You would be a great help to someone. It's difficult to keep everything straight and I read somewhere that some fans have kept track of things so that when a writer decides to do a sequel they have all the previous stuff."

Donna beamed. Chase was rather pleased with herself. She was being downright social.

Delia arrived with Chase's Dos Equis. "You're not pestering her." She eyed Donna.

"No," Chase and Donna said simultaneously.

Delia's surprise exploded on her face. "Really?"

"Donna would be a great asset for us. Look at this." Chase handed her Donna's notes. "She could write jacket copy and she keeps great notes."

"I do research too. I'm very good at accessing just about anything."

Delia looked skeptical. "We couldn't afford it." She sipped her beer.

Chase raised an eyebrow. She took a swig off her beer and waited.

"Gratis. I'd do it gratis," Donna said.

"Acknowledgments, free copies—you don't know what it

could lead to. It would look great on your resume," Chase said.

"I'll do it," Donna fairly screeched.

Delia studied Donna's notes. "She is good. I'm sold."

"So what do you do...normally?" Chase asked, suddenly wondering how she had so much available time at her disposal.

"I'm a communication major at the U of NM, work part-time at the college radio station and I volunteer at the Literacy Project," she said brightly.

"Oh, my," Chase said, glancing at Delia who appeared in equal awe.

"I don't sleep a lot. Three hours a night, two if I'm busy working on a project. It gives me between two and three extra months in a year. I really want to be a literary agent," Donna said. She picked up Delia's empty beer bottle from where she had carelessly put in on the nearest table and deposited it in the thirty-gallon trash can standing right next to them.

"Aha! The true motive comes out," Delia said.

"I need to understand the job from the bottom up," Donna said.

"I'll sign," Chase said.

"Me, too," Delia said.

"Thanks," Donna said. She smiled big and looked at both of them with what can only be described as utter and total glee. "I better let you go. I don't want to be accused of monopolizing." She left them.

"Your group is out back," Delia told Chase.

Graciela was standing next to Gitana on the red brick patio. The backyard was just as overgrown as the front. The fence was barely visible for the yellow and orange trumpet vines. Everywhere there were pots of marigolds, zinnias and pink petunias. Chase wondered who had the stability in the house to remember to water the plants.

Graciela was dressed as a cave woman complete with a plastic wooden club. Delia kissed her on the cheek and handed her a Dos Equis, even remembering the lime stuffed in the neck of the bottle.

"That's a fitting outfit," Chase said, eyeing the fake fur dress held together at the shoulder with a white plastic bone.

"It is if you're planning on dragging a certain someone back to your cave." Graciela tucked her arm around Delia's waist which was neatly accented with a pink belt that held up the slightly ruffled tutu skirt. She looked like a ballerina who'd gone on a binge and not fared well as her slightly askew tiara indicated.

Gitana gave Chase her best it-looks-like-someone-might-be-settling-down look.

Chase smiled and sat down next to her at the round rusted metal table that had once been white as slivers of the original paint attested. She scanned it to make sure there weren't any exposed edges. She tried to recollect whether Gitana had had a tetanus shot in the last ten years. She saw that Nora and Eliza were talking to two women, their backs turned to Chase, one dressed in a Victorian suit and the other in a smart business outfit with a short blond wig.

She watched Graciela and Delia as they fondled each other in a manner that for them was discreet. It was good her friends were settling down. For the longest time, she and Gitana were the only steady couple. Their friends were always dating or living together temporarily, planning ceremonies for life partnerships that didn't work out. Chase had stopped getting roped into being the best person at these ceremonies because she would rent a tux only to discover that the union had disintegrated shortly after the reception. She liked the food though. The way she figured it Gitana had a ring and they called it good. She liked to think there was a redemptive quality to long-term relationships and she wished her friends and relations would stick it out long enough to discover it.

"I'll be right back," Graciela said, untangling herself from Delia's embrace.

She went up to the two women Nora and Eliza were talking to. She pointed in Chase's direction and then returned to the table. "They'll be over in a minute," she said to Chase.

"Is that my mother?" Chase said, staring hard at the woman in the Victorian suit.

"Payback for this summer." Graciela gloated.

They came over.

"Oh, this is so much fun," Peggy said.

Stella glanced at Chase. "Graciela invited us," she said as if Chase needed an explanation.

"You look good with a mustache," Chase said. Her mother's hair was slicked back and dyed black. Temporary dye, Chase hoped. She didn't want her mother going from Victorian to Goth. She wore a black coat, gray trousers and a gray and black pin-striped vest with a gold chain. She'd gone to a lot of trouble, Chase noted.

Mother and daughter seemed shy with one another. It was weird, Chase thought. She could tell everyone was waiting for her reaction, including Stella. "Who are you, exactly?"

Instead of being insulted, Stella was thrilled as if being in costume meant being in disguise. "Why, I'm Hercules Poirot."

"Agatha Christie. You do look just like him," Delia said.

"Let me get a snap," Gitana said, pulling a small digital camera from her bag.

"Who are you?" Chase asked Peggy as she linked arms with Stella and posed for Gitana. Her mother actually looked like she was having fun.

"I'm DCI Jane Tennison," Peggy told her as she smiled for the camera.

"I love that show," Delia said, bringing Gitana a paper plate of cashews, radishes, carrots, celery and Bing cherries.

"Lovely, thank you," Gitana said, taking the plate.

"Yeah, Prime Suspect, DCI Tennison is..."

Delia stopped.

Chase just knew Delia was going to say something horribly sexual.

Instead, she finished, "Smart and strong and looks fabulous in a business suit."

Chase smiled and nodded at her in relief. "I've never heard of the show."

"It's on PBS," Stella said.

Her mother watched PBS? Chase didn't know anything about this. How many other things did she not know about her mother? Did she need to sit her mother down and get her to reveal all her secrets? It was completely and totally fucking bizarre. She imagined herself as an interrogator probing the recesses of her mother's mind. She'd take notes and still she would never really know her mother. It was all back to the lexicon of memory—the splashes of scenes, the remembering of one thing—and why that one incident instead of another had made the imprint. It didn't make sense. She felt herself rather peeved. How could she not have known that her mother was also a woman called Stella—a person in her own right—like Dr. Robicheck was a therapist, a divorced woman and now dating a man she loved. It was mind-blowing. She'd have to peruse her mother's media interests and interrogate Stella's lexicon of memory, gathering as much information as she could.

Eliza and Nora came back with plates laden with snacks. "For the group," Nora said, seemingly defensive about the heaping plate.

"And don't worry about Hantavirus. The kitchen was thoroughly disinfected," Graciela said.

"It's too late now," Gitana said as she finished the plate of snacks that Delia had brought her.

Chase was instantly mortified. She'd been so engrossed with her mother that she'd not screened Gitana's food consumption.

"Dude, you need to relax," Graciela said, putting her hand on Chase's shoulder.

"Hey, they're playing our song," Delia said, grabbing Graciela's hand.

Chase listened. It was some bump-and-grind techno thing that she didn't recognize.

235

Stella looked over at Peggy. "Want to give it a try?"

"I'd love too. I haven't danced or had this much fun since I don't know when," Peggy said.

They hightailed it into the house.

Nora and Eliza plopped down in two half-rotted green lawn chairs and smiled happily at each other.

Chase looked over at Gitana. "Fucking weird is all I have to say." Chase took a handful of jalapeno stuffed green olives from Nora's community plate.

"And there's been no mention of butt darts," Gitana said.

"What are butt darts?" Eliza said.

"I don't think you want to know," Nora said, taking her hand.

Chapter Twenty-Six

When Chase stepped into Dr. Robicheck's office and didn't scream, "What the hell!" she chalked this up to her new more flexible approach to life. The Halloween party had done much to dispel a lot of her preconceptions. It was like she'd been given another set of eyes and the world looked truly different.

"What do you think?" Dr. Robicheck asked.

"Uh, wow," Chase replied, not knowing where to sit.

"Over here." Dr. Robicheck pointed to one of the burgundy leather chairs that surrounded the round oak table located in the center of the room.

Chase sat down.

"Coffee or tea?" Dr. Robicheck said.

"Coffee, please."

"Cream and sugar?" Dr. Robicheck looked at her expectantly.

"Lots of cream, please—like the French do it."

"Very good." Dr. Robicheck reacted like Chase had made the

correct choice. "There, then." She set down two cups.

Chase sipped hers. "Thank you."

"Do you like the new arrangement? Do you feel more comfortable, more at ease?"

Chase thought for a moment. It was weird. It was new and indirectly, it had been her doing. These changes appeared to make Dr. Robicheck more enthusiastic about her career.

"I do. I do feel more at ease. I'm no longer fish-bowling." She leaned back in her chair and sipped her coffee. She suddenly wished she had a biscotti like the ones they had at Starbucks. She'd get some at Costco. She could do Costco now. There were a lot of things she could do now.

"Fish bowling?" Dr. Robicheck queried.

"You know, having someone look at you like you're a goldfish swimming 'round and 'round your glass prison, big eyeballs staring in at you making faux gulping gestures. I've always felt sorry for goldfish."

"I see. That's a good term. I will remember it."

Chase noticed she didn't have a yellow legal pad or a pen. "You aren't writing things down anymore?" She couldn't decide if she should be pleased or disappointed—like what she had to say wasn't important anymore.

"No. I decided that was intimidating as well, that I used to concentrate more on my notes than really listening to my patients. I have a strong memory and if I don't remember I can ask."

They then proceeded to have a visit, for it was more like that, than a session of picking Chase's brain for traces of neurosis.

Afterward, Chase drove home in the finest of moods. The sun was bright, the air crisp with the shadow of winter lurking about. The first snow would be coming soon, she thought.

When she got home she gave the dogs their treat, each a Jumbone, which they took with them reverently up to the writing studio where they would happily munch on them. Gitana had waddled off to work in the care of Nora to do the books for the month's end report. Chase sat in her ergonomic chair and the dogs leapt up on the couch and began chewing their bones.

She spun around in her chair as an idea hit her. "You know, girls I'm having a good day—let's ruin it and call my editor."

She dialed the number.

Ariana picked up immediately. "Oh, my God! What's wrong? You didn't lose another notebook."

"Technically, that one was stolen," Chase said, reminding her.

Sometimes, Chase disliked caller ID. It dispensed with the prologue. She had lost a notebook once. She'd gone to pick Gitana up at the airport after she'd been to an orchid convention in Phoenix. She took her notebook everywhere and had been writing while she waited. Gitana arrived and she got up to give her a hug. She turned back around to find her knapsack had been stolen. The thief must have been disappointed as it contained one black and white marbled composition book, a pocket Webster's dictionary and a mechanical pencil.

"What's wrong then?"

Chase took a deep breath. "I've written a book."

"Already? Another one isn't due."

Chase heard her flipping through her desk calendar. For ten years they'd both spent many phone calls flipping through their various desk calendars negotiating dates. "It's not. I wrote it while I was doing my assigned one."

"What kind of book?" Ariana's voice was tight.

Chase imagined her face drawn, eyes narrowed so the pupils resembled peppercorns allowing no brown of the cornea to be visible. Ariana was not a beauty. She was stout with short spiky blond hair. She had a pointed chin and thin lips that made her look like one of the masks of the Comedia d'Arte.

"It's a mystery novel with straight people in it." Chase's mouth was dry. She grabbed for the bottle of Dasani that sat on her desk. She took a quick sip.

"Really?" Ariana's voice lifted.

Chase took the plunge, grabbing from the recesses of her

spirit for courage. "I'd like to send you a précis, outline, whatever you want so you could tell me if I should submit it. I trust your judgment."

"Is it good?"

Chase glanced at the manuscript as it sat piled on her desk, all four hundred and twenty-five pages. "I think so. I workshopped it with my writer's group."

"Send the whole thing. I'd love to read it."

"For sure?" Chase said.

"Chase, I've been waiting for you to realize that you're talented enough to write other fiction. You've got a great imagination and so switching genres is a logical move for you. You can still write lesbian fiction but why not expand your audience with some different stuff. I'm thrilled. It's time. Send it Express Mail, will you?"

"I'll send it this afternoon." Chase was completely taken aback.

"Great. When's the baby due?"

Now, this was really different. Ariana seldom thought of anyone other than herself. "The second week of December."

"She'll be a Sagittarius like me. How fortunate. Ta-Ta." She clicked off.

"Okay, that's fucking weird," Chase said, putting the phone down.

"What's weird?" Gitana asked.

Chase whirled around in her chair. "You know for a waddling pregnant gal, you sure are sneaky." She surveyed the dogs. "Great guarding, by the way."

Annie opened one eye, wagged her tail and went back to sleep.

"I think they knew it was me." Gitana kissed her on the cheek. "You didn't answer my question." She eyed the manuscript on the desk.

"Ariana asked about you and the baby." Chase didn't meet her gaze.

"That's unusually kind of her. What else?"

How did Gitana know her so well? "And she'll look at the book." Chase had taken to calling it "the book" as if to differentiate it from her other books. Chase put her hand on it as if in blessing. She thought of Jacinda. Did she have some rosary beads or prayer or relic to give the book good vibes?

"Oh, Chase that's fantastic." She hugged her. "I'm so proud."

"Wait until she rips it to shreds." Chase frowned.

"She wouldn't even look at it if she didn't think it was worth her time."

This was true. Ariana never went out of her way. No sympathy, no pity, the word "altruism" had been banished from her lexicon like it was a salacious oath.

"You're right."

"Are you going to do some work?" Gitana inquired.

"Not really."

"Want to take a nap?" Gitana said, running her finger across Chase's collarbone.

"As in a nap-nap or a naughty nap?"

Gitana smiled. "The latter."

Chapter Twenty-Seven

It was the second week of November and snowflakes the size of quarters were gently covering everything with complete disregard for size or shape. The landscape was a monochrome white sky with white falling stuff, on white ground—like a gallon of paint poured over the world.

"This is so beautiful," Gitana said, lounging on the couch, sipping hot cocoa and gazing out the window. She looked beatific.

Chase was on the phone dialing the transportation hotline. "No, this is dangerous," she said as she glanced outside. She listened intently to the recorded message. "For Chrissakes, they've closed the fucking airport and I-40 from Santa Rosa to Grants."

"Don't worry. It can't snow forever," Gitana said. "Drink your cocoa and relax."

Chase sat next to her and looked out the large front window in utter panic. She popped back up. "I'm going to check the weather on the Internet." She tromped upstairs and shortly tromped back down.

"What's wrong?" Gitana said, looking up from her copy of the *Collected Works of Emily Dickinson*. She read out loud every day for Bud's benefit. "Maybe she'll grow up to be a poet," Gitana had told her.

"The satellite dish must be covered in snow. If I don't come back, send out the dogs."

"Why don't you take them along?" Gitana suggested.

Annie and Jane both jumped up from where they were sleeping on the floor.

"All right, let's go."

Chase put on her yellow Gore-Tex parka and her Sorel boots. She was dressed for the Arctic.

"Don't forget your hat," Gitana called out as Chase and the dogs went for the back door.

"She'll make a fabulous mother," Chase told the dogs who were only interested in getting outside. They barked furiously at the sunroom door in anticipation of release. Chase grabbed her blue knit hat and followed them out.

The dogs raced around in sheer happiness. Chase checked the snow gauge she had constructed of a one-by-one board with a three foot measuring stick glued to the front of it. The stick read thirteen inches. No wonder the airport and the freeways were closed. The freeway, she thought panicking. The freeway that connected to the other freeway that led to the hospital that contained the maternity ward and a qualified physician. This was not good.

She brushed off the satellite dish. The snow was almost up to her kneecaps. What if there was a storm like this in December? What if they couldn't get to the hospital in time? She tried not to panic, but her heart raced and it thumped in her head. Just breathe, she told herself. But what if? Town. They'd have to stay in town until the baby was born.

She ran through the possibilities as she rescued the buried

snow shovel from beside the potting shed. She made a path from the front door to the gate, then from the sunroom door up to the writing studio. The dogs bounded and played, diving their snouts into the ever-increasing drifts and coming up with beards and mustaches of snow. They played while she attempted to stave off dread. She looked at them plaintively. They would have to be boarded. She hated to do it as they viewed the kennel as time spent incarcerated, but at least they'd be safe.

When she got inside, Gitana was asleep on the couch. She covered her up with a pink and blue fleece throw that said "My mommy's the best" on the front. The dogs stayed outside and romped. Chase sat down at the kitchen table and made a list of all the things they would need to take with them to her mother's.

It was a horrid reality, but it would have to be done. Jacinda's house wasn't an option. Chase knew she'd kill Graciela inside a week and besides Jacinda's house was too small for all of them and sleeping in the living room with the relic cupboard creeped her out. For Bud, she would prostrate herself to her mother.

When the roads cleared and they could get out two days later, Chase took Gitana to the orchid nursery. She was worried about the effect of the snow on the greenhouses. Nora would meet her and Gitana was to stay put until Chase got back from town.

"Why do you have to go to town?" Gitana asked, as they pulled out of the driveway and before Chase, with great effort, got the gate open. She hopped back in the car.

"I need to get some composition books and I want to get some emergency supplies. I read on the Internet what we should have."

"Like?" Gitana put her seat belt on and adjusted the seat cushion that Chase had purchased for her for lower back pain.

Chase peered down the road which contained one set of tire tracks. She put the Hummer in four wheel drive low. "Candles, water, medications, canned goods, etcetera." She took a deep breath and set out, telling herself it's a Hummer, she can handle anything.

"Chase, it was a fluke storm. The news said the Sandia

Mountains haven't had this much snow in fifty-nine years."

"Which means everything is out of whack and out of whack is an inconsistent state of being thus anything is possible." She exhaled. They'd made it to the county road. First obstacle overcome.

By the time Chase got to the greenhouse, clouds once again covered the sky and the radio forecast announced another cold front was on its way. "Fucking great!" Chase snarled.

"Get lots of soup," Gitana said as Chase helped her out of the car. She was so bundled up, at Chase's behest, that she resembled a two-year-old with an overprotective parent.

"Do not leave here. I mean it," Chase said.

"I promise," Gitana said, holding up two fingers in homage to the Girl Scout pledge of honor.

As she drove into town, it started to snow but only lightly. She did pick up office supplies at OfficeMax, three black and white marbled composition books, a cartridge of black ink for her Epson 2000 and three packets of number five millimeter mechanical pencil lead. Once she had gone to Mazatlan with Gitana and forgotten to bring an extra pad. It was awful. She'd had to write on the back side of every page and the whole thing was a mess to straighten out later. She vowed then never to be caught padless again.

Then she went to Smith's. It was confusion and crowds like something out of New Orleans and the broken levees extravaganza. She grabbed the last two gallons of water, a case of tomato soup and two boxes of Saltines. She raced through the self-checkout before she had a panic attack brought on by claustrophobia. She hurried to the Hummer and sped out of the parking lot like she was pursued by goblins.

Getting across town was no better. According to the radio, Albuquerque didn't have enough snowplows. This meant that all secondary streets would go unplowed until the major arteries had been cleared. The schools had been closed down and people were urged to remain at home if possible. Chase clicked off the radio and thundered through the snow toward the Banter residence.

She pulled the Hummer through the iron gates of her mother's house. The manicured gardens all looked the same—the snow giving them the air of homogeneity. She parked in the drive, walked up the steps which had been shoveled, but noted that the Hummer tracks were the only ones in the driveway. Chase hoped this meant her mother was at home.

She really wished she didn't have to do this, but she had no option. She let herself in and crept back to the kitchen to find Rosarita—the compass in her mother's house. Rosarita always knew what her mother was up to, how she was feeling, and whether she was in the mood for a chat. She slunk into the kitchen where Rosarita was preparing lunch. She was making grilled cheese sandwiches or rather panini as Stella referred to them. In this case, they were reuben paninis and Rosarita was heating the sauerkraut with obvious disdain.

"I thank God, we do not have this stuff in my country." She must have been talking to herself because Chase startled her.

"Oh, mija, you scared me." She gave Chase a hug and then pulled back. "What is wrong?" She stared hard into Chase's face as if the secret would be revealed there.

"Nothing. Everything is fine."

"Oh, blessed be the Virgin." She put her hands together in supplication.

"I need to talk to my mother about us maybe staying here until the baby is born—you know the weather and all." Chase waited for her reaction.

"Oh, yes. I think that's a very good idea. Very...prudent."

Chase liked when Rosarita learned a new word and the reverence with which she used it, carefully like it was a Royal Doulton teacup that must be cherished and respected for its value.

"I'm going to ask her."

"She's in her office, working, working very hard. She works

246

all the time." She shook her head with gravity and then poured Chase a cup of black, thick as oil coffee. "Sumatra, very strong." She got the half and half out of the fridge.

Chase poured until the black tar became a milk chocolate color. "In her office?"

"Sí."

First off, her mother didn't have an office and second, she didn't have a job.

Rosarita seemed to comprehend Chase's apparent confusion. "The old nursery. Now it's all fancy. You'll like it."

Chase nodded, took her coffee and made her way down the hall. The nursery had been hers until she moved upstairs into a larger and more remote room with its own bathroom. Her mother had never done anything with the nursery other than strip the sheets and shut the door as if that chapter of their lives was finished and needed no further consideration.

She stood in the hallway, looking in. All fixed up nice was right, Chase thought. The walls were painted a shade of mocha. The room was filled floor to ceiling with cherry bookshelves that were actually full of books rather than the bric-a-brac she'd seen on HGTV where expensive bookcases were installed in the "library" but contained precious few books. Her mother was ensconced behind an impressive mahogany desk, wearing aquamarine half-moon spectacles and poring over a thick hard-bound manual. She looked like she should have been a professor at Hogwarts going over a lesson plan for an incantations class. Behind her was another smaller desk with an iMac laptop poised on Google.

"What's all this?" Chase said.

Her mother looked up, quickly recovered from her surprise and announced, "It's my new office. Do you like it?"

Chase hadn't meant the room but rather her mother's activity. Still to be polite she said, "It's very nice, downright posh." It made her writing studio look like a pit of cast-off furniture. "But what exactly are you doing?"

247

"It's my new business venture and these are its accoutrements." Stella behaved as if she were a venture capitalist and this "new venture" were one of many.

"Which is?" Chase asked. Her eyes wandered to the bookcases and took in the titles. Where had all these books come from? Most of the titles were literary—a complete set of *Jane Austen*, *War and Peace*, *Wuthering Heights* as well as many other classics. Had her mother read them all? If she had she was extremely well-read, an intellectual powerhouse.

"A private detective. Peggy and I are starting a business. I'm studying for the exam. I've passed my firearms test and got a conceal carry permit."

"You've got a gun?" Now, Chase was alarmed.

"A nine-millimeter Glock, to be exact."

"I see." Chase felt like Dr. Robicheck trying to connect the dots and determine if the patient was a nut job or not.

Her mother must have read her mind. "I'm not crazy. This is something I'm interested in and we've already had calls. See, here's our business card. We've notified our clients that we are not currently licensed but will be shortly. Most don't mind. They feel comfortable with women."

"Because *they* are women?"

"Yes. We're doing cheating spouses at the moment, but I expect we'll branch. It's very lucrative. After all, how much is a divorce settlement based on adultery worth?"

Chase sat in a chair across from her mother. "That's really cool. I'm impressed." She studied the business card—*I-Spy Detective Agency*. It had a silhouette of a person dressed in a trench coat and a fedora encased in a large eyeball. "I like the graphics."

"Peggy did it. Addison helped. She's a smart kid. She reminds me a lot of you when you were a child."

Chase missed Addison. She was busy doing the scenery for the Thanksgiving Pageant at school so Chase hadn't been able to see her.

"So what brings you to town? I didn't think with all the snow you'd come in. They were saying on the news that there hasn't been a storm like this for fifty-nine years."

"I know. That's what I wanted to talk to you about." Chase fingered the edge of the oak office chair.

"Snow?" Stella raised her eyebrow.

"Indirectly. They closed the freeway this time."

"That's right. You can't stay up there. What if you got stuck when Gitana goes into labor and can't get to the hospital?"

Both of them looked out the window. It had started to snow again.

"You should come stay here. She's due in a month or less. Nora can take care of the greenhouse and Gitana can rest up. It'll do her good. The last month of pregnancy is absolute hell. We'll put the queen size guest bed in your old room and turn the den into an office for you. We'll get a router for the Internet so you'll have access." Her mother sat back and nodded like she was checking things off her mental list. "I mean, if that's all right with you."

"That's what I came to ask you." She didn't exactly look at her mother when she said this.

"You did?" Her mother sounded incredulous.

It was odd to be on the same wavelength, Chase thought. "I'll board the dogs."

Her mother looked affronted. "Nonsense. They hate the kennel. They can stay here."

"Mom..." They were both startled. Chase hadn't called her that since she was six. Chase tried again, "Mom..." This time it came out better. "They're holy terrors. Remember how they plowed you down at the barbeque?"

"That was an accident."

"They'll destroy the yard," Chase countered.

"I have gardeners. Besides, it's winter and everything is dormant and at the moment covered with snow. You can help Rosarita with cleanup. Your house always looks good so you obviously manage. Chase, the dogs are part of the family. We'll get through it."

"If they're really bad, they will go to the kennel," Chase said firmly.

"Let's give them the benefit of the doubt for now."

Chase studied her. It was if aliens had abducted her mother and replaced her with someone really nice.

"Thanks, Mom."

"You're welcome. Shall we shoot for this weekend?"

"That'll work."

Stella glanced out the window at the falling snow. "It's so beautiful."

"And dangerous. I better get going." She got up to leave. "I promise to behave."

"So do I," Stella said.

The lightly falling snow had become a blizzard by the time Chase picked up Gitana. Chase helped her into the Hummer.

"I take back everything I ever said about the Hummer." Gitana pulled on her seat belt and brushed off her coat.

"She was absolutely amazing coming up the canyon. There were cars off the road everywhere. I bet money they close the canyon by tonight." Chase pulled out of the parking lot observing that indeed Nora's truck was still there.

"Maybe we should have planned for a spring baby," Gitana said, rubbing her protruding stomach.

"We didn't exactly have a choice, but I don't regret a single thing." Chase made the first tracks out to the county road. All traces of their previous journey on the road had been erased by the insistently productive snowfall.

"Nora is leaving soon, right?" Chase said as snow plopped down on the windshield like mud patties from on high.

"Yes. She was waiting for you. I can't believe this weather."

They were both quiet for a moment, the only sound being the wipers slapping the snow away.

"Chase, I'm a little worried."

"About what?" Chase turned onto the 441 and made for home.

The state road had been plowed, but the snow was accumulating so quickly that it was almost a moot point.

"The delivery and…"

"The weather," Chase added.

"I mean, it probably won't snow." Gitana stared out the window.

"But what if it does?" Chase glanced at her.

They watched as a Ford Focus in front of them fishtailed out onto the highway.

"I talked to my mom. We can stay there. In fact, she insists."

"What about the dogs?" Gitana said morosely.

"They can come too."

The Ford Focus had gained control and sped off. Chase wondered how long the small car would stay on the road.

"Has she lost her mind?"

"No, but I think aliens abducted my real mother and lent us a better one." Chase saw the sign for Cedar Meadows indicating one mile and eased her knuckles off the steering wheel.

"Are you okay with this?" Gitana asked.

"It's only a month. I can be good for a month—for Bud."

"Maybe Jacinda can give us some holy water," Gitana suggested.

"For me and the dogs?" Chase inquired.

"Blessings from above can't hurt."

Chapter Twenty-Eight

"You're doing what?" Lacey asked.

"Look, are you coming to Thanksgiving dinner or not?" Chase said. She had somewhat expected this response from Lacey, but this was nothing compared to the next bombshell she was going to drop, the emotional equivalent of the bombing of Dresden.

She'd been forced to have an emergency session with Dr. Robicheck who kindly pointed out that what Chase viewed as drastic was a progression that had been steadily plodding along since she'd been aware of the pregnancy. She was changing so she could be a decent parent. Chase figured the doctor was right. Most of her swearing had stopped. She was more tolerant and she shopped at Costco. Perhaps, the biggest change was reconciling herself with her mother followed by her close ties with Addison. It was all so unlike her, she often didn't recognize her own thoughts. She approached her life now in an almost benevolent fashion. It was positively frightening.

"We're staying here until the delivery."

"You're staying *here?*" Lacey's tone shrieked of incredulity.

"Yes, what's wrong with that?" Chase rearranged her pencils in the desk drawer. Her makeshift office still needed some fine-tuning. She was going through Ariana's notes on her mystery novel. She found them quite helpful. Her animosity toward her editor had lessened. This was another oddity.

"You despise your mother and where'd you put the dogs?"

Chase whirled a perfect three-sixty in the expensive office chair her mother had purchased. She relished her next statement. "They're here."

"What!"

This was good. Rich like the espresso pie at The Flying J Café. She should really take Gitana there for lunch. Temporarily living in town had its benefits. She'd been to the library several times getting books, CDs and movies. They were listening to Bach, Vivaldi and Mozart so Bud could bone up on classical music in the womb. Gitana was reading Garrison Keillor's *Lake Wobegon Days* so she'd have an idea of small-town life with its glories and travails. All this was done in an effort to keep Gitana entertained.

"So are you coming for turkey or what?"

"Can I bring Jasmine?"

"Of course. 'You' now includes your partner," Chase informed her.

Chase could almost see the beaming look on Lacey's face.

"We'd love to."

Later that day, Chase availed herself of her mother's library. She pulled out Baudelaire, D.H. Lawrence, Vonnegut, Norman Mailer and J.D. Salinger. Her mother walked in. Chase looked up. "I didn't know you had such a library. Where have all these books been?"

"In the attic. Your father thought books were tedious and a waste of space."

Chase was mortified. It was absolutely scandalous.

Her mother nodded. "You know," she said, sitting on the edge of what could only be called the reading table—a long narrow table with two straightback chairs, two bookstands and green shaded reading lamps so that Chase imagined being in an Oxford or Cambridge library. "We've never really had a talk about your father."

Chase didn't immediately know where this was going—then, she got it. In the figurative sense she was going to be a father. "Yes."

"What do you remember of him?"

She dutifully thought back. She'd been eight when he died. Leaning back in her chair, she decided he was a shadowy figure—a coming and going blur. He was never present in her mind at the breakfast table like fathers in the movies or TV. There was the occasional, mostly silent, family dinner. She remembered her mother at one end her father at the other of the ornate dining room table and that she couldn't wait for dinner to be over. She didn't remember watching him shave, the smell of his cologne, bedtime stories, being hiked up in the air—he was nothing but a cipher in her child's mind.

"Truthfully, not much. I'd have to see a photo to recognize him."

Her mother smiled. "Good."

Chase wasn't certain if her mother said this out of conviction or spite. "I won't be like that."

"I know you won't." She touched Chase's shoulder.

Chase felt herself blush so she changed the subject before things got mushy. "Why are so many novels written by men obsessed with genitalia?" She'd just finished *Villages* by John Updike and another book by Philip Roth. She'd learned more about penises and what they did than she ever cared to know.

Stella laughed. "Now that you mention it—you're right, at least in twentieth century literature."

"That's why I'm a fan of the nineteenth," Chase said.

"I as well. I imagine that their perspective on the world is primarily viewed from behind a pair of furry golf balls and a

254

bratwurst." She laughed.

Chase didn't laugh. She was worried. "What if Bud has a penis?"

"There's a fifty-fifty chance. You'd better bone up on your ball skills." This started a whole new rash of laughter.

Chase buried her head in her hands and moaned.

When her mother had regained her composure, she patted Chase on the back. "Don't worry. We'll make him into a multi-cultural, gender-informed, strong yet sensitive man. He'll see through the veil of his little head and steer on without further thought to his nether regions." Stella burst into apoplectic spasms of laughter.

Chase wondered if her mother had lost her senses.

"My, we're having a good time in here," Peggy said as she stood in doorway.

"She is," Chase said disgustedly as she looked around Peggy for a sighting of Addison.

"She's in the kitchen with Rosarita. She wants to make this smores pie thing for Thanksgiving so she's getting pointers from Rosarita," Peggy informed her.

"You're still coming to dinner?" Chase asked.

"Of course. The pie is Addison's personal contribution."

Stella wiped her eyes. "I haven't laughed like that in years."

"I'm glad I could be of service," Chase said, getting up.

"But seriously, Chase, if Bud is a boy we'll make him a good one—so don't worry."

"Oh, honey, you and Gitana are going to be the best parents on the planet. Don't give it a second thought. Besides, Addison is chomping at the bit to give you all a hand." Peggy took off her blue blazer with gold buttons and draped it over a chair. She looked dressed for the club with her khaki trousers and penny loafers.

"Thank you, Peggy." As Chase left she overheard Peggy tell her mother "I was at the club and met with Evelyn Myers. She wants us to tail her cheating no-good husband. According to her he's worth a lot."

Their voices trailed off. It seemed the detective agency was never short of cheating spouses. Those two will be making a fortune, Chase thought.

In the kitchen, Addison and Rosarita were going over the cut-out recipe from the food section of the newspaper and adding its required ingredients to the already daunting grocery list. The three of them were doing the shopping.

Addison lit up when she saw Chase. "Look at this. Isn't it fabulous," she said, giving Chase the recipe.

"Wow, that does look good," Chase said.

"It's not overly complicated. Rosarita says it's okay not like a chocolate mousse, double boiler thing."

Rosarita clucked and shook her head. "Simple is better."

"Exactly, especially when there's already a lot to do. Are we ready?" Chase asked.

"Sí," Addison and Rosarita said in unison.

Chase handed the clipboard with the grocery list to Addison. "You're in charge of inventory accumulation."

Rosarita cocked her head and looked at Addison. "I'm in charge of checking stuff off the list. I know simple is better, but she's a writer and it's an occupational hazard."

Chase strode quickly to the door. Rosarita grabbed Addison's arm. "Come, before her big brain gets her in trouble."

Three shopping carts later they returned to the Hummer. With some difficulty and several attempts they got the groceries in the back.

"Be careful, those are the crescent rolls," Addison said as Chase attempted to shut the tailgate on them.

"Right." Chase pulled them out of the plastic grocery bag and threw them in the backseat.

"That's much better," Addison said, rolling her eyes.

They climbed in the car and Chase got out of the parking lot as quickly as possible as it was beginning to resemble a bumper car ride. As Chase merged onto the freeway, heading toward her mother's house she questioned Addison about the grocery list, making her reiterate it several times.

"Are you going to do these holiday things a lot?" Addison asked, putting the clipboard under her seat.

"I suppose so, especially once Bud arrives." She found herself thinking about Bud like a guest or long lost acquaintance soon to arrive. "Why do you ask?" She exited the freeway and turned on Mountain Avenue.

Addison didn't reply instead she readjusted the teddy bear's seat belt that had gone askew since being knocked in the head with the packet of buns.

Chase glanced in the rearview mirror. She must watch things like that. It could have been Bud's head. "All right, I'm a little nervous which tends to make me neurotic. I'll work on it."

"All will be fine, mija. No worries," Rosarita said, touching Chase's arm.

"I know." She took a few deep breaths. She almost chewed a cuticle, but Addison reached forward and grabbed her wrist.

"Don't, you're doing so well."

Chase put her hand back on the steering wheel. They pulled up into her mother's driveway. Chase swung the Hummer around the circular driveway so she could back up to the garage. The Hummer didn't fit into the garage, being too tall, an engineering snafu, Chase thought ruefully as the three of them stared at the load.

"I know," Addison said, hopping out. She pulled out a green metal garden cart from the depths of the garage.

"Brilliant," Chase said, and they began loading the cart and dragging it to the kitchen.

When they got into the house, Gitana and Stella were playing Scrabble. The game board lay between them on the white couch with the dogs curled up on either side of them.

Boy, things have really changed, Chase thought.

Gitana looked up and smiled. "Your mother is smoking me."

"I don't wonder. She used to drill me on vocabulary every

257

night at dinner. Thank God, she didn't go in for the National Spelling Bee."

Stella smirked. "It did cross my mind." She put down six tiles to spell "radical."

"Thirty-five points!" Gitana screeched.

"I could help," Addison offered.

"No way, you're on kitchen duty," Chase said.

Addison ignored her. She reached over and rearranged Gitana's tiles.

Gitana smiled slyly and then plunked them down against an existing word, spelling out "callously."

Stella and Chase peered down at them.

"Fifty-five points," Chase said.

Stella smiled savagely at Addison. "You're next. If a nine-year-old can beat me, it's back to the dictionary."

"I only play for money," Addison said, rubbing her fingernails on her T-shirt.

"A nickle a tile?" Stella queried.

"I'll keep score," Gitana said, sliding over to let Addison slip in.

Chase put her hands on her hips. "There goes my kitchen help."

No one paid any attention as they set up a new game.

Chapter Twenty-Nine

"This has been the weirdest nine months of my entire life," Chase said.

"Does that include puberty?" Lacey asked.

Chase thought for a moment. Puberty was boobs, periods, sex, lust and desire. "Okay, the second weirdest but a close second."

They were in the kitchen peeling and dicing potatoes for the big turkey day celebration. Chase pondered the value of these family rituals, but it always came back to Bud.

"Sex and driving a car, that's what I remember," Lacey said.

Her distracted look led Chase to believe she was reliving those moments. Lacey was in charge of dicing while Chase peeled. She had a sudden concern for Lacey's fingers. Chase brought her back. "Like it's any different now. Puberty is still all about a pounding clitoris and being behind the wheel of a potential killing machine. Sixteen is really too young to be driving."

"Oh, no, poor Bud won't be allowed to drive until she's

259

twenty-five." Lacey dumped a pile of neatly diced potatoes into the enormous stainless steel pot Rosarita had given them.

Chase glanced at the endless pile of potatoes she was required to peel. "Are you implying that I'll be an overprotective parent?"

"Yes."

"I know. I'm hoping I'll ease up."

"Gitana will make you." Lacey glanced at the twenty-pound bag of potatoes. "Are we really going to need all these potatoes?"

Chase glanced over her shoulder at Rosarita who was making the masa for the corn tamales. That was the problem with living in New Mexico, too many cultures crammed into one place— the triculture. They were having Anglo, Hispanic and Native American food. Too much food for one table.

Rosarita, with their help, was essentially making three Thanksgiving dinners. This was blatant overfeeding, Chase decided. Something must be done for the sake of the planet. "Quick, open that cupboard," she whispered to Lacey.

Lacey, being an expert at shirking, understood immediately. She took the bag of potatoes and shoved it in the Tupperware cupboard, knocking over some of the containers but with no other consequences. Rosarita hadn't heard the noise.

"That was brilliant," Lacey whispered.

"I thought so." Chase dumped the cut and peeled potatoes in the boiling pan of water and wiped her hands on the blue and white twill apron Rosarita had insisted she wear.

Graciela came in with three bottles of Cabernet Sauvignon precariously perched atop of case of Modelo beer.

Lacey lunged for the wine. "Those are expensive. Have you lost your fucking mind—two trips, duh."

"Don't I know. I had to detail a Benz and a Land Rover just to foot the liquor bill," Graciela declared.

Chase pulled out her wallet. "I'll get it."

"Don't worry. I got it covered." Graciela set the case of beer by the inset wine fridge next to the stainless steel one. She opened the wine fridge and pulled out two bottles of Modelo from the cardboard box. They fit perfect in the rack.

"You're not putting beer in there," Lacey said.

"Why not? It keeps the beer at the perfect temperature."

"Like you would know," Lacey said.

"I work for rich people, remember. I have knowledge of their finer habits."

"Whatever," Lacey said, handing Graciela back the bottles of beer and putting the wine in their place.

"Fucking wine snob," Graciela said.

Rosarita looked up from her masa. "No bad language—baby coming."

"Sorry," Graciela said. She opened the fridge and attempted to put the case of beer into it, unceremoniously shoving important side dishes every which way.

This time Chase intervened. "You're like a bull in a china shop. Get out of here before you destroy Thanksgiving."

"All right, already." She snagged a beer and made a hasty exit.

Gitana poked her head in the kitchen. "How's it going in there?"

"You mean between the language police and the stress monkeys—fantastic," Graciela said, stomping past her.

"You're supposed to be resting," Chase said.

"I'm bored," Gitana said.

"You sit here. You help me with the tamales," Rosarita said, pulling out a stool at the kitchen island.

Chase frowned.

"It's good," Rosarita said.

"All right," Chase conceded unwillingly.

"Can I help? It looks like fun," Lacey said.

Chase smirked. Fun, ha! Lacey must be entertaining thoughts of domesticity with Jasmine.

"Oh, yes. Gitana show you how. I must do the posole now."

Chase's intestines did a loop at the mention of posole—that stuff was so hot it would melt lead—not to mention the driving force of the hominy. The whole mess cleaned you out like Draino.

261

A bowl of Rosarita's posole would make you crap for a week.

"I'll get Addison and we'll set the table." Chase had to get out of the kitchen. She was reaching overload.

"Use the good," Rosarita said.

"No, not the china," Chase moaned.

Rosarita raised an eyebrow. "Special day."

"I know." Chase left the kitchen and went in search of Addison. She found her sitting at the dining room table surrounded by strange dried floral things of unrecognizable origins and a hollowed out pumpkin.

"What the hell?" Chase said.

"More like what the fuck? It's a stupid centerpiece."

"Addison, language. I hope you didn't get that from me."

Addison rolled her eyes. "Sorry. My mom and Stella put me in charge of the awful centerpiece."

"How does it work?" Chase said, staring at the bits and pieces of dried flora.

"You're supposed to stick all this stupid stuff into the pumpkin—artistically of course, and then the whole gross ensemble goes on the table and gets in the way of the food. My mom saw it in that Martha Stewart magazine, which I am going to start intercepting because it gives her strange ideas about crafts."

"Why isn't she doing it?"

"She's busy helping Stella catch some cheating bastard husband in the act." Addison bounced some odd looking dried spore thing on the table.

"We're going to have to teach Bud the earmuff thing."

"I can tell you right now, Bud is going to swear," Addison said.

"I know," Chase said, plunking down in a chair next to Addison. They stared morosely at the unmade centerpiece.

"What am I going to do?" Addison said.

Chase brightened. "I know. Close your eyes. I'll hand you things and you stuff them in the pumpkin."

Addison looked dubious. "What if it turns out ugly?"

"You're suffering a creative block. If you get it started then we can always fix it later. Besides, do you really care?"

Addison considered this. "No, I don't. Just because I drew pictures when I was five and stuck them on the fridge does not make me Picasso. I'm literary. Words are my art. I'm not some floral arranger."

"Precisely. Let's make a go of it."

When they were done, it wasn't exactly hideous, but it was close.

Graciela came in, gasped, laughed hysterically, held her sides and left. Gitana was kinder. She attempted to help. It did look a little better when she was finished.

"I should have brought some orchids. Where did you get all this stuff?" Gitana inquired.

"Hobby Lobby. I hate that place. My mom is always trying to get me to try some craft thing."

"Like what?" Chase asked.

"Like make little bracelets with multicolored plastic beads or paint designs on flip-flops. I pretty much cured her, though. I convinced her to buy me a Shrinky Dinks kit and I almost burned the house down. It was beautiful. The house stunk like burnt plastic for weeks." Addison gloated.

Chase made a mental note not to force crafts on Bud. If she had an artistic bent they would assist.

Just then Stella and Peggy walked in talking animatedly. They stopped.

"Oh, Addison, you did a great job. It looks just like the picture," Peggy said. She patted Addison on the head.

Addison muttered, "She's big on things looking like the picture."

Chase nodded sympathetically. She did not admit that when she cooked she liked things to look like the picture. It was a character flaw, but she couldn't help herself. She found it comforting.

Delia and Jasmine came in.

Graciela rushed out of the kitchen and nearly flattened Delia. They fell together on the couch. Jacinda, who'd been picked up as well in the Jasmine-taxi, came toddling in with the menudo. Chase took it from her. Jacinda, upon noticing Graciela being overly physical with Delia, whacked Graciela with her rosary beads, and called her something horrid in Spanish that ended in El Diablo. She smiled apologetically at Stella and Peggy and followed Chase into the kitchen.

"That child," Jacinda said, shaking her head.

"I know. She'll grow up someday," Chase said half-heartedly. "Ha!"

Rosarita cried out, "Mi amiga, come taste this. I need your help." The rest of the conversation was in Spanish.

Chase set the menudo on the counter, wondering at this strange extended family. She'd gone from being a hermit to arranging a feast. She sighed heavily and took four Modelos and a grape juice for Gitana out to the living room.

It seemed like an eternity before the food was on the table. Chase sat at one end of the long cherry wood table with its awful centerpiece and her mother at the other end. Chase was to do the toast. Stella gave her the look—the one that said this is the culmination of all your handiwork—do not fuck it up.

Chase wanted to dive gracefully into her now clear pool of complete understanding. Instead, she figuratively jumped, held her knees to her chest and executed a gargantuan cannonball. Had there been water the dinner guests would have been soaked. "Here we are one conception later, my straight best friend now a raging lesbian, my sister un-in-law almost tame and my mother has morphed into a ball-busting sleuth."

Everyone was silent. They stared, seeming to await the brick through the window.

"And I think it's absolutely marvelous—the best year of my life and I love you all."

Stella smiled. "That wasn't exactly what I had in mind but it will do."

"Grace and subtlety are not part of my make up. You must beg my pardon." Chase bowed and sat down. Glasses clinked.

Fine bone china with a delicate pattern of pink primrose was filled and happiness like a blanket wrapped itself around her. Jacinda and Rosarita were still praying. Graciela got impatient.

"Damn it, Chase pass the f—uh, the posole."

Chase reached over their bowed heads. She put turkey and tamales side by side—indicative of her two families. She was pondering the cultural melting pot as she cut her turkey. She looked over at Gitana who was staring into her lap. Chase leaned over. So did Addison.

"She's leaking," Addison said, pointing to the mahogany wood floor of the dining room.

"Oh, fuck, your water broke. Fuck! Fuck! Fuck!" Chase had gone from bliss to panic.

"Chase, stop that foul language this instant," Stella said, getting up calmly.

Jacinda rushed to Gitana and held her hand, murmuring soothing words. "It's all right, mija."

Stella and Jacinda gently lifted Gitana out of her chair.

"I'm not ready for this," Chase said.

Addison kept staring at Gitana's protruding belly like she was waiting for alien spawn to rip open the flesh and jump onto the nearest bystander.

Lacey grabbed buns, cranberry sauce and turkey and began making little sandwiches. "Get the mashed potatoes," she commanded Jasmine. She wrapped the food into the linen napkins.

Stella looked at Lacey unperturbed as the cranberry sauce leaked through her best table linens.

"I'll buy new ones," Lacey said, stuffing a tamale into her mouth. "I promise."

Or that's what it sounded like to Chase. "How can you think about food at a time like this?" Chase shouted at her. Just then she felt an excruciating pain in her shin. She bent over and grabbed it, squealing in pain.

"I'm sorry. I had to," Addison said.

"Why?" Chase eeked out.

"You were in shock," she replied.

"Good call, Addison," Stella said.

"Maybe we should go to the hospital," Gitana suggested as a contraction made her double over.

"Hummer," Chase said.

"Chase, Jacinda, Graciela, Addison and myself in the Hummer. The rest of you follow," Stella said.

They instantly obeyed her. Chase hopped in the driver's seat.

"Dude, can you do this?" Graciela asked as she helped Stella load Gitana in the front seat, easing the seat back a little.

"Yes, I can do it. I need a focus."

Addison yanked the bear and car seat out and threw them in the back cargo area to make room for everyone. Chase started the car and calmly pulled out of the driveway. She pulled onto the street with equal care. It looked good. Then Gitana had another contraction. Everyone stared at Chase. She looked at Addison in the rearview mirror.

"Time them," Chase told Addison.

Addison nodded. She set her watch.

Aside from gripping the wheel tightly, Chase drove with care and efficiency. She pulled up into the emergency room driveway. She leapt out of the Hummer and before anyone could commend her efforts, she ran screaming into the emergency room. Before they had Gitana out of the car, Chase had an EMT, a fireman and a nurse in tow with a gurney.

Gitana was mortified. "I'm fine, really," she said as they loaded her on the gurney.

"I know, sweetheart, expectant..." The nurse paused and looked at Chase and she started again, "Expectant partners are always a little hyped-up." She took Gitana's pulse. Gitana had another contraction. She frowned. "I think we better get you inside."

Chase hung by her side, clinging to the gurney.

Graciela called after her. "Dude, the keys."

Chase looked at her blankly. Graciela pointed to the Hummer. Chase threw her the car keys, narrowly missing her mother's head.

"Don't try out for the softball team," Graciela said. She moved the car.

Stella and Jacinda came in with Chase. Addison went with Graciela. Chase fervently hoped Addison wasn't going to persuade Graciela to tell her dirty stories. She would've prevented this if Gitana's contractions weren't occurring at such quick intervals. At this rate, she thought as they hastily went down the hallway, Bud was going to blast out any minute.

Gitana gripped Chase's hand. "Chase?"

"Yes?" Chase eagerly gazed into her eyes, fully prepared to offer hope, praise and encouragement—to rise up to her utmost being.

"I don't want you there."

"What!"

"She's right, Chase. You'll only make a mess of it," Stella said.

"But I want to. I have to," Chase protested.

"She's right, mija," Jacinda said.

The nurse whispered in her ear things Chase did not want to know. Chase gagged a little. Stella gave her the you-know-when-you've-been-defeated look.

"All right. But anything," she said looking at Gitana, "unusual occurs I'm there."

Gitana squeezed her hand.

"We completely understand," Stella said. She glanced at the nurse. They all knew that if something went wrong nobody would be allowed in the delivery room except the professionals.

The medical team pushed Gitana through the metal doors into the delivery room. Chase stood watching as her mother and Jacinda followed her in. She felt shut out but pulled her resolve together and met the others in the waiting room.

267

She started pacing. Lacey had finished her supper in the car but had brought the pumpkin pie with her. Jasmine looked uncertain as Lacey pushed a forkful at her, smiling coyly.

Chase watched them absently. She paced from one end of the waiting room to the other. She thought she should be praying or chanting. She decided on "Please let them both be okay." She timed her words to her paces. So far she had managed to stave off the thoughts of something going wrong—but now they burst forth like a flock of bats exiting a cave.

"Dude, you're going to wear out the floor," Graciela said. She was playing rummy five-hundred with Delia. Addison, who seemed to have every conceivable thing in her backpack, had given them the cards. Everyone, it seemed, had found a way to wait except her. She stared at them, puzzled, and then resumed her pacing.

Addison nudged her mother. Peggy was reading her private detective manual that she kept within reach at all times. "Mom, can I have the car keys? I left something in the car."

Peggy didn't remove her gaze from the manual. "Sure, honey." She fished them out of her purse. Addison took them and got up.

Chase glanced at her. "You shouldn't be wandering around the hospital by yourself."

Addison pursed her lips.

"What I mean is no one should go about by themselves."

"Dude's right. Crackheads are in the ER. I could use a walk. Come on Delia, let's go with her." Graciela set her cards down.

Delia frowned. "We resume the same game when we get back."

Addison smiled. "I guess we know who's winning."

"I'm down five," Graciela said, pulling money from her pocket and handing it over.

"Does it normally take this long?" Chase said.

Lacey got up and touched Chase's hand. "It's fine. Come sit down." She guided her to the chair next to Jasmine and by Peggy. "Peggy can tell you."

Peggy looked up. "Oh God, I'm sorry. I'm so wrapped up in passing the PI licensing test, I can't seem to concentrate on anything else."

"When is it?" Chase asked.

"Next Thursday." Peggy closed the book.

"You really want to be a private investigator?" Chase inquired.

"Yes."

"You're sick of real estate?" Jasmine said.

Jasmine had an uncanny interest in why people discarded things. She wanted to know why a person quit this or that like it gave some clue to their personality. Chase wondered about that. She always concerned herself with the new or future plans of the person. One day, when her partner wasn't screaming bloody murder and trying to pop out a baby, she'd inquire about the why of this from Jasmine. She got back up again and resumed her pacing.

"Chase, she's fine. The doctor will let you know if there's a complication and so would Stella. Stop worrying. Come sit down," Peggy ordered.

"Maybe you could ask Peggy test questions," Lacey said.

Both Peggy and Chase scowled at her.

"Or maybe not," Lacey said.

Addison, Delia and Graciela returned. They were smiling. The kind of smile that belies innocence, Chase thought. "You haven't been telling her bad stories," she said, eyeing them suspiciously.

Graciela held up her hand. "I swear."

Chase glared at Delia.

"She did ask, but we didn't indulge. Isn't that right, Addison?"

Addison was fiddling with something in the pocket of her red fluffy down jacket. Then she blurted, "Now."

Delia and Graciela grabbed Chase by each arm and sat her in one of the square wooden chairs with a thin mauve colored seat cushion. Addison made ready and in one quick movement took a bungee cord and tied fast Chase's struggling legs to the chair. Graciela held Chase's arms to the side of the chair while Addison did the same with her arms.

"There, now you'll have to sit still. You're working yourself into a fervor and you've chewed three cuticles already," Addison said.

Graciela and Delia looked pleased with themselves.

"Good plan, Addison," Graciela said.

Delia looked smug. "I should've brought one of my crappy stories so we could edit it while you're still."

Chase glowered at them.

Lacey and Jasmine regarded her.

"Help me," Chase said, looking at them imploringly.

Lacey appeared to contemplate the plea and then shook her head. "This is better."

Peggy was mortified. "I don't think it's legal."

Addison piped in. "According to English law, upon which our legal system is based, something is not considered illegal unless forbidden by law—in contrast to the European standard that all behaviors are sanctioned by law. Bungee-cording a lunatic to a chair in the waiting room of a maternity ward is not on the books."

"Damn, that kid is smart," Graciela said to Delia in a low voice.

"I am not a lunatic!"

"At present you are behaving like one," Addison said.

Chase calmed herself. Leave it to a child, she thought. "All right, this is probably better albeit unorthodox."

Everyone seemed to sigh with relief. Cards were resumed and Lacey and Jasmine went back to their pumpkin pie.

Peggy seemed mollified. "I suppose it is better than wearing out the floor and your nerves." She went back to her studies.

Chase knew she'd lost her only ally. She sat quietly. Then, she looked over at Addison. "The least you can do is read to me."

"Great. You'll like the play I'm reading, *Two Gentlemen of Verona*."

Chase groaned. "How close are you to the dog part?"

270

"Pretty close."

"All right then." Chase respected the playwright but dreaded the mental calisthenics his work demanded.

Addison dug out the *Riverside Shakespeare* from her backpack.

"That thing is huge. You're going to need a chiropractor," Lacey said.

"I'm working on my biceps. There's this girl at school…"

She was interrupted by the arrival of Stella who strode through the double doors as if she were Moses parting the Red Sea. She stopped. "Why is she tied up?"

"She became a public nuisance," Addison said.

Stella nodded. "Good work."

"Good work. It borders on treason not to mention laborious." Chase cocked her head toward Addison's mammoth edition of Shakespeare.

"Which play?" Stella asked.

"*Two Gentlemen of Verona.*"

"The one with the dog?" Stella said.

"Yes. We're almost to that part," Addison replied.

Peggy intervened. "Do you have news?"

They all sat upright, eyes set on Stella.

"Yes, of course. Gitana is doing as well as can be expected. Did you teach her to swear like that?" Stella said, frowning at Chase.

"I claim the Fifth Amendment."

"She's nearly shocked Jacinda into heart failure. The doctor insisted she desist in her spraying of holy water. They got into a screaming match over the salubriousness of holy water."

"Ha! Miss Goody-Two-Shoes is getting hers now." Graciela leapt to her feet and did a little jig. She looked at Addison to whom she now obviously assigned the title child genius, "What does salubriousness mean?"

"Healthy."

Chase jumped up and down in her chair, making it rock precipitously. "But she's okay, right? She's not going to—well, you know."

"Oh, for goodness sakes, Chase, this isn't the Middle Ages. Mortality rates are hardly worth mentioning," Stella said.

"Stella!" Peggy was again mortified.

"That's what she was asking."

Lacey got up and held Chase's shoulders. "Sit still, before you hurt yourself."

A very nervous group of six Hispanic men, one wide-eyed, obviously the father-to-be, took seats at the opposite end of the waiting room. They stared at Chase.

Jasmine offered, "Did you know that it was the advent of hospitals that raised mortality rates in Medieval times because the doctors didn't wash their hands between patients? When midwives were used in the home the infection rates were low and thus there were fewer complications."

"How do you know that?" Lacey asked.

"I took a Medieval lit class in college."

Chase glared at her mother. "Did he wash his hands?"

"Who?"

"The fucking doctor!" Chase screamed.

The nervous men in the corner of waiting room gaped at her.

Stella leaned toward her. "Any more obscenities out of you and I'll personally duct-tape your mouth as well. The entire room, including the doctor's hands, is sterile. Do you think I'd let anything happen to Gitana?"

"No, I'm sorry. It's nerves."

Stella put her hands on Chase's shoulders and said, "Everything is fine." She leaned over and kissed her forehead.

Everyone stared at this mother-daughter moment. Lacey dabbed the corner of her eye with a leftover napkin.

Stella strode back to the maternity room, calling out over her shoulder, "Don't let her go."

Addison stared at Chase.

"What?" Chase said.

"That was almost touching," Addison said.

Chase looked away. It was kind of touching but she turned

272

brash, "Let's get on with the damn story."

Addison smirked and began reading aloud.

Chase sat perfectly still. The moment had come, she knew it in her bones before the clatter of the doors drew everyone's attention. There was an unearthly silence like the world was holding its breath.

The doctor looked at them queerly. He called out, "Chase Banter." He searched their faces.

"Here, I'm right here," she said, hopping up and down. She moved with such force that they all watched as the chair began to rock and sway.

Lacey and Graciela leaped up to stop it, but it was too late. Chase fell flat on her face. A pool of blood began to seep out from where she lay.

Amid shrieks of alarm from everyone in the room, the doctor and Lacey lifted her up. Addison dug in her pack furiously for Kleenex.

"Nurse!" the doctor called out. He peered at Chase. "I don't think your nose is broken, but you'll have quite a knot on your head. I need to make sure you don't have a concussion." He pulled out his penlight and peered at her pupils.

The nurse brought a white towel. The doctor noticed her confusion. He looked at her now horribly embarrassed cohorts. "Perhaps, you should untie her."

Delia and Graciela got right on it. Addison held the towel on Chase's nose until she could do it herself.

"What about the baby?" Chase was finally able to say.

"What?" the doctor said.

"The baby," Chase muttered through the towel.

"Oh, yes, the baby. It's a girl."

Chase leaped around screaming, *"It's a girl, it's a girl!"*

Stella peeked through the door. "Well, aren't you going to come see her?" Then she grimaced. "What happened to your face?"

"She fell. She doesn't have a concussion," the doctor said. He left them and went over to the Hispanic men who looked more amazed about the menagerie of strange women than the child-bearing news he was about to relay.

Stella took Chase's hand and led her to Gitana's room. As they walked down the hall, Chase thought, her mother hadn't held her hand since she was a small child being restrained from dashing into oncoming traffic. She looked over at her mother. "Does she have...all her parts?"

Stella smiled. "She's absolutely perfect."

Chase smiled. Then, she felt like she was a human-parts bigot. "I wouldn't love her less if she was missing a thing or two."

"But you're glad about one part she's missing," Stella said.

Chase stiffened as they passed open doors with rooms filled with adoring parents and baby cries.

"Yes, well, fathers want sons whether they admit it or not. Why can't a woman-father-person-parent want a girl?"

Stella pushed her through a door. "You can and don't ever be ashamed of it."

Chase smiled back at her. She turned slowly to see Jacinda stroking Gitana's forehead, cooing softly in Spanish. Gitana was holding the baby.

Chase was holding the towel back up to her nose which was still bleeding, due to her vehement declaration of parentage.

Gitana looked up. "What on earth happened to you?"

Chase didn't answer. She was peering down at Bud.

Stella said, "They tied her to a chair and when the doctor came out she got so excited she fell on her face. She doesn't have a concussion."

"Makes perfect sense. Come here." Gitana held out her hand.

Chase pulled the towel from her nose, touched it, testing for bleeding and satisfied that she wouldn't be a biohazard to her new child, she leaned over and kissed Gitana's forehead, never taking her eyes off the baby.

"Are you okay?" Chase asked, tearing her eyes away from the tiny blue eyes that stared up at her.

"Yes. I can't say I ever want to do that again. I think Bud's going to be an only child. And I don't think Jacinda will ever recover."

"I heard you swore like a sailor."

"You would've been proud." Gitana took Chase's hand and put it on the baby's head.

It was so soft and smooth. It was the most incredible thing Chase had ever felt. She looked at Gitana in amazement. "Wow."

"You want to hold her?"

"Is it all right?"

"Of course." Gitana inched up to a more upright position with Jacinda's help.

Jacinda picked up the baby. "You're a papa now." She stroked the baby's head, cradling Bud's tiny head in her palm. "Hold her like this," she instructed.

Chase took her gently. Bud looked up at her with her seemingly unblinking blue eyes and curled her finger around one of Chase's strands of loose hair. Her hand was no bigger than a quarter. Chase's adoration was promptly broken by the sensation of something wet on her torso. Carefully, she lifted the baby. "She peed on me."

Stella laughed. "Welcome to being a parent."

Chase studied the angelic eyes. "I hope this isn't an indication of our future relationship."

Bud made a cooing noise. Jacinda took her to get cleaned up. She patted Chase's shoulder.

Chase looked down at her starched white shirt especially purchased for the holiday event. It was covered in urine and blood. "I'm not having a good day. I'm having a *great* day. "

"You can have my shirt and bring me another one later," Gitana said.

"Thanks, sweetie."

Jacinda fetched it. Chase went into the bathroom to change. She peered at her bloody nose and the lump on her forehead. She'd get Graciela and Delia for this and then she remembered

Bud. Revenge fantasies were no longer an option. She didn't want Bud to pick up any bad habits. She hoped Bud, whose real name was to be Angelica, wouldn't remember their first meeting. She'd already subscribed to *Parenting Magazine* and was rapidly memorizing the cognitive states of baby development. Bud, having just entered the world, was most likely still a little out of it. From womb to fresh air had to be a rather sudden shock—like when you hold your breath underwater and then burst forth as your lungs threaten certain mutiny.

Chase cleaned up and came out. She kissed Bud and Gitana on their collective foreheads. "I better go talk to the urchins. Can they come in?" She glanced at Jacinda and her mother and then Gitana.

"Are you up to it?" Stella asked.

"Sure. They're part of the family too."

"Tell Graciela one bad word and I drown her in holy water," Jacinda said, furrowing her brow.

"Yes, ma'am," Chase said, certain this threat would be followed through on instantaneously.

Epilogue

Chase sat with Bud in the nursery. Gitana was napping. She rocked Bud gently in the new oak rocking chair she'd purchased after learning that babies liked to be rocked. At first, she'd rocked Bud a little too aggressively and she'd spit up everywhere and Chase, herself, felt ill. Jacinda gave her a lesson and all was going well now. No one got sick.

She'd had a lot of lessons in the two months since Bud had been born. Bud's face had lost that just-been-squeezed-through-a-small-aperture-and-it-hurt look so that she no longer resembled an alien. Now she was a baby with a lot of dark hair. Chase desperately hoped she wasn't going to grow up to look like Eddie Munster, but she did have Gitana's full lips and a cute turned-up nose. She was fat and soft and Chase adored every inch of her except maybe her intestines which excreted the nastiest stuff she'd ever seen or smelled.

Diaper changing was simply horrid, but she'd learned to do it.

Spitting up was another horror. Chase had gone to Thrift Town and bought an array of T-shirts that had become more or less disposable depending on the amount of stain and the color that Bud had the uncanny ability of producing. It was a good thing babies where so cute and helpless or the experience would be much worse. One had to find one's better nature to get through it. Bud was not a fussy baby at least. Jacinda told her stories of the fussy cantankerous kind who stayed up all night and cried all day. Chase suspected she did this to fortify her. Gitana was the perfect mother and seemed to have implanted notions about what to do in any situation. Chase did a lot of researching and experimenting.

She rocked Bud who, due to Chase's choice of a prenatal moniker, was still being called "Bud" despite the name on her birth certificate. Chase figured Bud could come up with her own name if she didn't like the others when her cognitive abilities had more fully developed. Other cultures did it so why not American lesbians?

Looking down at Bud with her wide blue eyes staring up at her, Chase talked to her frequently. It was if Bud seemed to comprehend things even if the literature on baby brains stated the contrary. Chase didn't care. She told Bud things. So what if she had to tell her the stories again later. Kids liked repetition. They watched the same movies over and over again according to Gitana's cousin, Esmelda, who had four children and seemed to know everything. Chase had not been the best relation, but now she needed this extended family and they embraced her. They didn't behave like she was super odd so she figured she was doing okay.

"Today I am going to tell you the story of my redemption. I know some of it is chemical, but my neurotransmitters fire too quickly so the anti-convulsant drugs keep them in line. You'll like me better this way believe me."

Bud burped and some white gooey stuff came out. Chase wiped it away. "I wish you'd give me a little advance notice, but since you're still at that phase of digestion I'll cut you some slack. Now back to the story."

Chase rocked. Bud burped and together they worked through the story until Bud nodded off. Chase hoped it wasn't because she was a poor storyteller. Writing was one thing, live entertainment was another.

"I know you're not listening, but I hope you appreciate all my hard work in recreating myself into a decent human being."

She put Bud in her crib and went to take a nap with Gitana. Before she fell asleep next to her beloved partner she thanked the powers that be for this amazing chance to raise a future Nobel Prize winner. All right, she'd settle for bachelor's degree and hope for a doctorate.

The End